HEARTS IN HIDING

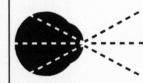

This Large Print Book carries the
Seal of Approval of N.A.V.H.

HEARTS IN HIDING

PATTY SMITH HALL

THORNDIKE PRESS

A part of Gale, Cengage Learning

Detroit • New York • San Francisco • New Haven, Conn • Waterville, Maine • London

GALE
CENGAGE Learning®

LIBRARY OF CONGRESS CATALOGING-IN-PUBLICATION DATA

Hall, Patty Smith
    Hearts in hiding / by Patty Smith Hall. — Large print ed.
      p. cm. — (Thorndike Press large print gentle romance)
    ISBN-13: 978-1-4104-5299-3 (hardcover)
    ISBN-10: 1-4104-5299-9 (hardcover)
      1. Women engineers—Georgia—Fiction. 2. German American women—Georgia—Fiction. 3. World War, 1939-1945—Veterans—Georgia—Fiction. 4. Nazis—Fiction. 5. Large type books. I. Title.
    PS3608.A54783H43 2012
    813'.6—dc23   2012030645

Published in 2012 by arrangement with Harlequin Books S.A.

Printed in the United States of America
1 2 3 4 5 6 7 16 15 14 13 12

Be kind and compassionate to one another, forgiving one another, just as God also forgave you in Christ.

— *Ephesians* 4:32

To Jennifer and Carly. God blessed
me so much when He sent you
both into my life. I love you.

To the editorial staff at Love Inspired
Historical, especially Rachel Burkot.
It takes an extraordinary staff of
talented people to produce a book —
Thank you!

ACKNOWLEDGMENTS:

It takes a group of giving, selfless people to help me write my books. Thank you to ACFW, my Seeds (Ane, Julie, Anita, Barbara D., Barbara K, Nora and Jim) and Laurie Alice Eakes.

CHAPTER ONE

Marietta, Georgia
Early spring, 1944

Maybe coming through the front door would have been a better option.

Beau Daniels glanced up at the bundle of cotton ruffles standing over him, the cold press of metal against his chest, the light scent of vanilla drifting around him. Whoever she was, she smelled of freshly baked applesauce cookies, his favorite.

"What do you think you're doing, coming through the window?"

The woman jabbed him lightly, the dull point barely creasing the muscles of his chest. If this woman thought to defend his aunt Merrilee's home with what — a poker? — she was sadly mistaken. "Well? Are you just going to sit there like a bump on a log?"

"Would you give me a second here?" If he had any sense, he would yank that pole out of her hands and toss it out the window, but that might not be wise. He wouldn't put it past the woman to crack his skull with the thing. He tugged at the thick canvas twisted around his legs. "I don't know if you've noticed, but I'm in a bind at the moment."

"Well, serves you right!" she let out, her voice as unyielding as the metal rod she had pointed at his chest. "Breaking into someone's house like that."

Defenseless! Beau scoffed at the description of the situation. If General Patton had this woman in his ranks, the Germans would be retreating back to their blessed Fatherland. "I wasn't breaking in."

"Really?" Her throaty chuckle twisted his gut into a pleasant knot. "The next thing you'll be telling me is that window was unlocked just for you."

"That's right." Untangling the curtains from his legs, Beau pushed the blackout material to the floor and stood. "When I was a boy, they couldn't afford an extra key so my aunt told me to always check the windows."

"Really," the woman answered with a hint of sarcasm. "Well, if that story's true, I'm Tokyo Rose. Pleased to meet you."

Beau tilted his head and studied her. Light from the low-hanging moon streamed in through the uncovered window, swirling around the woman, her black hair a velvet river spilling over her slight shoulders, the long sleeves of her shapeless robe falling down just over the tops of slender knuckles. She wasn't anyone he knew, and he pretty much knew everyone in the town — or at least he had until ten years ago. "What's your real name, Rosie?"

"That's none of your business."

Though he enjoyed the friendly push and pull with her, he didn't have time for games. "Look, miss," he replied, leaning back against the wall and straightening his right leg out in front of him. "I knew who I was fighting when I shipped over to North Africa. Figure the same holds true here at home."

She was silent for a moment, as if giving that idea some thought. "I live here."

Beau shook his head. "Sorry, but I don't believe that."

The poker trembled slightly in her hand. "Well, it's true!"

"My aunt owns this house, has owned it since her husband bought it and signed it over to her a few years ago."

"Everybody in town knows that."

Beau gritted his teeth together as the cramp in his leg increased. *Lord, I know bet-*

ter than to ask for patience, but I could sure use it with this woman. Maybe if he yanked her weapon out of her hand . . . "Well, I know about it because I was there. I saw Merrilee's husband sign the contracts."

"*Former* husband." Pressing the steel tip against him even harder, the woman took a step toward him. Her light scent filled his lungs, making him hunger for something, only for what, he didn't know. "So you know where John Davenport is?"

Not anymore, Beau thought, though up until eighteen months ago, John had been with him, working in San Diego. That was before John had been approached by the Navy to supervise operations for the Seabees at Port Hueneme. Which had led to the promise — watch over Merrilee.

A promise he intended to keep. This time.

"So Merrilee's your aunt?"

"Yes," Beau ground out. The cramp in his knee had quickly turned into an ache. He touched his affected foot down on the floor and lifted up a quick prayer that he didn't fall flat on his face.

She eyed him for a few seconds before nodding toward his leg. "Are you all right?"

The concern in her voice caught him off guard. Well, he didn't need or want her compassion. Beau straightened. "I'll manage."

"Are you sure?"

There it was again, that tiny note of worry. Maybe she wasn't the murdering sort after all. "You think you could ease up on that poker. I haven't spent the last couple of years ducking German snipers just to get clobbered in my aunt's front parlor."

His statement made her blink, the weapon wobbling slightly in her hands. "Is Ms. Merrilee really your aunt?"

Finally they were making some headway. Maybe now, she'd put that poker down. "I'm Beau. My father is her older brother."

Instead, she dug the sharp point firmly into his chest, tipping him back against the parlor wall. "You're James's son."

Grudgingly, Beau nodded. So she knew his father. Well, wasn't that just a kick in the pants? Meaner than a timber rattler, his old man, and always making trouble. Had been for as far back as Beau could remember. "What is my father up to now?"

But the woman ignored him. "Merrilee didn't say anything about you coming home to anybody here in the house."

"I wanted to surprise her." Pins and needles raced up his leg in a flash of heat. Beau dug the palm of his hand into his thigh and rubbed the contracting muscle.

"Really."

There was a note of disbelief back in her voice. Gracious gravy, at the rate this night was going, Beau wasn't sure he would believe his story, either. "My aunt loves surprises, and she'd see me being here in Marietta as nothing short of a miracle."

"I can't imagine any miracle coming from James's side of the family."

He drew in a frustrated breath. "We're getting nowhere with this. Why don't you just go wake Merrilee and ask her yourself?"

"And leave you down here to grab whatever you want, and run off before Merrilee has time to even make it downstairs? I don't think so."

"Lady, I'm not going anywhere." Beau took a step forward, then fell back against the wall. "I don't have any place else to go."

Head down, he massaged the strained muscle in his thigh and grimaced. How pathetic was he, telling a total stranger the truth like that? Must be more tired than he thought.

He stole a glimpse at the woman. She had moved closer, her free hand extended as if worried he might topple over at any second. "Are you sure you don't want to sit down?"

"No," he bit out, then admonished himself. She might be only trying to help, but it was too late. He didn't need her help, and neither did Merrilee. That was his job now, to take care of his aunt, make sure that she was provided with a steady income.

Clenching his lower lip between his teeth, he glowered at her and stretched up ramrod straight. "Look, I couldn't go anywhere right now if I wanted to. So why don't you run upstairs and get my aunt so that we can clear this mess up, okay?"

The woman hesitated for a moment, then began looking around the room. "I don't think so, mister. But tell you what — I'll be happy to go get Merrilee just as long as I know that when I come back, you haven't hightailed it out the window."

"I give you my word."

She scrunched up her nose as she focused her attention on the couch next to them. "That's just not good enough, what with a war going on and everything."

He really shouldn't have asked God for patience, at least not tonight. "What do you suggest then?"

Her lips turning up into a pretty smile, she tugged, pulling a length of rope from the cushions. "I knew Claire left her jump rope down here.

"Can't have you running out." She

glanced at him, pulling the rope into a tight line. "If you're as innocent as you say, you won't mind being tied up while I get Merrilee."

"And if I refuse?"

"Then I'll have the police on the phone before you make it out the window."

For Pete's sake! The Germans didn't give him this much trouble! But if agreeing to her demands brought this evening to a quick end, he'd do more than agree. He stretched out his legs, crossing one ankle over the other. "Here."

The shadows masked any surprise in her expression. She slid a measure of rope between his legs and pulled the cord tight before knotting it. "Are you comfortable?"

He shrugged off the tightness in his chest at the note of concern in her voice. "This is ridiculous."

"Maybe." A faint wave of awareness shot up his arm, then receded as she looped the rope around his wrist. "But I figure if you want to see Merrilee bad enough, being tied up for a few minutes won't be such a hardship."

Beau balled his fists, tugging on the ropes. Blast the woman! Already, he could feel his windpipe closing up, almost as if the cords dug into the tender flesh of his neck, cut-ting off what was left of his air supply.

It wouldn't do any good getting worked up like this, though he hated it nonetheless. The doctor told him he'd have these moments when the memory of his imprisonment overwhelmed him. But if he wanted to see his aunt, he would have to find a way to get through this. He blew out a sharp breath, but it did nothing to calm him. "Fine. Just be ready to get me out of these when Merrilee recognizes me."

"Deal. But if she has any reason for not wanting you here, I have to call Sheriff Worthington. You understand?"

There was no accusation in her words, but a consideration that calmed his battered senses. Beau glanced up at his captor. Starlight dusted the circumference of her dark eyes, turning them the color of sweet tea, and for the briefest moment, he wished he could trace the gentle slope of her chin, feel the warmth of her skin beneath his fingertips. Would that chase the chill from his soul?

What nonsense! Beau gave her a smile he didn't feel. "So Mack's finally the sheriff. I figured he would have moved on to something different by now."

"On a first-name basis with the police." She snorted softly. "Why doesn't that surprise me?"

"Well, you know," he answered with a shrug. "The rotten apple doesn't fall far from the rotten tree."

She hesitated for a fraction of a second before lowering her head, her fingers fumbling with the corded knot. "I hope not."

"You don't?"

"No," she answered, ducking her head. But he could have sworn he heard her whisper more. Something that made him wonder.

If that's true, then there's not much hope for me."

Beau stopped fighting against the coarse cotton of the rope. What exactly did she mean? What had happened to cause this woman to consider herself doomed? The question sat at the tip of his tongue, but when he looked up, he found her staring through the darkness at him and his breath caught in his lungs. Blast, if the woman's loveliness didn't give the stars a run for their money.

She drew in a shallow breath, then stood. "I'll be right back."

Beau watched as his captor quietly turned and left, the slight creaking of the footboards mapping out her path down the hall and up the stairs until finally drifting out of earshot. He leaned back against the wall, stretching the ball of his right foot toward him. The cramp gathered strength behind his knee, and he gritted his teeth against the onslaught of pain. What had he expected, a brass band to greet him at the county line? A cloud of suspicion had followed him out of town years ago. It only seemed fitting that he would return to the same.

The crickets chirped a soft melody outside the open window, lulling him with their bedtime serenade. He closed his eyes and drew in a deep breath, the fierce cold that had held him in its icy grip for the last nine months thawing slightly. He was back in the only place that ever felt like home, thanks to Aunt Merrilee. He only prayed she wouldn't toss him out before he had the chance to prove himself.

Beau breathed deeply, the pain in his calf easing a little.

Welcome home.

Edie Michaels moved through the dimly lit hallway outside of her landlady's bedroom as quietly as she could. Why hadn't she simply called the police instead of confronting the man she'd tied up in the parlor? Now the entire house would probably wake up, an occurrence too common in recent weeks.

But the man had claimed to be Merrilee's nephew, not that Edie believed him. No one in his right mind would acknowledge James Daniels as his father, not after all the trouble that man had caused of late. Which made the man she'd hog-tied downstairs that much more suspicious. So why hadn't she called Mack to carry the man off to jail?

I don't have any place else to go.

Edie grimaced. His statement, the way he'd said it so matter-of-factly, had hit a nerve. But why? She pressed her hand against the pocket of her robe, her fingers tracing the well-defined creases of the pages she carried with her. She knew all too well what it was like to wander the streets, praying for a way to go home. Well, maybe Beau Daniels deserved a chance, but if he upset Merrilee in any way, Edie wouldn't think twice about calling the police.

She stopped outside of Merrilee's door and, curling her hand in a fist, raised it but didn't knock. Gracious, she hated waking the woman up. Merrilee probably hadn't had a full night's sleep in weeks, but Edie didn't have a choice. Rapping her knuckles softly against the oak door, she whispered, "Merrilee?"

"Hmm?"

Edie cringed. Poor woman sounded so tired. "I'm sorry, Merrilee, but we've got a problem in the parlor downstairs."

"Claire?"

"Claire's as snug as a bug." Edie leaned against the doorjamb, thinking of her landlady's ten-year-old daughter. "This problem says he's your nephew."

Edie heard the sound of bare feet slapping softly against the wooden floor, then suddenly, the door opened. Her hair in a soft tangle of burnt copper at her shoulders, Merrilee stared at Edie as she pulled the two sides of her robe together. "But all my nephews are in the service."

"Well, this guy says he was in Europe," Edie answered, not sure why she felt slightly disappointed by her landlady's reply. "I don't know why I didn't just call the police in the first place when I caught the man climbing in through the parlor window."

"The window nearest the front door?"

Edie nodded. "It must have been unlocked."

"It was." Merrilee's answer came out in a hoarse whisper. She grabbed the ends of the robe's belt around her and tied them into a tight knot at her waist. "I've left it open for him for the past few years."

Him who? But before Edie could ask, Merrilee rushed to the stairs, taking them two at a time like a kid excited for Christmas morning. Edie hurried after her, praying neither of them missed a step in their rush. Merrilee had dealt with so much disappointment lately. What if the man tied up in the parlor wasn't her nephew, but just an intruder bent on robbing her instead?

Soft light bathed the hallway in a velvety glow as she reached the bottom step. Edie gently touched Merrilee's shoulder. "Are you sure we shouldn't call Sheriff Worthington?"

Pools of moisture glistened in Merrilee's dark green eyes. "Only one person on this earth knew I kept that window unlocked, and if it's Beau, it's an answer to years of prayer."

Beau. Her friend Maggie had told her about her arrogant lot of cousins. All males and all bent on making poor Maggie's childhood a miserable existence. More than likely, this Beau character shared the secret of the unlocked window with someone he knew without a thought to his aunt's safety.

Edie followed Merrilee to the wide doorway of the parlor. Merrilee held up the lantern and gasped. "Beau!"

"Aunt Merri." Tenderness infused his

voice, catching Edie off guard.

Merrilee flew across the room, dropping to her knees beside him, her arms cradling him like a child. He closed his eyes, his chin nesting into her shoulder as if he'd found home in the curve of his aunt's neck. A rush of warmth gathered behind her eyes.

Oh, mercy! The knots she had tied still held him captive. "Here, let me undo those ropes."

Beau opened his eyes and stared up at her, but instead of the anger she expected to see, his gaze held an emotion she didn't expect. Gratitude. "Thank you."

Her stomach did a little flip. Nerves, Edie thought as she kneeled down at his feet. Her fingers fumbled with the rope. "I hope you understand. I was just watching out for Merrilee."

"I appreciate that, Ms. . . ."

Merrilee leaned back, laughing. "Oh, where are my manners? Beau, this is Edwina Michaels, but most folks around here call her Edie for short."

"Ms. Michaels." Even with his hands still tied, he tilted his head with the grace she'd come to recognize in the men from this region of the country.

"Edie, please." She felt her cheeks go warm, though she wasn't sure why. "We're

25

very informal here."

His mouth quirked up at the corner as he rubbed his freed wrists. "Okay, Edie."

She'd never liked the nickname, not that she would tell Merrilee after all she'd done for her. But the way Beau said it, like a gentle caress, made her midsection take another pleasant tumble. She shoved her hands in the pockets of her robe, her fingers brushing over the thin parchment she'd shoved there when she'd first heard noises from the parlor.

Mom and Dad.

Edie swallowed hard, the flutterings in her stomach replaced by the cold hard truth. No one would want anything to do with her once they learned what her parents expected her to do for their homeland.

"Goodness me, are you all right?" Merrilee placed a hand on Edie's shoulder. "You're as pale as a ghost!"

Edie drew in a shaky breath. "I'm fine."

Merrilee pushed away from Beau, swiping at her cheeks before giving him a tender slap. "You scared poor Edie half to death."

"I think you underestimate your houseguest, Aunt Merri. She's pretty handy with a poker and some rope."

Edie glanced over at him. Big mistake. His green eyes, a shade lighter than his aunt's, danced with laughter. And his crooked smile guaranteed heartbreak for any girl, whether she be six or sixty.

Well, that just wouldn't do. She schooled her features into what she hoped was an icy stare. "I wouldn't have to be if someone would use the front door."

The humor in his eyes dulled and he nodded. "You're right, of course. It was never my intention to scare anyone."

"Really?"

"Really."

His apologetic answer rumbled through her. Edie stood and took a step toward the door. "I think I'd better go to bed."

"Are you sure you're all right?" Merrilee eyed her with the concern of a mother hen examining a nest of newly hatched chicks. "I'd hate to think that you might not sleep tonight. You've got such a busy schedule right now."

"I'm fine." Edie didn't have the heart to tell her that others at the plant were just as busy as she was. She cast a quick glance at Beau before turning back to Merrilee. "Are you going to be okay?"

Merrilee linked her arm through her nephew's. "We'll be just fine."

"Okay, then," she answered with a nod. "Good night."

Edie turned then, a slight tingle running up her spine as she walked across the room. He was watching her; she could feel his eyes follow her to the wide door frame.

"Ms. Edie?"

"Yes?" She turned, but her foot caught beneath the hem of the Oriental rug. She stumbled forward, slamming her eyes shut, her arms stretched out in front of her waiting for the hardwood floor to reach up and meet her.

Warm hands closed over her waist, sliding around her before pulling her back against a solid wall of muscle.

Turning, Edie opened her eyelids. The lines of concern bunched around Beau's mouth and across his forehead, his arms tightening around her, sending a pleasant warmth across her chest and into the pit of her stomach. He really had the most lovely set of eyes, green like his aunt's but shot with threads of amber that appeared to darken with his mood.

Pulling out of his grasp, she drew in a shaky breath. "I'm fine, Mr. Daniels."

His mouth turned up into a faint smile. "Beau."

She nodded, irritation bubbling up inside her. Well, he might be Merrilee's nephew but that still didn't explain why a grown man would sneak in through an open window. Beau was probably more like his reprobate father than Merrilee even knew.

Let he who is without sin cast the first stone.

Edie turned and headed toward the hall, her hand slipping into her pocket and settling over the old letter she kept there. No, she didn't have any reason to think badly of Beau's dad, not when her own parents had returned to Germany to do the unthinkable. Would have forced her to use her skills for the Führer, too, if she hadn't slipped out of her bedroom window in the middle of the night and taken the first train out of Detroit.

Because there was no power on earth that would make her follow her parents' wishes and cast her lot with Hitler and his plan for Germany.

CHAPTER TWO

Beau watched Edie as she headed for the stairs. He'd been wrong about her hair. It wasn't black, but a thick veil of darkest brown, the color of ripe pecans, the palest strands capturing the spark of lantern light, falling over her shoulders in silky waves. And her eyes weren't the light brown he'd envisioned, but a startling shade of blue-green that reminded him of the seas off the coast of Africa.

So this was Merrilee's protector.

"Pretty, isn't she?" his aunt said, stepping into place beside him. "And smart, too. Do you know that she's a draftsperson over at the bomber plant?"

Hadn't even been home two seconds and Merrilee was trying her hand at matchmaking. Well, she'd have to be disappointed. He had too much to do at the moment. Looping his arm around his aunt's trim waist, he turned to smile. "Well, I've only got time

30

for one beautiful woman right now."

"Yeah, right," Merrilee scoffed. "The least you could have done was to let me know you were coming."

"And ruin the surprise?" Truth was, he wasn't sure he'd come home to Marietta, but there was nowhere else to go, and he'd promised to look out for his aunt.

Merrilee laughed, her hand at the crook of his arm, her fingers tightening against his elbow as if she thought he might disappear. "I can't believe you're home."

"I missed my favorite aunt."

"You silly boy!" The light swat to his arm reminded him of when they were kids. "I'm your only aunt!"

Beau chuckled then, startling himself with the sound. When was the last time he'd laughed? Too long, probably sometime before the war. Certainly not once during his time at the prison camp in Moosberg, though he had found reasons to smile at times. After all, the Lord was with him even there.

"I'll confess." Grabbing her hand, Beau pulled her down into the chair opposite his. "My stomach missed you. After all, you are the only one in the family who knows how to cook."

"Oh, my goodness! I haven't even asked if

you were hungry." Merrilee gestured to a table laden with covered bowls and plates against the far wall. "And if you can't find anything there, I've got some leftover chicken out in the kitchen."

"Maybe later. Thanks."

The muted creaks and moans of the house filled the silence. Should he bring up what had really brought him back home, the promise he had made concerning her?

"I guess you heard about your daddy?" Merrilee asked.

Beau felt his insides tighten. He didn't give a hoot what James Daniels was up to. But he couldn't tell Merrilee that, not without breaking her heart. His aunt probably still loved her brother despite his obvious transgressions. "He's not dead, is he?"

"Don't say such a thing," she whispered, her cheeks suddenly pale.

Beau nodded. Of course his father wasn't dead. A man that mean wouldn't do everyone a favor and just die. "So what's going on with Dad?"

"He's in jail."

The way she said it, barely above a whisper, made Beau sigh. People from good families didn't go to jail, or at least that's what most people believed. Well, James might have come from a good family, but he'd never been a good person. "I can't say I'm not surprised. Dad's been tiptoeing around the law for as far back as I can remember."

"Beau!"

"Aunt Merri, you know it's the truth. My old man's been bootlegging whiskey since I was a kid."

"He wasn't always like that." She pressed her lips into a quivering line. "When we were little, James was the one who would give you the shirt right off his back."

Yeah, he'd heard Dad was once a good man, just hurting deep down in the black of his soul. Beau wouldn't know. He'd been too busy running from the beatings his dad deemed necessary after Beau's mother left home. "What did he do?"

"I don't even know where to begin." She hesitated, then the words poured out of her like one of those geysers he'd seen in his time out West. By the time she finished, even Beau was stunned by the magnitude of his father's supposed crimes. "He would have killed that girl if she hadn't landed that plane when she did."

"Is the woman okay?"

Merrilee nodded. "Last we heard, she was back home working with a doctor to strengthen her leg, but yes, she's fine."

33

"Maybe you could get me her address. I'd like to see if there's anything she needs."

Merrilee studied him for a moment, the brittle lines around her eyes and mouth softening. "I've been praying you would come back home for years, ever since that day you ran off with the Civil Conservation Corp. You were always so determined to be anywhere else but here."

Beau couldn't deny it. He'd never wanted to come back to Marietta, not as long as his father still lived. He'd been honest with Ms. Michaels. If it hadn't been for Merrilee, he probably would have headed back out to California. But he had made a promise to John at the shipyard before the older man had sailed off to the Pacific: provide for Merrilee, keep her safe. It was the only thing John Davenport had ever asked of him. "When the army decided to cut me loose, this was the place I wanted to be."

"So what are you going to do, now that you're home?"

"I don't know. I was a medic in the army and thought maybe I'd volunteer at the hospital before I made any decisions."

"That's a wonderful idea. And you know —" Merrilee smiled at him "— Edie volunteers over there a few days a week. I bet she'd be happy to introduce you around."

34

Beau wasn't so sure about that. "You'd better ask her first."

"Sure, I will." His aunt eyed him from head to toe. "Didn't they feed you over there? You're as skinny as a rail."

His gut clenched into a ball. No need to tell her about the prison camp right outside of Moosberg he'd been held at for the last year. The muscles in his cheeks hurt from the smile he gave her. "Folks don't join the army for the grub."

"I know, but . . ."

"I'm fine, Aunt Merri. And if there was something wrong, it's nothing that your home cooking won't cure."

"Then you need to eat." Merrilee stood and bustled over to the table. "Are you sure you don't want me to fix you a sandwich?"

Beau glanced over at her, bustling over plates and bowls of food. This was the Merrilee he remembered, always the mother hen caring for her brood. "Truth is, I'm ready to hit the sack. That is, if you've got a place for me."

She answered with a smile. "I've already got a bed made up, as long as you don't mind sleeping in the attic."

It beat the slatted planks he'd been forced to use as a bed this past year. "Sounds perfect. I'm going to grab a glass of milk, then head on up."

"If you need anything, just let me know." Merrilee cupped his face in her hands and brushed a soft kiss across his brow.

"Thanks, Merrilee. And good night." Beau stood, watching her go, the lamplight flickering down the hall before fading into darkness.

Pouring himself a large cup of milk, Beau walked across the room and slid down into the high-backed chair. He was home, but now what? He made a short list in his head of things he needed to check into around town before his thoughts turned back to his father.

Wrapping his hands around the cool porcelain, Beau took a long draw of milk. Surely, Merrilee didn't expect him to find his father a lawyer. Last thing he wanted to do was put any effort into helping his dad, but how could he not? Merrilee had been so upset, worried James wouldn't have anyone to defend him. Maybe she hadn't considered that James had used up all his second chances.

If that's the truth, then there's not much hope for me.

Edie's words came back to him. She seemed like a good sort, but what had she meant by that? Had someone in her life let her down so much that she didn't think she deserved a break?

It didn't matter. Beau had bigger problems to take care of and a promise to keep. He swallowed the last of the milk then stood. He needed sleep right now, or he wouldn't be able to function tomorrow.

As he walked toward the table to deposit his glass, he noticed a scrap of paper, torn around the edges, peeking out from under the table. Reaching down, he picked it up and unfolded it. It looked like the first page of a letter.

Scanning the text, Beau's heart went into overdrive, the air in his lungs trapped in a vise. No wonder Edie Daniels thought she was doomed. He'd escaped one enemy only to be met by another, more beautiful one. Well, he wouldn't be suckered in by a pretty face, not when he had a promise to keep. His eyes slipped over the scribblings once more. Though it was written years ago, the language and the person to whom it was addressed was undeniable.

Meine tochtor, Edwina.

Blast, Beau Daniels!

Edie leaned her cheek into the palm of her hand, her elbow resting on her dressing table as she stared into the beveled mirror, the pressed powder she'd applied doing little to mask the dark smudges under her eyes. The sheets on her bed lay in a tangled heap from her constant tossing and turning in the hours after she had gone to bed last night.

Why couldn't the man use the front door like a normal person rather than climb in through the window like a thief in the night? Granted, it had been left unlocked for him, but she couldn't help feeling he was up to something, sneaking around like that.

I don't have anywhere else to go.

Edie frowned at the memory. The words had sounded so sincere, as if Beau had just grasped the truth in his statement as he said it. An odd sort of tenderness welled up inside her. It must have been hard, living under the same roof as James Daniels, horrible man that he was.

And Beau probably picked up some of his father's meanness, too.

A quick glance at the clock on the hearth sent her rushing to put the last touches on her hair before she stood up. Grabbing her purse, hat and gloves, she was barely across the room when the door slid open.

Claire Davenport, Merrilee's ten-year-old daughter, poked her head inside. "Momma wanted me to see if you were still in bed.

She thought you might have overslept."

"No, just running late this morning, that's all." She grabbed her sweater from the hook off the back of the door.

"I doubt you'll need a sweater. It's going to be another scorcher today."

Edie bit back a grin. It hadn't taken her long to figure out that Claire's biggest wish was to be older, or at least old enough to matter. But this time, the young girl was right. Spring had arrived with a vengeance, bringing with it sweltering heat. Throwing her sweater on a chair, Edie followed Claire out into the hall, shutting the door behind them.

"I heard you met my cousin last night," Claire said as they reached the staircase. "What's he like?"

Edie stared down at the girl. "Don't you know him?"

"No." Claire slid her hand along the smooth surface of the oak banister. "But Momma told me stories about him."

The slight curiosity she felt annoyed Edie. "What kind of stories?"

"You know." Claire pursed her lips together in a childish pucker. "Like he was smart and that he played first base in high school before he ran away."

"Your mother told you that Beau ran away

from home?"

The little girl dropped her chin to her chest. "I didn't mean to listen, but Momma was talking to my cousin Maggie about my daddy and she mentioned how hard it was when Beau ran away." She looked up at Edie through pale lashes. "I'm sorry."

"I'm not the one you need to be apologizing to, sweetheart."

"I've got to tell Momma?" Claire whined.

Edie draped her arm around the little girl's shoulders and brought her close. "You know it's the right thing to do."

"I just wanted to know more about my daddy." Claire sighed. "At least now, I'll have Cousin Beau around — to ask him questions. He was really good friends with Daddy."

Edie's throat tightened at Claire's words. Ever since it was discovered that John Davenport had signed over the deed of the Daniels homestead to Merrilee, Claire had developed an insatiable curiosity about her father. Hopefully, Beau Daniels would have enough sense not to fill the young girl's head with nonsense about her absent father.

A tug at her sleeve drew her attention. "So? What's my cousin like?"

"I really didn't get the chance to talk to him, honey." She started back down the stairs, Claire close behind her.

"Is he handsome?" Claire asked when they reached the bottom.

Butterflies fluttered around her midsection. Edie walked to the ornate mirror Merrilee had hung near the front door and dropped her purse and gloves on the bench. "Why in the world would you ask something like that?"

"Momma says that the only way you can learn anything is by asking lots of questions," Claire replied quietly. Pale green eyes stared back at her in the mirror, her warm body pressed close to her side, the scent of Ivory soap and sunshine reminding Edie just how young Claire was.

Lord, keep her heart safe. I'd hate to see it get broken like mine. She bent to brush a kiss against the girl's soft hair. "Your mother's right, Claire Bear. It's always good to ask questions."

Claire leaned back to stare straight up at her, giving her a hopeful smile. "Then is he handsome?"

Edie lifted her hat to her head, moving it from one side to the other, trying to decide how to best answer Claire's question. It annoyed her that Beau Daniels was so attractive. Even in the dim light of the lantern, he had been devastatingly handsome. But as

Merrilee was fond of saying, the physical was just packaging. What was Beau like on the inside, where it counted?

"I guess some would say that your cousin is a nice-looking man." Edie pushed her hat pin into the gray felt. "Not that it matters."

"I guess you're right." Claire sighed. "Though I like the idea of coming from a good-looking family."

Turning, Edie cupped the young girl's chin in the palm of her hand. "You know what your mother says. Beautiful is only skin deep, but ugly goes clean to the bone."

"Sounds like Aunt Merri."

Edie and Claire looked toward the stairway to where Beau Daniels occupied the bottom step. How long had he been standing there? And more important, how much had he overheard?

"Cousin Beau?" Claire took a step toward the man, then stopped.

There was no mistaking the confusion in his eyes when his gaze met Edie's over the little girl's head. Claire had told her that Beau had left before she was born. Was it possible the man didn't know anything about his aunt's child? "I don't believe you've been properly introduced. Beau Daniels, this is Claire Davenport, Merrilee's daughter."

"Merrilee's . . ." His voice drifted off. He covered the short distance between them, then knelt in front of the child, his gaze moving over Claire's oval face. "*Claire.* That's a beautiful name."

"It's my grandma's name."

"Yes, I know. She was my grandma, too."

Claire giggled. "Of course she was. We're cousins, silly."

The smile Beau gave the girl made Edie's heart pound like rivets against steel that filled the air outside her office door at the bomber plant. "Except I think you're a bit prettier than I am."

Claire giggled again, her cheeks turning a delightful shade of pink. "You really think so?"

Beau nodded. "Yes, I do. You look the spitting image of your momma."

"What about my daddy? Do I look anything like him?"

Edie's chest tightened. How was Beau going to handle Claire's endless stream of questions about the man? A father who had betrayed her, much like Edie's own.

Beau touched the tip of the little girl's nose. "You've got your daddy's smile."

Edie let out the breath she had been holding. So far, so good. But what would happen when Claire's questions got tougher?

Would Beau fill her head with useless fairy tales about a man who'd never had anything to do with her or her mother? Sure, he'd signed over the house to Merrilee, but it should have been hers in the first place. Edie would have to keep an eye on him. She wasn't about to stand by while Beau Daniels broke Claire's tender heart.

CHAPTER THREE

"Did you hear that?" Claire stared back at Edie, her green eyes shining. "I have my daddy's smile."

"That's lovely, sweetheart."

The slight edge of concern in her voice told Beau that Edie Michaels wasn't crazy about the direction this conversation had taken. Well, that was too bad. One look at this little girl who shared Merrilee's eyes and her father's impish grin, and he'd been lost. At least, his aunt wasn't as alone as he'd thought, but now the promise he'd made to John took on more importance. There was a child involved — John's daughter. A protectiveness he'd always felt toward Merrilee grew with each girlish giggle from Claire.

"Don't you need to get ready for school?" Edie asked.

Claire's face fell. "But I still have a lot of questions to ask Beau."

45

Beau cupped her cheek in one palm and tilted her chin up to meet his gaze. "I'm not going anywhere anytime soon, sweetie pie. So I'll be around for you to ask as many questions as you want to."

Claire flung her arms around his shoulders and buried her face in his neck. "So you'll tell me more about my daddy?"

Beau wrapped his arms around her slight body and glanced up at Edie. Why did the woman look so worried? Was something going on here that he didn't know about? He pressed a kiss into Claire's hair, then pulled back to look at her. "You need to hurry. Don't want you missing the bus and getting me in trouble with your momma, now do we?"

She hopped out of his embrace, then leaned back in to give him a wet kiss on his cheek. "I'm glad you're home, Cousin Beau."

"Me, too, kiddo." Beau watched the little girl race up the stairs, stumbling over her feet like a newborn colt yearning to break out in a run. John would be so proud. His daughter certainly knew how to wrap someone around her little finger.

"Do you think that was such a good idea?"

Beau glanced over his shoulder at Edie. The housecoat she had worn the night before hadn't done her justice. The sky-blue shirt tucked into a slate-colored skirt complemented her lithe form and shapely legs. A dove-gray hat sat nestled above a loose knot of chestnut curls gathered at the nape of her neck. The woman really was a looker, probably one of the loveliest girls he'd ever seen.

And German.

Meine tochtor, Edwina. The phrase had played through Beau's mind well into the early hours of the morning. He knew enough of the language to know it was an endearment, something a mother or grand-mother might write. But what if the whole thing was just a cover, to send everyone chasing the wrong rabbit down the hole while Edie gave plans for the B-29 to her German comrades.

Beau grimaced. He'd tended to men ripped apart by Nazi bullets, carried the stains of their blood on his soul while he'd tended to their wounds as they died on the enemy's soil. No, something about Edie's letter bothered him, and until he found out more about her situation, he planned on watching her like a hawk.

Beau shook the thoughts from his head as he stood to face her. "Don't you think Claire needs to know a little something about her father?"

Irritation flashed in her blue-green eyes. "Not if she's going to be hurt."

Hurt Claire? Beau clenched his hands into tight fists. He'd no more cause pain to that little girl than he would himself. "Now why do you think it would hurt Claire to know a little about her father?"

"It's just that ever since we learned John Davenport bought this house and signed it over to Merrilee, Claire's talked of nothing else but her father." She hesitated, a glimpse of pain streaking across her face then, just as suddenly, gone. "The man abandoned her and her mother."

Heat flooded Beau's veins, and it took everything inside him not to lash out at her. "There are two sides to every story, Ms. Michaels."

Edie crossed her arms over her waist, digging her fingers into the cotton material of her shirt. "Well, he's not here to tell us his side, now is he?"

No, and with good reason. Beau glanced around the room, choosing to ignore her question by asking one of his own. "Why hasn't Merrilee told Claire anything about her daddy?"

Edie shrugged. "I don't know. Probably

felt that the less Claire knew about him, the better."

Beau scrubbed a hand over his face. This didn't make sense. John had loved the idea of having a child with Merrilee. It was all he talked about on those long days, shoveling asphalt along the winding highways near Hoover Dam. How he couldn't wait to get home to start his life with Merrilee.

Then one day, everything changed, and John never spoke of Merrilee and home again.

And what about Merrilee? His aunt had never been the type to harbor bad feelings for ten minutes, much less ten years. So why hadn't she told Claire more about her father?

"I don't understand." The words came out before Beau could think to stop them.

"Most people don't when it comes to a parent giving up on their child."

Grabbing her purse from the bench, Edie opened the latch and rifled through it, as if looking for answers that eluded them both. But there had been no mistaking the hitch in her voice. This situation with Claire bothered her, but it hadn't caused the faint lines that had settled in the corners of her eyes. Had Edie experienced that kind of rejection? Did it have anything to do with

49

the letter he'd found last night?

He shook the thought aside for the moment. "What if John doesn't know about Claire?"

"Maggie says your aunt sent him letters every week, right up until he served her with the divorce papers."

"We were all over the West Coast, Ms. Michaels. Letters get lost."

"Maybe one or two, but Maggie said there were dozens." She grimaced. "Why are you so determined to think John doesn't know about Claire?"

"Because I know him. He's like a brother to me. And if he knew he had a kid, John would do whatever it took to get home, whether Uncle Sam liked it or not."

Her chin raised a notch, almost as if she were throwing down a challenge. "You seem so sure of yourself."

"I am."

"Then tell me, Mr. Daniels. Why do you think John has never heard about his daughter?"

Beau couldn't decide whether to shake that smug look off her face, or kiss her. He compromised. His fingers gently clamped over the soft curve of her chin. "Because until I saw Claire a few minutes ago, I didn't know about her myself."

■ ■ ■ ■

Beau entered the dining room, feeling cleaner and more rested than he had in the month since leaving the hospital. Usually, the nightmares woke him, but last night, he'd drifted off to sleep, the German words from Edie's letter chasing him around until he'd finally succumbed to a dreamless sleep. Better than the nightmares of the prison camp.

His stomach gave a painful growl at the heavenly aroma of fried bacon and strong coffee filling his lungs. He could get used to three squares a day after months of gnawing hunger, wondering where his next bite of food was coming from.

If only he could hold his tongue with Edie Michaels. Frustration ripped through him. Women had never given him much trouble, but this one . . .

This one was something else.

"I've got you a seat right here, Beau." Claire pulled a high-back chair from under the table, the wooden legs making a low thud against the scratched hardwood floors.

"All right, squirt." Beau nodded before his gaze drifted to a young woman eyeing him from the end of the table. "Maggie?"

"How are you doing, Beau?"

Beau smiled. He hadn't heard that voice since the night he'd left, and while it had taken on a more feminine tone, he could still picture the stubborn little wildcat with the reddish-gold ponytail that Maggie had been. He gave a low whistle. "Wow, Magpie. I bet Uncle Jeb has to beat the men off with a baseball bat."

"Would you please not call me that?" Her lips quirked up in a faint smile. "I am, after all, an engaged woman."

"Old Man Bailey down at the train station told me." Leaning forward, Beau grabbed the coffeepot from its spot on the table and poured himself a cup. "Said you were marrying you a pilot."

"Captain Wesley Hicks," Claire answered, pressing up against Beau's side.

"Thank you, squirt." Beau smiled at the little girl then turned his attention back to his older cousin. "Margaret Hicks. It's got a good sound to it."

"I like it."

Beau turned toward the doorway. A man, tall with blond hair, stood wearing the dark green uniform of the United States Army.

Stuffing his hat under his arm, the man held out his hand. "Wesley Hicks. Merrilee told us you came home late last night."

"And liked to scare poor Edie to death," Maggie added.

"Really?" Claire asked, her eyes sparkling.

"No." Beau gently squeezed Claire's shoulder before turning to shake Wesley's hand. Firm grip. Maggie had done well for herself. "Ms. Michaels did a pretty good job of holding me off with a fire poker."

"Poor girl. Everyone interrupts her during her quiet time." Maggie snorted out a girlish laugh. "First Jimbo and his nightly drunks, and now you breaking in through the front window."

"The window?" Wesley looked first at Beau, then at Maggie.

"My cousin doesn't enter a room like normal people," Maggie said over the rim of her coffee cup. "He's been climbing in through Merrilee's parlor window since he was nine."

Beau shot a glance at Maggie. He probably deserved that dig for all the times he'd tortured her growing up. He'd only realized later how horrible it must have been for her. A case of monkey see, monkey do. An apology was in order the next chance he got. Beau picked up a cup and handed it to Wesley. "So you're the guy marrying my cousin?"

"As soon as I can get her to the altar."

Wesley took the coffee cup from Beau. His gaze settled on Maggie, and a faint smile played on his lips. "Though it can't be fast enough for me."

Maggie smiled back at him. "Me, either."

Beau busied himself pouring cream in his coffee, all the while stealing glances at the couple. Maggie glowed with happiness. They both did. Was this what real love looked like? Not that he would know. Mom had left years ago. Said living with Dad and a houseful of boys was too tough.

Beau took a deep breath. Well, good for Maggie. She'd always been a good egg, putting up with all the tricks he had played on her when they were growing up. Maybe, just maybe she had a chance at finding real happiness.

"Congratulations to you both," Beau said.

"Thank you. We appreciate it." Maggie pushed back from the table and stood. "I hate to cut this little reunion short, but I've got to get going. I'm supposed to meet Edie in an hour."

Beau watched her round the table and place her dirty plate in a dish pan. Maybe Maggie could answer some questions he had about Edie Michaels.

Like why someone would write to her in German?

When he pushed back from the table, a small hand covered his sleeve. "Where are you going?"

Leaning forward until his forehead touched hers, Beau brushed his nose against Claire's. "I'll be right back."

Her girlish giggles chased him out into the hall. Maggie stood in front of the mirror, a bobby pin clenched between her teeth as she tucked a curl behind her ear, pinning it there. Her green eyes met his in the glass. "Couldn't get enough of me at breakfast?"

That was Maggie, always teasing. "I've got some questions for you if you don't mind."

She stuck the last pin in her hair and turned to face him. "What's up?"

He stuck his hands in his pockets. "How well do you know Edie Michaels?"

"Why do you ask?"

Typical Maggie. Even as a kid, she always answered a question with one of her own. But he couldn't tell her the truth, that he had Edie's letter, that he intended to keep it until he knew some truths.

Like was the woman a patriot or a traitor?

"Just wondering," Beau finally answered.

Maggie cocked her head to one side, a vague smile playing on her lips. "You're interested in her, aren't you?"

Yes, but not for the reasons his cousin

thought. "I'm always partial to a woman who takes a swing at me."

"You deserved it, sneaking up on her like that." Maggie folded her arms across her waist. "Why don't you ask her yourself?"

"And give her the chance to take another swing at me? No, thanks!"

"She really spooked you, huh?"

"Let's just say I'd like to know her without the poker in her hand."

"Fair enough." Maggie laughed. "So what is it you'd like to know?"

"Anything."

"Well." She tapped the tip of her index finger against her chin. "She's from some small town just outside of Detroit, but moved down here when Abner Ellerbee hired her on as his secretary over at the bomber plant."

Beau grimaced. Ellerbee wasn't as bad as his father, but he came in a close second. "Why would she do that? There are tons of war industry jobs in that part of the country. She could have stayed closer to home."

"Not if she wanted the kind of opportunities Bell's been willing to give her."

"A secretary?"

"Edie got a promotion a couple of weeks ago," Maggie replied, her voice filled with pride. "She works in the drafting department now, drawing the technical sketches for the assembly line."

Dear Lord! Was that what Edie Michaels had been hoping for from the start, to maneuver her way into a position with complete access to the most intricate details of the United States's greatest hope to win the war?

A knock at the door fragmented his thoughts. He glanced at Maggie. "It's kind of early for folks, isn't it?"

Maggie walked over to the front door. "Not since the war. We get visitors at all hours of the day or night." She threw him a teasing smile. "And occasionally through the front window."

"Very funny. You're never going to let me live that down, are you?"

"Not until we're old and gray." Maggie opened the door just enough for Beau to see the flash of tin and a gun harnessed in black leather at the man's hip. She stepped out of the way. "Come on in, Mack."

Beau hadn't seen Mack Worthington since their days at McEachern High School, playing baseball for Coach Fuller. While most on the team dreamed of playing in the big leagues, Mack had a different goal. To be Marietta's sheriff.

"Well, look at you." Beau glanced down at

the badge pinned to his friend's shirt and smiled. "I can't believe they gave you a gun. You couldn't even throw straight."

"Home run hitters didn't need to know anything besides hitting the ball and running around the bases." His old friend clapped him on the back. "Which is more than I can say for you. I heard you were back in town."

Mack never pulled any punches. "Figured it was time I came home."

"If you gentlemen will excuse me, I have a job to get to." Maggie tugged on the knot holding her scarf in place, then grabbed her lunch bag and purse.

"Thank you, Maggie." The lawman fumbled with his hat, circling the felt rim with his fingers. "I'm sorry to barge in, but I thought I might have a word with Beau."

"Sure." Beau nodded toward the dining room. "You want some coffee?"

"That would be good."

"Merrilee's just made a fresh pot before she left."

A few minutes later, they settled around the table, steaming cups of Merrilee's brew making misty swirls above the rims of the china cups. They settled around the dining room table, the lawman at the head of the table, Wesley and Beau flanking his sides.

Wesley had had the good sense to send Claire upstairs to finish dressing for school. No telling what the sheriff had to say.

Mack reached for the miniature pitcher of milk and poured a generous helping in his steaming cup. "I'm sorry to bother you on your first morning home, Beau, but this just couldn't wait a minute longer."

Beau leaned back in his chair. "What has the old man done now?"

If Mack was surprised, he didn't show it. He picked up his cup, curling his fingers around the dainty china. "He knows you're back home and he wants to see you."

Ten years Beau had been gone, and the minute he hits town, the old man starts making demands. Well, Beau had some business to take care of — getting a job, for one thing, so he could take care of Merrilee and Claire, fulfilling his promise to the only man who'd cared for him like a son.

Beau shrugged. "Dad's going to have to wait."

Resting his arms along the edge of the table, Mack leaned forward. "I figured that's what you'd say, but Beau —" He paused. "He's made some threats, promised he'd make our lives at the jail a bit rough if you don't come by and see him in the next day or two."

Beau laughed over the rim of his coffee cup. "Since when did an old man's threats scare the Marietta police force?"

"He doesn't, but the last time your daddy started trouble, we had to transfer six prisoners down to the federal pen for medical care, most of them Negroes. Almost had a race riot all because he didn't think he got his mail quick enough."

Beau ground his back teeth together. So Dad had figured out the reason he'd left home all those years ago, and even now, wanted to use it against him. Controlling . . . Beau forced the curse that came to mind out of his thoughts. *I am a new creature in Christ.* So why did his dad's threats still bother him? Because now, as then, lives hung in the balance.

Beau stood up and paced across the room to the window. "Do you think he's bluffing?"

"I don't know." Several seconds passed as Mack lifted his cup to his lips and took a sip. "He put up a pretty good fight the day he got arrested."

"Don't I remember!" Wesley chuckled. "Gave me a nice sock in the eye."

Beau pulled back the curtain and looked out over the front porch. "Why can't the old man just stay out of trouble?"

There was a silence, as if the two men were giving serious thought to his ridiculous question, before Mack spoke again. "Any thoughts about who's going to represent him?"

Turning back toward them, Beau shook his head. "Not really. I'm not even sure he's got the money to hire a lawyer."

"Has your father got any savings?" Mack asked, placing the cup back in the saucer.

"Hasn't trusted a bank since the Crash." Beau scrubbed the back of his neck. "I've got a little, but nothing compared to what he's going to need."

"What about his house?"

Wesley stared at Beau. "I didn't know James had a house. I mean, he's lived here since before I moved in."

"He probably thought it was his best shot at keeping an eye on Merrilee." Beau blew out a deep breath, then looked at Mack. "You think I could get enough from his house to pay for a lawyer?"

Mack shook his head. "Not the way it is. James let it go to waste after you boys left."

"That bad?" But Mack didn't have to answer. The hard downward pull of his mouth spoke volumes. Beau chewed on the tough skin around his thumbnail. Why was he worrying over this mess? It wasn't his problem to clean up. And he'd never intended on helping his father escape punishment — not after what that man had done to Merrilee and Maggie, and if he was completely honest, to their family. If convicted, James Daniels would spend the rest of his life rotting in jail. He lowered his gaze to the tablecloth, brooding over the intricate stitches. The old man had done it again, putting Beau in an impossible situation, counting on his son to get him out of it.

Well, Beau was done with him. He might take a look at the house and see what he could repair to get the place sold, but that was it. No more cleaning up his father's messes. No more.

I am a new person in Christ. The old has passed away.

Beau pushed the palm of his hand into the aching muscles of his leg. He'd been on the same path as his father and the Lord had changed him, loved him, made him new. Could God work the same sort of miracle in James's life as well? "I'll go out to the house and see what needs to be done."

Mack leaned back in his chair. "You can always asked for a court-appointed lawyer, Beau."

But Beau shook his head. If he wanted

God to work in his father's life, he had to be willing to do his part, too.

"You might want to get someone who knows something about houses. Just from looking at it, I'd say you may have some problems with the weight-bearing walls," Mack said. "An architect could tell you what the problem is."

Beau plowed his fingers through his hair. First a lawyer, now an architect. "Where am I going to find one of those around here?"

"God must be smiling on you, my friend, because there's one living right here in Merrilee's boardinghouse." Wesley leaned to one side, resting his cheek on his fisted hand. "And you've already met her."

CHAPTER FOUR

Edie bit the inside of her lip as she placed the slide ruler on the crisp sheet of parchment, quickly casting a glance at the anchors that held it to her angled desk. Pressing the sharp edge of the protractor against the metal, she traced the tip of her pencil lightly across the page, then stopped to study it. She couldn't afford to make any mistakes in the updated drawings, not when the fighting men of the Army Air Force depended on it.

"Edie?"

She peered over the top of her desk and smiled as Maggie stood at the door. "Well, hey, you."

Maggie studied the layout of the room, much like Edie imagined she did while in the cockpit of the B-29. Once she had the target in her sights, she headed toward her, her purposeful stride chewing up the floor until she stood at the edge of Edie's desk.

She glanced around the empty room. "Where is everyone?"

"The dining hall." Edie leaned back, stretching her crossed legs out underneath the desk. "Ruthie Clark made several of her juicy chocolate cakes from Major Evans's private stash of Hershey bars. First come, first serve."

"A piece of that cake's worth a month of rations," Maggie replied, rubbing her hands together. "So when are you going to take a lunch break?"

"Not today." Edie released the screws of the anchors holding the blueprints until the paper popped free. Carefully, she rolled it into a tight scroll and placed it into its protective case. "Got to get these changes out."

"You've got to eat."

"I know. This is the third set this week and it's only Tuesday." Edie blew out a deep sigh. "And I don't want to disappoint Mr. Ellerbee."

"He's blessed to have you."

She nodded, though she wouldn't exactly call herself a blessing. Abner Ellerbee had taken a chance on her. As one of the few women draftsmen at the plant, military documents crossed her desk on a daily basis. If she'd chosen Germany like her parents . . .

"What happened to your test flight this morning?" Edie took out another sheet of clean paper. "I figured I wouldn't see you around for the next couple of days."

"A problem with the preflight check. Nothing big, but Wesley wanted one of the mechanics to take a look before he gave the okay."

Edie shot her friend a sideways glance. "He's very protective of you, isn't he?"

"Yes." Color infused Maggie's cheeks, giving her a subtle glow that only complemented her girl-next-door good looks. "And the funny thing about it is, I'm actually enjoying it."

Edie leaned forward, resting her elbows on her desk. "I think it's kind of sweet."

"Merrilee was right. Love changes everything."

Edie lowered her gaze to the blank paper, the happiness radiating from her friend's face a reminder of her own dim future. Hope lit Maggie's smile. Edie could only pray she never lost it.

"Oh, Edie." Warm, slender fingers closed over her forearm. "When you meet the man God has just for you, you'll know it."

The image of Beau Daniels, his russet hair slicked back, his green eyes filled with gentle concern at her pitiful attempt to hold him off with an iron poker flashed through her mind. She didn't even know the man, except that he was James Daniels's son — and that wasn't saying much.

Who was she to judge? The pencil in her hand trembled against the paper. Her parents had abandoned their home, left everyone they knew, all for the ravings of a madman.

Edie stared at a collection of dust bunnies gathered in the corner. At least Beau knew what his father was capable of and had adapted.

Unlike herself.

She shut her eyes, the memories of that morning almost four years ago flooding through her. Shattered plates. The acrid smell of burnt toast. Even now, breakfast turned her stomach. Her ears still rang with the anger in her father's voice. Edie reached up and touched her cheek where her father had struck her when she refused to go to Berlin.

"Don't think you can hide from us forever, Edwina! The Bund is a very powerful German American group, and we will find you!"

Edie swallowed. *Keep me hidden, Lord.*

Silence hung in the air for the next few seconds. "I heard you met my cousin last night. Merrilee should have warned us that she always kept the front window unlocked for him."

"It was fine once I knew who he was," Edie answered, stealing a glance at her friend's face. If Maggie thought it odd that her cousin entered the house through an open window, her expression didn't show it.

"Good," Maggie replied. "I think he might be worried that he made the wrong impression on you."

Edie glanced over at her. "Why would you say that?"

"He asked me some questions this morning, and I couldn't help feeling that he wanted to know more about you."

Her heart sped up to a nervous rhythm in her chest. "Why would he do that?"

"Because you're absolutely wonderful, that's why!"

"I don't think he got that out of our conversation last night." Or this morning, for that matter.

"You never know." Maggie gave her a sly smile. "I had to go before we had a chance to talk. I figure we'll catch up once I have a break."

Edie's stomach knotted in panic. Why would Beau Daniels be nosing around her? What would he do if he learned the whole truth? That there were people after her, ready to send her to Germany?

"What's wrong?"

"Nothing." Edie's hands shook as she slipped her drafting tools into their case. "I just don't think it's such a good idea to encourage him."

"Why not? He's obviously interested in you."

Edie's heart skipped a beat, and she grimaced. "I don't know, Maggie. It's just that I'm not interested in a relationship right now."

"But I thought . . ."

"I've just started a new job." Edie's heart began to beat faster and for once, she was glad of her bulky desk so that Maggie didn't see her trembling legs. "Plus, you've always complained about how your cousins bullied you."

Maggie ran her hand down the long angle of her drafting table. "I know, but Beau was different. He looked out for me even after he left home."

Her eyebrows furrowed in confusion. "What do you mean?"

"A couple of weeks after he went into the Civil Conservation Corp, I started junior high school. I must have told him how nervous I was because when I went to my locker that first morning, I found a note from him. He was so encouraging. For the next two weeks, he made sure I had a note in my locker." Maggie smiled softly. "I've still got those letters."

Edie cleared the sudden knot in her throat. "That was very sweet of him."

"That's the kind of guy Beau is."

Edie nodded, not sure how to respond. This piece of information seemed to contradict everything Beau Daniels had hinted to her the night before about his unscrupulous life. And yet, it didn't strike her as out of character. If he would go to such lengths to comfort a teenage Maggie, what would he do to protect his family from someone like her? A hunted woman?

"Then he shouldn't have any problems finding a date around here." A vague sense of melancholy drifted through Edie.

Maggie nodded, her shoulders slightly rounded in surrender. "I guess you're right. I was just hoping the two of you might hit it off."

"Of course," Edie answered. "You're marrying the man you love, and you want everyone else in the world to feel that way, too."

"Not everyone, just my best friend."

Tears pricked Edie's eyes. She'd left so

much behind when she'd taken this job — not only family, but friends she'd known for most of her life. Maggie's friendship meant the world. Edie patted her arm. "So tell me. How are the wedding plans coming along? You and Wesley set a date yet?"

Maggie's face lit up with a bright smile. "That's why I'm here. I figured since I'm not flying out today, maybe we could start looking at material for my wedding gown, at least see how many rations I'm going to need to make a decent dress."

"You couldn't come up with a parachute?"

"Wesley's still working on it, but I'm not holding my breath. The man is chomping at the bit to get married." Maggie grabbed her hand, her mood infectious. "So what do you say? Want to come with me this afternoon? Merrilee is going to meet us at Goldstein's if she can find someone to watch Claire."

"Why doesn't she ask Beau? He and Claire seemed to be getting along well when I left them this morning."

"He can't," Maggie answered. "Said something about having an appointment this afternoon."

How could Beau Daniels already have some kind of engagement when he hadn't even crossed the county line twenty-four hours ago? "Did he say what it was?"

"Why?" A knowing grin slanted across her face. "Are you more interested than you let on?"

Maggie's remark hit too close to the truth. Edie smoothed down the rough edge of the paper. "I just think it's odd, that's all."

"Oh." That answer seemed to take the wind out of Maggie's sails. "So will you come with me?"

"I wish I could." Resting her elbow against her desk, Edie cupped her cheek in her hand. "But I'm scheduled to work at the hospital this afternoon."

"Oh, come on. Can't you just play hooky this once?"

With her free hand, Edie reached out to touch her friend's arm. "I would, but we're expecting a new batch of soldiers in, and I don't want to leave them shorthanded."

Maggie glanced up at her, her eyes luminous. "You're just the sweetest thing."

"I don't know about that." Edie laughed, the hard knot of guilt in her throat causing her short chuckle to be harsher than she'd like. "Tell you what. Why don't I meet you over at Goldstein's after I finish? Maybe we could go out for a bite to eat or something."

"I'm supposed to meet Wesley for supper." She bit the pink flesh of her lower lip. "Maybe you could meet up with us and have some dessert."

"You go ahead. By that time, I'll probably just want to go home anyway."

"Are you sure?"

No, but it had to be this way, at least until those determined to send her to Germany were out of the way. "Go. Have fun with your fiancé."

"Edie?"

She looked toward the masculine voice coming from the doorway. She'd been so deep in conversation with Maggie, she hadn't noticed her boss, Abner Ellerbee, walking toward them. "Yes, Mr. Ellerbee."

The older man stopped in front of her desk, his head and shoulders peering out over the angled desk top. "Maggie."

"Mr. Ellerbee," Maggie acknowledged, then turned back to Edie. "I'd better scoot. See you this evening back at Merrilee's."

Edie nodded. "You guys have a good time."

Maggie made her way across the room. Only when the door clicked shut did Mr. Ellerbee turn to face her. "How is everything going with the new job?"

"Very well, sir," Edie answered, unable to keep a smile from forming. Every day in the drafting department felt like a blessing.

"Anyone giving you a hard time?"

She understood his concerns. Some of the men hadn't taken too kindly to a woman doing what was generally thought of as a man's job, but she wasn't about to complain. "No, sir. In fact, I never worked with such a nice bunch of guys."

"Good." The older man's lips turned slightly upward into one of his rare smiles. "You're a hard worker, detailed and meticulous. Which is why I brought you this." Mr. Ellerbee held out a manila envelope. "The War Department sent me these this morning and asked me to put my best team on it. I'd like you to lead the group."

Edie didn't know how to feel. Thrilled out of her mind, of course. After all, this was what she had been working toward her entire career. But there was a thread of terror running through her, too. What if her father and the group of thugs he associated with found out she was working on the plans for the Super Fortress? Would they step up their efforts to find her and send her to Berlin? "Are you sure I'm the right person for the job, sir?"

"We knew what we were getting when we hired you, Edie. Your work speaks for itself." The soft smile he gave her reminded her of her father. "And we know how far you've gone to prove your loyalty to our country."

She nodded. "I'll do my best."

"I know you will." He dropped the envelope on her desk. "If you have any questions, just come by my office and I'll see if I can answer them."

"Yes, sir."

Edie waited until he'd left to pick up the envelope and tear open the seal. Mr. Ellerbee had always had so much faith in her — Maggie and Merrilee, too. If only she could believe everything would work out in the end. A verse Merrilee had read during one of their nightly devotionals quietly stole across her thoughts.

I can do all things through Christ who strengthens me.

Edie extracted the document and studied it. She knew the verse to be true, but sometimes, in the inky darkness of her bedroom, she found herself wondering if God would give someone like her the strength she needed to get through this war.

Or had God turned his back on the Germans, too?

Pushing her thoughts to the side, Edie reached for her pencil. Too bad she'd already promised Dr. Lovinggood she'd be at the hospital today. From the looks of things, she'd have to cut her shift at the hospital short just so she could come back later tonight to get a jump on this new project. She pulled out a sheet of paper and began making notes.

"I don't want a shot!"

A set of bright, fevered eyes stared up at Edie as she clasped the little girl's hand between hers. "I know, sweetheart, but let's wait and see what the doctor has to say, okay?"

Dr. Lovinggood linked his stethoscope around his neck. "Have we got a free bath-tub right now?"

"I'm sure I can find one."

"Good." The man rolled up his shirtsleeves as he walked over to the sink. "We've got to get her cooled down as soon as possible."

"Yes, sir."

"Before you go, I have some swabs over there on the countertop that need to go down to the lab." Lovinggood turned on the spigot and shoved his hands under the water. "Tell the lab assistant I want to see it once they've got the slides ready."

"Yes, sir." Edie stood back, her pencil flying over the paper, writing down instructions as Lovinggood barked them off like a general commanding his troops. No please or thank-you to anyone. Just more work.

When the lock on the door clicked shut behind the doctor, the girl turned to Edie. "He scares me."

"You want to know a secret?" Pocketing the instructions, she leaned close and pushed a piece of damp hair out of the child's face. "He scares me sometimes, too."

The child broke out in a smile despite her discomfort.

"Ready?" Edie gathered her up in her arms, concern racing through her at the warmth coming off the girl's fragile body. "I'm going to go get your momma, okay?"

The child gave her a slight nod.

Edie set the girl down gently, grabbed the swabs on the countertop behind her and turned toward the door. "I'll be right back, pumpkin."

She slipped into the hallway, her stomach churning like the propellers of a Super Fortress ready to fly at full speed. It had been the same in all three children admitted through the emergency room today — high fever, muscle weakness — and with this heat. She didn't like the diagnosis she kept coming back to. Polio.

"What are you doing here?"

Edie snapped her head toward the familiar male voice. How was it that she'd known Beau Daniels less than twenty four hours yet knew the cadence of his voice? "I could be asking you the same question."

"I'm here for an interview with Dr. Lovinggood." He fiddled with his tie, making it even more crooked than before. "One of the nurses told me he was up here."

"I haven't seen him in the last few minutes." She couldn't let him meet the doctor looking like that. Edie reached out and gently tugged him by the blue silk of his tie. "Come here."

He stretched his head back, giving her room to work. "I thought I'd done a pretty good job with it."

"Only if you were looking in the mirror cockeyed."

His laughter brushed against the backs of her fingers as she adjusted the knot. "I was supposed to keep my eyes open?"

Edie bit her lower lip. He really could be funny when he wanted to be. "Didn't anyone ever teach you how to do your own tie?"

"Never needed to working with the Civil Conservation Corp." He lifted his head again, but this time she felt his gaze following her. "By the time I got out of basic training, the army was shipping us out. Only use any of us had for a tie was as a tourniquet."

Edie gave the scrap of silk one last tug, her throat closing up at the thought of Beau or anyone else lying in a field somewhere with only a piece of fabric between them and death. She pressed her fingers gently against the silky knot at his throat. "Well, every man needs to learn how to tie a Windsor knot."

"Maybe you could teach me?"

Edie's midsection fluttered. If she had any sense at all, she'd step back from him, give herself a little room to think but her feet felt glued to the floor. "I'm sure Merrilee can help you."

"She's as out of practice as I am."

Beau was probably right. But Edie couldn't chance being that close. She was more than a little attracted to him and worried that the more time she spent getting to know him, the more difficult it would be when he learned the truth about her. "If you don't ask her, it may hurt Merrilee's feelings."

His brow furrowed into a straight line. "I don't want to do that."

Why did his concern for his aunt's feelings only make her like him even more? She had to get away from him. Edie headed toward the stairwell. "I'll see you later."

"Wait a minute," he called out, catching up to her in two long strides. "Where are you going?"

Why wouldn't he let her get back to work? So she could fill her mind with cheering up patients or running errands for Dr. Lovinggood, not wondering about the effect Beau Daniels had on her. "I was on my way down to the laboratory."

He held open the door for her. "Mind if I walk with you? Maybe we'll run into Lovinggood downstairs."

Oh, right, Beau's interview. A vague sense of disappointment flowed through her. What was she thinking? Of course, he was looking for the doctor. Why else would he want to walk with her? "Sure."

The door had barely shut behind them when a swish of stiff cotton turned her attention to the woman in white hurrying toward them. It was her friend, Gertie, a nurse from the Negro floor.

"What's got you running like a house on fire?" Beau asked, the corner of his mouth pulled up into a crooked smile.

Gertie's smooth brow wrinkled in confusion. "Beau? You're back home?"

Beau nodded beside Edie. "Came back last night."

Her friend's face lit up in a sudden smile. "I'm so glad."

Beau returned her smile with one of his own. "How's your mom and dad?"

"About the same. Daddy's driving the bus for the bomber plant and Momma still works for the Hendersons."

"I figured your momma would have quit Old Lady Henderson before now."

"A person's got to work."

Edie realized that Beau didn't just have a passing acquaintance with Gertie and her family, but an intimate friendship. But how? Edie spoke before she realized what she was doing. "How do you two know each other?"

"Beau and my brother George used to get into trouble when they were kids."

Beau leaned toward her, his breath warming her cheek. "We were friends."

Edie nodded, not quite sure what to make of this information. One thing she'd learned in the year since moving to Marietta was that whites and Negroes could be friendly to each other, but not friends. She stole a glance at Beau. But this man had bucked the norm, going against everything his society deemed proper and right.

Beau spoke before she had a chance to think any further. "So what's the rush?"

Gertie drew in a deep breath then blew it out before looking at Edie. "When was the last time you gave blood?"

Edie frowned. When one of the nurses asked that question, someone usually needed a transfusion. "Who?"

"One of the soldiers that just transferred in from Crawford Long is hemorrhaging pretty bad. He needs a couple of units and we've only got one."

Beau pressed his lips into a straight line. "Have you checked the floor's records to see who you could call that has the same blood type?"

Gertie nodded her head in disgust. "I've called the ones who have phones but so far, no one wants to donate right now. I'm writing up a letter and sending it out with my pastor. Maybe he can round somebody up."

"Why not call the other people on the list?" Edie met the young woman's gaze.

Gertie exchanged a look with Beau before turning back to Edie. "Most white folks around here don't like the idea of donating blood to a Negro."

"But that's silly. I mean, what does one thing have to do with another?"

"Dr. Lovinggood strikes me as the kind of doctor who wouldn't like to lose his job," Beau interjected with a sense of authority. "And I'm betting that there's a policy in place that restricts the use of blood from a white person in Negroes." He glanced at Gertie. "Am I right?"

Gertie's dark eyes met hers. "Beau's right.

It's against hospital policy."

Edie stretched her neck to the side. Stupid rule. From her reading on the subject, there appeared to be absolutely no sense behind such policy, only fear. She slid a sideways glance at Beau. The man puzzled her. He had gone against every social confine to be friends with Gertie's brother, yet now, stands silent against a rule that puts lives in jeopardy. Edie turned to Gertie. "Come on, Gertie. We've got to scrounge up some help for your patient."

"What are you going to do?"

"Talk to the people in the lab. See if they have any ideas that could help." When Edie glanced back at Beau, his expression spoke of suspicion and concern. She braced herself against further questions. "I hope everything goes well with your interview."

Beau grimaced, then turned to Gertie. "Don't do anything foolish." He glanced at the door, then back at them. "I need to find Dr. Lovinggood. I don't want to lose this job before I've even been offered it."

His quick steps echoed against the cinder blocks as he walked to the door. With the click of the door opening, he was gone.

Probably best this way. Beau wouldn't approve of her next move, not that she should care. It had been only a few days since her last donation to the blood bank. To give again so soon would leave her feeling weak for the next few days, maybe a week, but what was that compared to the service this young man had done for their country?

"We don't have to look any further for a donor." Edie pushed away from the wall. "I'll do it."

Gertie's eyes narrowed. "Are you sure about this? I can always send messengers out to the Negro communities until someone steps forward to help out."

But that would take time, time this young man might not have. Edie shook her head. "Why do that when I'm right here?"

The way Gertie glanced up and down the hall, you'd think she was on the lookout for German spies. "You can't breathe a word of this to Dr. Lovinggood."

"What would he do anyway, fire me? I'm a volunteer." Edie chuckled. She might like Robert Lovinggood — he was a decent doctor — but he had some issues that disturbed Edie. Like the way he shied away from the Negro patients who came to the hospital, assigning their care to the nurses and only looking in on them when pushed to do so.

"Well, as long as you know what you're getting yourself into."

Threading her arm through Gertie's, Edie

glanced at her coconspirator. "Then let's get these specimens to the lab and get this transfusion done before Dr. Lovinggood has a chance to find out."

CHAPTER FIVE

"So you served as a medic?" Dr. Robert Lovinggood asked, leaning back in his chair, studying Beau over the wired rims of his reading glasses like he was a germ under the microscope. "I can't say I'm not surprised."

Beau chuckled, his ankle crossed over the top of his knee. "Well, you and me both. Most folks figured I'd be in jail by now."

"You were a wild kid, always into something." The man tsked, shaking his head. "Just like that daddy of yours."

Heat raced through his veins. Beau needed this job, but he wasn't sure he was ready to grovel just to get it. "No denying I was a handful, sir."

"Then running off just like your mother." The man tsked again. "My patients need dependable care."

Beau mashed his lips together. God may have forgiven him, but obviously there were still those in town who felt the need to judge him. "I'm not like my parents, sir."

"Why do you say that, son?"

"Because I chose not to be like him."

The man straightened, his eyes bright with what Beau thought looked like respect. "Good to know. You're going to need that strength, especially with your father's trial coming up. But then, I figure with what you've already had to deal with over in Germany, James's legal issues shouldn't be much of a problem." Lovinggood sat back again. "So what can I do to help?"

"Well," Beau started, "I'm looking for a job. A position that will allow me to work and maybe squeeze in some college classes."

"Classes?"

Beau felt like a schoolboy, saying the words out loud to this respected man. "I'd kind of like to get a degree, eventually go to medical school or something."

"Hmm." Dr. Lovinggood seemed to ponder that statement for a moment. For a brief second, Beau thought the doctor might turn him away. "I could use someone to help the nurses. The army's taken to shipping injured soldiers to us if they have family in any of the nearby towns. I can't offer you much pay, but I'll be happy to write you a recommendation for school when the time comes."

Relief flooded through Beau. He hadn't realized how much he'd wanted this job. "Thank you, sir. All I want is the opportunity to learn."

Laughter echoed through the tiny office. "Oh, you'll learn all right. Nurse Arnold may be older, but she's tougher than anything the United States Army could ever throw at you. If you listen to her, she'll teach you quite a bit."

Beau smiled, a feeling of purpose seeping through his veins. "Sounds like just the person I want to work with. When can I get started?"

"How about tomorrow morning?" The doctor pulled open his desk drawer. "Unless you have time to fill out some paperwork now?"

"Yes, sir," Beau answered, raising his hand to the silk knot at his neck before skimming his fingers down the length of his tie, Edie Michaels's face suddenly flashing into focus, remembering the touch of her fingers at his neck, the scent of warm vanilla floating around him.

Beau frowned. He didn't have time for this attraction to the beautiful Ms. Michaels, not when his concern was protecting his family.

A woman, her nursing cap teetering on

the back of her head like a white flag of surrender, peeked around the door. She glanced first at Beau before focusing her attention on Lovinggood. "Doctor, we have a situation in the emergency room that needs your attention immediately."

"Be right there." The doctor stood and made his way around the desk. "It's as good a time as any to introduce you to everyone. That is, if you're not too busy."

"I'm free all evening." Beau pushed himself out of his chair. Maybe he'd catch up with Edie again. Find out how the search for a blood donor had panned out.

The doctor already had one arm shoved into his white coat before Beau moved toward the door. Moments later, the scent of iodine and antiseptic filled the air, burning his nose and mouth as the men walked in silence down the hall. Funny how the familiar combination of odors was an odd comfort to him. He turned a corner, increasing his pace when Dr. Lovinggood pushed through a set of double doors, then moved to the side to hold one open for him.

The emergency room was small, not quite half the size of the bunkhouse he'd been assigned to along with most of his platoon at Stalag 7B. Three beds hugged the wall, allowing for a narrow pathway for hospital

89

personnel to work. A thick white curtain gently swung with each movement around what Beau surmised must be another bed.

An older woman approached them, the starched, white cotton swishing in time with her every step. "Who gave you permission to come into my emergency room, Beauregard Daniels?"

His face flushed hot. Only one person outside of the United States Army had ever dared to use his full name. His lips lifted in what he hoped was his cockiest grin. "Since when did you start working at the hospital, Ms. Arnold? Last time I saw you, you were terrorizing the kids at the high school."

"And now I'm busy running this hospital."

"Which is the reason I've hired Beau here to help out," Doctor Lovinggood interjected. "He served as a medic in the army."

"He looks kind of puny to me." Ms. Arnold gave him a quick once-over before meeting his gaze, her expression stern. "You sure you're up to this?"

"Don't worry about me. Aunt Merri's home cooking is all I need," Beau answered.

"So you've already been to your aunt's house. Guess that means you plan on sticking around this time."

Ms. Arnold never minced words, one of the reasons he'd liked her so much. Beau nodded. "As long as she's got an available room."

The older woman gave a little smile, seemingly satisfied with his answer. "Well, every bed in here is full for the moment, and more are standing in the waiting room. So the sooner you can get this girl out the door, the better. Then we can use that bed for someone who's really sick."

Beau followed them to the closed-off section of the room, listening as Ms. Arnold gave Dr. Lovinggood a report on their patient. He didn't catch a name, but gathered that whoever it was had passed out.

"All I can figure is she must have skipped lunch again," Ms. Arnold said, pulling the curtain to the side. In the bed lay a woman, her familiar gray hat perched on the bedside table.

Edie Michaels.

She looked so serene, her hair an ebony fan spread out against the pillow, her hands folded neatly across her midsection. The rosy color he'd noticed in her cheeks less than an hour ago had drained from her face, leaving her the palest shade of white. Without thinking, he picked up her hand and examined her fingertips. Cool to the touch, but pink.

Beau glanced over at Nurse Arnold. "What

happened?"

"Stood up after giving a pint of blood and passed out." The woman shook her head. "Knowing her, she probably hasn't had a bite to eat all day."

Beau's gut twisted into a tight knot. Despite what he suspected about her, he couldn't bear the thought of anyone going without food or water. He'd seen enough emaciated bodies on both sides of this war to last until his dying breath.

A faint intake of air drew Beau's attention back to the bed. Edie's eyes fluttered open, her unfocused gaze searching the area before coming back to him. "Beau?"

There was something so tender in the way she'd said his name, almost as if she had expected him to be standing there waiting for her to wake up. He squeezed her hand tighter. "Hello there."

The muscles in her neck contracted as she swallowed. "What happened?"

Ms. Arnold pressed two fingers over Edie's wrist and studied her watch. "You passed out."

"That's impossible," Edie whispered, giving her head a slight shake.

"Fell harder than Clark Gable did for that Carole Lombard," the woman answered, dropping Edie's arm. She flipped open a chart and began writing.

Edie sank farther into her pillows, a pale pink hue coloring her cheeks. "I've never fainted before."

"It can happen." Beau laid her hand back down on the bed and stood up, the sudden urge to comfort her racing through him. Why would he want to help her when she might very well be the enemy? "It's easy to pass out after giving blood, especially if you haven't eaten anything today."

"I was so busy with work and everything." Her cheeks flushed a faint pink. "I forgot."

Nurse Arnold blew out an aggravated breath. "I swear these girls today don't have the sense the good Lord gave them."

Why couldn't Ms. Arnold just be quiet? Couldn't she see how embarrassed Edie already was? Beau glared back at the older woman. "She was only trying to help someone who needed blood."

"I don't remember any of our patients needing a transfusion." It was Dr. Loving-good from somewhere behind him.

"One of the new transfers was bleeding out, and no one could be found to come in and donate a pint. I'm a universal donor so I figured . . ." Edie's voice drew his gaze. Her coal-black lashes fluttered down, caressing the slope of her cheek.

She'd given her own blood to the Negro soldier. But for some odd reason, it didn't surprise him, remembering how she'd been protective of Claire even when there had been no reason. Not exactly what you'd expect from the enemy.

But Germans were crafty, sliding into any persona to get what they wanted.

"Just who is this soldier?" Dr. Lovinggood bit out, reminding Beau of a drill sergeant ordering a platoon of grunts. "And why wasn't I told of the situation?"

Gertie stepped forward from her post at the foot of Edie's bed. "I was on my way to tell you when I ran into Edie. When I told her the problems I was having getting a donor, she volunteered to help."

"So Ms. Michaels's blood is being transfused." Was it Beau's imagination, or was the doctor gritting his teeth so hard, they might break? "Into a patient on your floor?"

Gertie nodded. "Private Benjamin Watson of the 92nd Infantry Division."

"Nurse Stephens, I want to see you in my office," the doctor snapped.

Beau stole a glance over his shoulder at the doctor. Even if rules had been broken, what was done was done. Edie and Gertie had ensured the well-being of their patient.

"Go home, Ms. Michaels." Lovinggood

gave Edie a distasteful look, then turned to the young nurse, anger blazing in his gaze. "Now, Nurse Stephens."

He wouldn't like to be in Gertie's shoes right now. *Lord, rein in Lovinggood's temper. Let him see that they were only trying to help.*

"How did your interview go?"

He turned back to the bed to find Edie's clear blue-green eyes watching him. Laid out in a hospital bed and the woman was concerned for his interview. Beau's heart skipped a beat. He cleared his throat. "Just like a woman. Always asking questions, aren't you?"

Her lips quirked to one side. "Claire says it's the only way to learn the answers."

"You two know each other?" Nurse Arnold asked.

He nodded. "I had the pleasure of meeting Edie at my aunt's boardinghouse early this morning."

"He broke in through the front window." There was no condemnation in her voice like he might have expected, but no other emotions either.

"That doesn't surprise me none." Ms. Arnold shot him a sideways glance as she shook her head. "He's been pulling stunts like that since he was just a runt of a boy."

Beau ignored the nurse. "Are you feeling

any better?"

"I could use a glass of water."

"How about some juice?" The older woman fussed with the covers at the foot of the bed. "Apple or orange?"

"Apple, please."

"Be right back." The nurse hurried across the room and disappeared behind the door.

"So," Beau started. "When's the last time you had anything to eat?"

A flash of white teeth nibbled at her lip, drawing Beau's attention to her soft mouth. "I had one of Merrilee's cookies last night before I turned in."

Foolish woman. Or too kind for her own good. "You know you need three square meals when you donate blood."

Her cheeks flushed a bright pink now. "With work and everything, I guess I just wasn't thinking."

Blast, but the woman looked so contrite, with her dark brows furrowed in a worried line. Made him almost wish he could forget the letter in his pocket and explore this sudden protectiveness he felt toward her. "I think it's time for some supper then, don't you, Ms. Michaels?"

"Supper?"

"Beau Daniels." Nurse Arnold's voice cut through the haze of his straying thoughts.

She held out a paper cup of juice to her patient. "Are you asking this young woman out on a date while she's under my care?"

A date? He shook his head. It had been years since he'd been out with a woman, before the Lord had stepped in and saved him from himself. Until he got his life on a more even keel, he had no intention of getting involved, particularly not with a woman who could be the enemy.

"I just figured that I should keep an eye on her and make sure she gets home okay after she's got something in her stomach."

"But I'm supposed to help with dinner tonight," Edie replied, a slight rise in her voice as if something had irritated her.

Well, he didn't want her running away, at least not until he was sure she was okay. "I'll give Merrilee a call and tell her what's happened."

"You can't." Edie shot him a pleading glance. "She's over at Goldstein's with Maggie, looking at material for her wedding dress."

"I'm sure they'll understand. And you know what? Maybe the saleslady will send them home with some samples so you can still help her pick things out."

She fell back against the pillows. "Oh, I just hate the thought of disappointing her."

Beau patted her hand, aware of the delicate bones of her knuckles. "They'll be more disappointed if you took a nosedive in the asphalt."

Edie laughed, a joyful sound that he found completely charming. "You've got a point there."

"Well, if you're about finished with your juice, let's see if we can get you up." Nurse Arnold looped an arm under Edie's shoulder. "I'm sure there are other people who need this bed more than you."

Beau stood. "I'd better go see if I can get a message to Aunt Merrilee before she heads out."

Her hand grasped his. "Would you please tell her I'm sorry about dinner?"

He gave her fingers a gentle squeeze before letting go. "There's nothing to apologize for." But her expression told him she didn't believe that. He nodded. "Sure."

Beau turned and headed across the ward, aware that Nurse Arnold followed close behind. As they passed the nursing desk, she spoke. "You've changed, Beau Daniels."

"Most people do, you know."

"What are you wanting to do now that you're home?" She gave him a smile.

The Ms. Arnold he knew never smiled at anyone. "I'd like to go to college, maybe medical school down the road."

"You've got a nice bedside manner, son. Kind, yet sure of yourself." Her white cap bobbed up and down on a bed of silver curls. "I believe you're going to be a great asset to us."

Turning to her, Beau held out his hand. "That means a great deal coming from you, ma'am."

Nurse Arnold snorted, giving his hand a firm shake before releasing it. "Fuss and fiddlesticks. Just be here first thing in the morning."

"Looking forward to it."

As he opened the door and stepped out into the sunlight, Beau scoured the landscape of Marietta's town square. With the influx of new people and businesses, it felt as if the town, with all its new construction, had grown up while he had been gone.

The heat radiating off the sidewalk chased the chill he'd felt since first seeing Edie Michaels so fragile and feminine passed out in the hospital bed. Something about the woman appealed to him, which didn't make sense. He didn't know her. Well, that wasn't necessarily true. He knew she loved his aunt and cousins, would protect them at the risk of her own life. That she was a hard worker, a volunteer willing to help anyone, black or white.

And she had a laugh that lit up her whole face.

A horn honked. Beau stared at the short line of cars waiting for him to cross then shook his head. Better to keep his mind on the letter in his pocket, on protecting his family. But as he stepped off the curb, thoughts of Edie Michaels wouldn't release their hold on his mind.

"I could have made it home, you know." Edie clasped the coffee cup in her hands, the heat from the porcelain warming the last of the chill from her fingers. "I wouldn't want to keep you from something important."

He rested his spoon against the edge of his plate and glanced up at her, his green eyes dancing with laughter. "But I am doing something important, Ms. Michaels."

She frowned. Why did it bother her that Beau was back to calling her Ms. Michaels? "And what would that be?"

"Protecting my future, of course."

Edie choked on her coffee, sputtering and coughing at the intimacy of his words. When she finally caught her breath, she glanced up to find him watching her. "How's that?"

"What would people say if my first patient passed out in the middle of Powder Springs Road?" He sipped his coffee. "Not much for confidence building."

Of course, he was protecting his career. What else could it be? But the thought didn't stop her from feeling like a bit of a knucklehead. "I would have thought breaking into someone's house in the middle of the night would have made people think twice before entrusting you with their health."

His warm chuckle surprised her, but it was a nice sound. Warm, husky, real. "You're never going to let that go, are you?"

Spearing a piece of Mr. Smith's delectable roast with her fork, she glanced over at Beau, remembering his words from the previous night. *I don't have anywhere else to go.* "I'm sorry. It's just that today hasn't gone exactly the way I had planned. I guess I was taking it out on you."

"It's okay." Beau's green eyes seemed a shade darker, more solemn. "It wasn't my intention to scare the living daylights out of you, coming in through the window like that. I hope you can forgive me."

Edie took another sip of coffee, watching him over the edge of her cup. She hadn't lied to Claire when she'd said Beau was a handsome man. His short hair had been combed back, fine threads of pale gold a stunning contrast to the dark auburn hues. The black suit coat he'd borrowed from Merrilee barely held the muscled shoulders and broad chest Edie had been too nervous to notice the night before. And she'd never felt as safe as when she woke up in the emergency room and found Beau staring back at her, concern in those pale green eyes.

"So? Am I forgiven?"

Edie set her cup down. If Papa hadn't been so strict, she'd know how to handle this attraction she had toward Beau Daniels. She'd just have to make sure she didn't encourage him in any way. Maybe she should just tell him the truth, that she was German. That would nip even friendship in the bud before he learned the whole truth of her parents' involvement with the Nazi movement.

But something deep inside, where she used to feel things, wouldn't let him go. "I'll forgive you on one condition," Edie said.

His brow wrinkled together. "And what would that be?"

"Use the front door from now on."

She hadn't expected him to laugh but it was a nice sound, one she found increasingly appealing. A rush of awareness skated down her spine. "I think that can be arranged, though old habits die hard."

Edie's gaze shifted to her saucer. "Sounds like you've used that window quite a bit."

"Merrilee wanted me to have a safe place to go when things weren't going too well at home."

Beau said it so matter-of-factly, she wasn't sure she'd caught his full meaning. "A safe place?"

"You may not know this, but my father has a bit of a temper."

Oh, she knew. In fact, the whole town knew. When James Daniels had been dragged out of the woods behind Merrilee's house, the trees behind him smoking embers from the explosion of his moonshine still, it had taken three officers to bring him down, so livid was he at his failed attempted to gain ownership of the family homestead. And as the police cuffed and put him in the back of the squad car, he had yelled out to whoever would listen that the homestead belonged to his heirs.

What if Beau was back after all these years to make a claim on Merrilee's home?

Edie cleared her throat. "You said something about patients. Are you a doctor?"

"No, not yet. I have to get through college first."

All the men her father had introduced her to may have been educated, and a few practiced medicine, but none had the natural people skills Beau appeared to have. She blotted her mouth with her napkin. "What got you so interested in medicine?"

Beau leaned back, his wide shoulders seeming to fill his side of the booth. "I guess you could say Uncle Sam helped me decide. I was a medic."

She broke off a small piece of her biscuit. "Where were you stationed?"

"Tunis first, then Italy."

"And now you're home. With the shortage of men, I'm surprised the army didn't reassign you."

His eyes darkened to a somber shade of emerald green. "I guess they just didn't need me anymore. At least, that's what they told me when they shipped me back home."

"The army really told you that?"

He gave a slight nod. "In so many words."

Something in the way he'd spoken made Edie think coming home hadn't been his idea. She guessed she could understand. The men she knew would want to fight to the very end. Maybe he was thinking about all the lives he could have saved as a medic

104

on the battlefield. But Beau had been hurt, and if truth be told, he could be as much use here as in Italy. With the shortage of medication and supplies, even a common illness could prove deadly. There were lives in Marietta that needed saving, too.

"So you're going back to school?"

"Not right away." Beau scooped some mashed potatoes onto his fork. "I've got to get Merrilee's place up and running. Got to get seed in the ground if we hope to cash in on the harvest next fall."

"You're a farmer, too?"

He chuckled again. "I don't know if I'd go so far as to say that. But I'm willing to learn, especially if it will provide a way to take care of Merrilee and Claire."

Edie pushed her green beans around on her plate.

Well, Merrilee didn't need Beau's help. From where she sat, her landlady was doing a pretty good job of taking care of her and her daughter. She had the boardinghouse, and she made a little pocket money by selling the extra fruit and vegetables from her garden to every diner in town. And her baked goods were always in demand. Edie glanced over at the counter where one of Merrilee's rare chocolate confections sat encased in a glass cake plate. So why did

Beau think he was obligated to provide for his aunt?

She put her cup down. "Well, I'm sure Dr. Lovinggood will be glad to have your help. We're always short staffed, especially in the evenings."

"You must volunteer at the hospital quite a bit to have Ms. Arnold hovering over you like she did." Beau gave her a smile that would melt all the snowdrifts back home in Michigan.

Edie felt herself go hot. "The folks around here have been so nice to me. I figure it's the least I can do."

"That's mighty kind of you."

Did she detect a hint of skepticism in his voice, as if he wasn't quite sure whether he believed her or not? A nest of butterflies took up residence in her midsection. It didn't matter what Beau Daniels thought. Though working with the sick wasn't something she planned on doing for the rest of her life, she found a sanctuary at the hospital.

Or a hiding place. She wasn't sure.

Edie swallowed against a tide of uneasiness. "So did Dr. Lovinggood give you a job?"

Beau nodded. "Even offered to pay me. Said it wasn't right for a man to come home from the war and not make an honest day's wage. I figure I can use part of it for seeds and equipment and put the rest back for school."

"You've got some mighty big plans."

He leaned back in the booth. "You sound surprised."

"I guess I just figured . . ." Edie broke off, her mouth suddenly dry as a summer drought at her unfinished thought. She should know better than anyone what it's like to live under the shadow of her father's horrible decision. And yet she'd judged him. *Lord, please forgive me. And help me see Beau the way I want others to see me.* She took a calming breath. "I'm sorry. I shouldn't have said that."

"Don't worry about it. You just said what everyone else is thinking."

"But that doesn't make it right."

He shook his head. "No, it doesn't. The only way folks are going to realize that I'm not like my dad is for me to show them I've changed."

Beau made it sound so simple, but was it? Would he ever convince people that he wasn't like his father, a man who had run moonshine, who had tried to steal his sister's home from her, who had almost killed another woman pilot while hoping to scare his niece away from her work?

And would she ever step out of the shadows of her parents' treason without it tainting everything in her life?

Shame ricocheted through her. She highly doubted it. Well, there was nothing else to do but try to be the best person she could.

Beau set his fork down. "What about you? Where are you from?"

She hadn't been expecting that question. "Right outside Detroit."

"Still got family there?"

Yes, but none who would claim her. "No."

His gaze turned soft. "That must be tough, being all alone like that."

She pressed her lips together, glancing around the half-empty diner. What if she told him the truth, that her father and mother wanted nothing to do with her since she'd turned her back on their beliefs? Would Beau understand, or would he only hear one word?

German.

"It was hard being alone at first," Edie said, remembering the nights she'd come home to an empty apartment. Sleep had not come easy in those days, just in fits and starts. "But it's gotten easier. I keep myself occupied."

"You mean your volunteer work."

"Yes, and living at Merrilee's is like being with family."

"Still, you must miss them."

She nodded, struggling to swallow against the knot in her throat. Yes, she missed her parents, her grandmother, too. More than she ever imagined. She longed for the old times, spending the afternoons running errands downtown with her mother. Sitting in her grandma's kitchen, the warm scent of vanilla from the fresh cherry pies they baked lightly perfuming the air. There had been no worries then, just the comfort of family.

But those days didn't exist anymore.

Beau's hand covered hers in a reassuring squeeze. "It's tough being on your own. Believe me, I know. But I also know that whether we understand it or not, God will make something good come out of your situation."

How she wanted to yell. Instead, Edie stared at him. "Is that what you thought when you left home at what? Fifteen?"

"Sixteen," he corrected. "No, I thought running away was the only answer."

Just a kid. "You were so young to be on your own."

"Well, it was either that or become a permanent resident of the county jail." One side of his mouth quirked up into a half smile.

Lowering her gaze to the table, Edie pushed a strand of hair behind her ear. "Just like your father."

"Yeah, Dad's always been as mean as a snake. Probably be good for him to spend some time behind bars." He laughed, a humorless sound, cold and unfeeling, leaving her to wonder what kind of pain James Daniels had inflicted on his son. "Maybe then he'll think about what he's done to his family and pull his life together."

"You think he can change?"

He shook his head. "I'm pretty sure he won't. But there are a lot of people who would never have believed I could change, either."

"Do you even know the charges against him?"

"Yes, but that's not what's important."

Not important? Had the man lost his mind? Edie threw her napkin on the table. "I think you need to speak to Mack Worthington about it. I'm sure he would be happy to talk to you about the severity of the charges, maybe even give you some advice."

"I'm sure he would. And he'll probably tell me that the possibility of Dad ever getting out of jail is nonexistent. But that doesn't mean he can't change."

The oddly gentle tone in which he spoke caused her to glance over at him. She could only imagine what Beau Daniels must be going through. Would he rethink his discussion about giving his father a second chance when he learned the truth, that James Daniels had been charged with one of the most despicable crimes a man could commit against his country?

The same charges her own parents would face if caught.

"Look, Beau." She cleared her throat. "The bottom line is, your father is going to have to face his punishment."

"I know, and I think he should be punished. But that doesn't mean he can't have a change of heart." Crossing his arms in front of his chest, Beau studied her. "You don't believe much in people changing, do you?"

Sure, she did. But she knew James Daniels, had witnessed his mean spirit firsthand. "Not when I know it's a lost cause."

The soft smile Beau gave her made blood race through her veins. "The way I see it, we're all a lost cause before God gets hold of us."

Dishes clinked quietly around them. Edie

didn't expect him to understand, though for the life of her, she couldn't figure out why Beau would *want* to help the man who had chased him out of town when he was just a kid. Well, it didn't matter. She'd prayed that God would — how did Beau say it? — get hold of her parents, while she waited for them to see how misguided their belief in Hitler was. No, no matter what Beau believed, God didn't give everyone a second chance.

Not James Daniels. And not her parents. *Not me.*

So deep in her thoughts was she that Edie barely noticed the man standing next to them until his hat came to rest at the corner of the table.

Sheriff Mack Worthington cleared his throat. "Hello, Edwina, Beau. Didn't expect to find you here."

If Beau was nervous about the sheriff's sudden appearance, he didn't show it. Instead he stood, smiling widely when he patted Mack on the back as if greeting an old friend. "We were both over at the hospital. Edie hadn't eaten anything all day, and I've been pining for some of Smithy's homemade meatloaf and mashed potatoes for years. What about you? On your dinner break?"

The man shook his head, his gaze shifting from Edie before settling on Beau. "Got some more questions for you, Beau."

Edie blinked. When had the sheriff had time to question Beau in the first place?

"Well, then here." Beau scooted over on the bench seat to make room for Mack. "Let me buy you a cup of coffee, and we can talk."

"No." Mack eyed Edie cautiously, as though she were too delicate to hear what might be discussed. Edie mashed her lips together in irritation. What did the sheriff think, that one conversation was going to make her faint dead away? "This isn't the kind of conversation that needs to be conducted in front of a lady."

Beau looked at her, his eyes questioning, a slight wrinkle creasing his forehead the only sign of any trouble. He turned back to Mack, this time his expression serious. "Of course. Where would you like to talk?"

"How about down at the station?"

Edie sat back in the booth. Of course, Beau may not have been back in Marietta but twenty-four hours, but there was no telling the damage he'd left behind when he had skipped town years ago. Maybe he'd been right, maybe he had changed. But if he'd committed a crime, he'd have to answer for it.

But something about Beau Daniels made her think that wasn't the case — that instead of taking after his good-for-nothing father, Beau had spent his life away from everything he loved to have a chance at becoming the kind of man James Daniels never would.

Edie shoved the thought aside as she pushed her plate away. "Well, I was finished with dinner anyway."

"Then let me walk you home. I'm sure Merrilee will let me borrow her car to drive back into town." Beau retrieved his wallet from his coat pocket. He shucked out some bills and threw them on the table.

"I'm sorry Beau, but I can't let you do that." Mack shook his head. "This can't wait."

"It's okay." Edie scooted across the slippery leather of the booth and stood. "I'm perfectly capable of finding my way home."

Beau stood up. "Then at least let me call you a cab."

"I could get one of my deputies to drive you home, Edwina."

She shook her head. "That's all right. A nice long walk home is just what I need at the moment." She turned to Beau, unprepared for the way her heart stumbled when their gazes met. Well, she refused to be

114

duped into believing another man. With a fortifying breath, she straightened. "What would you like for me to tell your aunt?"

"That I'll be home as soon as I'm finished with Mack. And to keep the front door unlocked, just in case." He gave her a tender smile. "Don't want to scare anyone when I come in."

Edie gave him a quick nod, then turned, not sure why his mention of the promise he'd made her caused a shaft of warmth to flood through her like a stream after a dry season. She walked toward the door and glanced back. Beau was on his feet now, his head bowed as if in prayer as he stared down at the sheriff.

But he wasn't praying. More than likely trying to talk his way out of whatever scrape had drawn Mack's attention in the first place. Well, she didn't need to borrow any more trouble than she already had.

Not when she had enough problems to last a lifetime.

CHAPTER SIX

Lifting his hat to his head, Beau stepped out onto the sidewalk. Although the muted colors of early evening had settled over the square, he peeled off his wool jacket and draped it over his arm. Spring had never been this hot when he was a kid — or maybe he had had too many other things on his mind back then.

Like living through another day.

He glanced through the paned-glass window of the diner then straightened. Where was Mack? He smiled. Knowing his old friend, he was probably talking Old Man Smith out of a cake doughnut and a cup of coffee to go. He had hoped to run into the sheriff sometime today, though the man's timing wasn't exactly perfect.

Beau looked down the street in the direction Edie had gone just a minute ago. Mack had sure scared her off, not that it would have taken much. Beau had been walking on thin ice with his aunt's beautiful boarder since he'd tumbled through the window the night before. Edie Michaels wasn't one for giving second chances — she'd said as much. And he'd blown his first one breaking into Merrilee's house.

But what had caused Edie to stop giving people another opportunity when they messed up?

Beau drew in a deep breath. Maybe the woman's position had something to do with the letter he'd found the night they'd met.

"I've got to tell you," Mack interrupted, blowing at the steam gathered along the top of the paper cup he was holding. "I love being a police officer. Only job that will keep your coffee cup filled at any hour of the day or night."

"That, and you get to hassle law-abiding citizens, too."

"What does that mean?"

For a brief moment, Beau felt the urge to knock the cup right out of the sheriff's hand. "Could you have scared off Ms. Michaels any faster? And what was all that stuff about hauling me down to the station?"

"Hey, take it up with Chief Muster. He's the one who wants you to play third base when we go up against the bomber plant in a couple of weeks."

"But did you have to make it sound like you were about to arrest me?"

Mack chuckled. "Yeah, that was a stroke of genius, wasn't it."

Beau started walking. "Not from where I'm standing."

"Well, if you think you've got a chance with Edwina Michaels, you'd better be thinking again," the man said, coming up alongside him. "I've walked the woman home from the hospital a couple of times, even asked her out once, and it's always the same. She's too busy with work."

And yet Edie had come to dinner with him. Granted, she was starving, but if she had truly not wanted to come, she seemed to be the type to throw out a made-up excuse. Only she didn't. The faint feeling of contentment slightly confused him. A relationship, particularly with someone like Edie Michaels, wasn't on his agenda, not with too many other pressing items weighing on him.

"So," Beau started. "What was so urgent you felt the need to interrupt my dinner for?"

"What do you think?"

My father. Beau lowered his head, his gaze settling on the cracks in the paved sidewalk.

"How's the old man doing?"

"Fine. Got into a bit of a fight today, but one of the prison medics was able to stitch him up." Mack looked over at him. "He keeps asking about you."

Not back home for twenty-four hours and already the old man was in more hot water. "What does he want to know?"

"If you're going to come see him."

"I will, but not yet. I've got some other things I need to take care of first."

"I hate to keep asking, but have you thought about a lawyer for him yet?"

Beau shook his head. "I figured I'd have to go to Atlanta to get someone."

"Probably not a bad idea. Too many people know too much about him around here." Mack drew in a deep breath. "Don't know how we're going to sit an unprejudiced jury."

So things were that bad. Well, Beau wouldn't give up. He couldn't. His father had to have an opportunity to understand what he had done in committing these crimes, to see how he had hurt so many, including his own kin. To reflect on his sins and ask forgiveness. And prison just might be the place for such soul-searching.

After all, it had worked for him.

"Anybody you'd recommend?" Beau

watched the plant bus pass. The men crossed the street in front of the courthouse, where the two bottom floors made up the police station and county jail.

"Not off the top of my head, but I'll ask around." Mack took a couple of steps then turned to face him. "Another thing. Right after I talked to you this morning, the judge gave us a warrant on his house down Powder Springs Road. I went out there this afternoon, but I couldn't get in. Thought maybe you had a key."

Beau shook his head. "Maybe Merrilee does. From what I've heard, Dad's been living at Merrilee's since Granddaddy died."

"The house, it was trashed, at least around the outside. Yard's waist-high in weeds. Afraid I was going to get snake bit. And that front porch is going to have to be reinforced before anyone tries to go through that front door."

Beau nodded. Just as he'd expected. Dad had left the house to rot.

"But that's not the oddest thing. I went out behind the house, just to take a look at the barn." Mack stared up at him. "There's a crop in the field."

Beau wasn't sure he'd heard the man right. "A crop?"

"Right beyond the back of the barn. Corn,

tobacco, maybe even a little wheat. And it looks as if it's almost ready to harvest."

"What are you saying, Mack?"

Mack's brows furrowed into a hard line. "Your dad may have been farming that land before he was arrested."

"That doesn't make sense." Beau scrubbed his hand along the tight muscles in the back of his neck. Even during his youth, he couldn't remember Dad ever planting crops. He thought it was beneath a Daniels to be working in the dirt. "Did you talk to Uncle Jeb or Aunt Merrilee about it?"

The sheriff nodded. "Neither of them knew a thing."

"Then what do you think it is?"

Mack shrugged. "If it was anyone else, I'd think that your daddy had rented out the fields. A lot of folks are putting in victory gardens to make up for the shortages."

"There are just as many people looking for a place to live, what with the plant here and everything, so why not rent out the house?" Beau thought for a moment. "Did you check the kitchen door?"

"No, can't say that I even looked for it. I was too busy noticing the fields."

"Then maybe Dad did rent out the place." Though Beau still had his doubts. Dad

121

would rather cut off his right arm than do something that generous. "Have you met anyone around town that might be living out there?"

"Trying to meet everyone that's moved in is like trying to count the stars in the sky. It's near impossible."

Same kind of odds that his dad had been renting out his house.

"You want me to keep trying to make contact?" Mack asked. "I can take the patrol car out there just to check up on things."

"That's okay." Beau shook his head. "I don't want to take up any more of your time than I already have. If there is someone living there, I need to meet them and let them know the situation with my father."

Mack's brow furrowed. "And if your dad hasn't put renters in there?"

Beau wiped at the beads of sweat on his forehead. "Then I may have to give you a call. If they've got a crop in the field, they're not going to take too kindly to being put off the land."

"So how are you going to handle this? Just go up and knock on the door?"

"That's how it generally works. Unless you've got a better plan."

"I don't know, Beau. I just can't shake the feeling that something is wrong over there."

"Well, you know me. Never been one to run away from trouble." He chuckled at the sheriff's concerned expression. "Face it, brother, if this person is on the wrong side of the law, your patrol car would send him running before we get any answers, and I need to know why he's there."

Mack tapped his finger against his lower lip. "So when are you planning this little surprise party?"

"Not sure. I've got some things to tend to around Merrilee's before I can break free. Maybe this coming weekend."

"Well, if you need me, you know how to get in touch with me."

Mack was a good man, and an even better friend. The kind of guy Beau would have appreciated standing next to him in the heat of battle. He held out his hand. "I appreciate all you've done, Mack, for me and my dad."

"Just wished I could have done more." With a quick shake, the sheriff started down the granite stairs before turning back to him. "Hey, what do you want me to tell Chief Muster about the ball team?"

Beau smiled. "Tell him I'll be happy to play for the men in blue."

"Good! I'll let you know when our next practice is." With a smile, Mack pulled open the wooden door to the police station and disappeared inside.

Beau turned, strands of light playing peekaboo between the pine trees that rose like chess pieces in the town square, the last threads of warmth slowly severed as the sun sank behind the water oaks lining Cherokee Street. He'd despised this town when he had tied what clothes he had in one of Mom's old sheets and walked out of his father's house all those years ago. Promised himself he'd never step foot in this place again.

But now, staring out over the square, he wondered how he could have stayed away so long. A group of kids took turns swinging on the swing set, while over at the fountain, a young man dressed in navy blues fished something out of his pocket, the woman beside him watching, her mouth curved into a tender smile.

The memory of Edie's blue-green eyes shining at him from across the table kicked his heart rate up. So he was attracted to the woman. What man in his right mind wouldn't be? But she was German, the very enemy he'd been sent to fight against. And he was tired of the struggle. For once, he didn't want to worry about his father's temper, or fighting an unseen enemy or battling his own worries. And he certainly didn't want to take on a woman whose eyes haunted him with their sadness.

Exchanging one prison for another.

No, he couldn't allow himself to be ambushed by a beautiful and intelligent woman. He had a promise to keep — providing a living for Merrilee and Claire, eventually getting his education. And, with God's help, saving his father from himself.

But as he turned down Main Street for home, an unfamiliar sense of emptiness he couldn't quite shake welled up inside.

What an absolute dope she was!

Edie kicked a piece of gravel across the freshly paved street, the heat from the setting sun rising from the asphalt radiating warmth up to her knees. What had she expected, that Beau Daniels would be completely different from his father, that he'd be respectable and kind, maybe even everything she admired in a man? Instead, he gets arrested almost the second he strolls back into town.

Well, not really arrested, she silently corrected, staring at a nearby oak tree. *But that doesn't mean he won't be in jail before the night is over.*

The newly blossomed leaves of the water

oaks — the same vibrant color of Beau's eyes — trembled in the last fading strands of sunshine. Well, Beau might be a handsome man but she couldn't afford to be caught up in trouble, and that's exactly what Beau Daniels was.

Trouble.

Only he'd sounded that way when he'd spoken of his desire to go back to school, to study medicine. Unlike a lot of the boys she'd known, Beau had seemed like a man who knew exactly what he wanted to do with his life. And she found that quality equally attractive.

Edie stopped and looked around. Goodness gracious, this didn't look anything like Fairground Street. Where was the old oak that spread out like an umbrella, giving workers from the plant a brief respite from the heat on their walk home? Why was the road veering left instead of right? Slamming her eyes shut, Edie had to grit her teeth to keep from screaming. She's been so deep in thought over Beau Daniels, she must have taken a wrong turn.

Blast the blasted man!

The only thing she could do now was turn around and head back into town. But night was settling over her quickly. Even now, long shadows of pine blended against the soft red clay, the last drops of sunlight hugging the new buds. Edie rubbed her arms, not sure if it was the evening air or her uneasiness that made gooseflesh rise on her skin. Well, standing here like some helpless ninny wasn't going to get her home any quicker. She'd better get a move on before Merrilee got worried and called the police.

Twenty minutes later, with the last light of day fading, Edie pulled up alongside a street sign and took a deep breath, wishing for the first time in a long while that she was back in Detroit. At least there, she could have grabbed a cab, but Marietta wasn't quite the metropolis her hometown was. She drew in a deep breath and sighed. Mack's offer of a police escort looked pretty good now.

Edie let her head fall back, gazing up at the first hint of starlight that glittered against the velvet of the purplish-blue sky. *Lord, if You could help me find a way home safely, I'd sure appreciate it.*

The sound of childish laughter dancing in the air like a playful tune drew Edie's gaze downward. Amid the blackness of the tree line, a patch of snowy white widened into a narrow path leading into a clearing. Maybe, if God was listening, the kids could take her some place where she could use a phone. With a perfunctory glance first one way, then the other, Edie crossed the road.

The jagged edges of rock against the soles of her saddle shoes slowed her down, a faint hint of honeysuckle filling her lungs with each breath. A line of pale yellow, soft and welcoming, lit the path some distance ahead of her. Edie hurried toward it, pushing aside the low-lying pine limbs in her way.

Letting go of the last branch, Edie stepped out into the clearing and stared. A nest of houses, each one identical to the last, dotted plots of land alongside the path, reminding her of the neat cookie-cutter homes that lined the streets where she used to live. Tall pines hung over yards made up of kudzu and dandelions, an occasional bicycle peeking out from the weeds. At the end of the dirt road, a group of boys played baseball, squeezing out the last few seconds of fun before night engulfed the day. A familiar longing welled up inside her.

Home.

The gentle slap of a rocking chair pushing against the wood drew her attention to her left. "Is anyone there?"

The rocker jittered like butter on a frying pan as its occupant rose. Faint light from the front room was enough for Edie to make out the familiar face of Harold Stephens. "Ms. Edie?"

"Mr. Stephens, I am so glad to see you." Edie let go of the breath she'd been holding, her heart slowing at the comforting appearance of the familiar bus driver. She hurried up the rock path leading up to the house. "Thank heavens, I wasn't sure if I'd even find someone to help me."

His footsteps pounded against the floor as he came to the top of the stairs. "You shouldn't be here."

Edie slowed her pace. What an odd thing for him to say. Almost as if just the thought of her presence here in his front yard bothered him. And here she'd thought they were friends. "I'm sorry to impose on you, really I am. But I got turned around coming out of town and managed to get myself lost."

"Oh, Ms. Edie." Mr. Stephens waddled down the stairs, hesitating at each step until finally he stood in front of her. "I didn't mean to bark at you like that. It's just, we don't get too many folks like you out this way."

Edie nodded. He didn't have to explain. After months of meeting Gertie in the back stairwell of the hospital, she knew the unspoken barriers between the whites and the Negroes in this town. It had never sat well with her, but particularly not now when she could see the worry in Mr. Stephens's expression.

Well, fuss and bother, this was an emergency. "If I could just use your phone, I'll wait out by the highway."

"We don't have a telephone."

"Oh." No phone. Just how far had she walked? How could she not have noticed the absence of telephone lines overhead? Her stomach fluttered at the answer. Too busy fuming over Beau Daniels.

The screen door squealed on its hinges as it opened. "Daddy, are you out here talking to yourself again? It may be how you think things through, but you've liked to scare Momma right out of her apron when you started answering yourself. She almost dropped a pan of hot pudding."

Edie grimaced. "I'm afraid I'm the one causing all the commotion."

A young woman stepped into the shadows and stood on the top stair. "Edie?"

"Gertie? I thought you had to work the late shift."

"Dr. Lovinggood sent me home. Thought I might need a little time off." The woman walked down the stairs, the starched cotton of her skirt swishing with each step. "What about you? Last thing I heard, you were on your way to dinner."

"I took a little detour and got lost. I had hoped to use the phone, but your father says you don't have one."

"Nobody around here does." Gertie joined them at the bottom of the stairs. "Phone company says it's too much bother to string lines into our neighborhood. Says we're a bad risk."

"Now, Gertrude," her father warned.

But Edie knew this look. Had seen her friend climb up on her soapbox enough times to know better than to pull her down. "But what's going to happen when someone needs medical attention? Will they finally put in the lines when someone dies?"

Gertie had a point. "Can't Dr. Loving-good help you? It seems to me that he would be the likely person to convince the phone company."

Father and daughter exchanged an odd look before Gertie turned back to Edie, her lips pressed into a straight line. "Well, I might as well tell you. Dr. Lovinggood fired me this afternoon."

Edie gasped. "Why?"

"Insubordination. Told me I shouldn't have talked you into giving blood to that soldier on my floor."

Edie laid her hand on Gertie's forearm. "But I made the decision to donate. Didn't you tell him that?"

But Gertie just stood, shell-shocked. "I still gave your blood to that boy on my floor, which is against hospital regulations."

This wasn't fair. She had to do something. "I'll talk to him. He's got to know this was my choice." Edie felt her voice catch in her throat. "He can't fire you. You're too good of a nurse for that."

"That's what her momma and I think, too, Ms. Edie." Mr. Stephens's deep voice rumbled as he draped an arm around his daughter and pulled her close. "Any hospital in the state of Georgia would be blessed to have my baby girl on their staff."

Gertie laid her head on her father's sturdy shoulder. "Thank you, Daddy."

Edie's heart constricted into a hard knot. She had always run to her dad when school or friends had let her down. And he had always held her, his arms cradling her while he assured her that everything would work out all right. She had felt precious beyond anything else on this earth.

But there would be no more hugs, no more assurances. Only loneliness.

And a sense of guilt that continued to grow with each life she touched. "What are you going to do now?"

Lifting her head, Gertie shrugged a shoulder. "I'm not sure. Probably apply to the hospitals in Atlanta. I could always enlist."

But Gertie was needed here, in Marietta. Dr. Lovinggood had to know that. "I'll talk to the doctor, tell him it was my idea. He'll have to give you your job back."

"Don't you go doing something so foolish. He'll just make it harder on you and the other girls on my floor." Gertie gave a brief shake of her head. "It might be best if I enlist. More opportunities."

"Your momma couldn't stomach all of her children gone." Mr. Stephens hugged her tighter.

Edie glanced at Gertie. "Oh, is George in the military?"

"No, I have a younger brother, Roy. He's off with the 128th in the Pacific."

Edie nodded, her thoughts fragmented. Another man fighting, possibly dying for his county while her parents . . . She refused to let her mind wander in that direction, not now. "You must be very proud."

The older man glanced down at his daughter, his dark eyes shining with pride. "Yes, I am."

Gertie gave her father a smile, then turned to Edie. "Now, what are we going to do about you? I mean, as much as I'd like a visit, this ain't exactly the best place for you to be."

Edie felt herself go warm. "I'm sorry. I'm beginning to think I should have just waited around until Mack finished up with Beau."

"What were you doing with Beau Daniels?"

"Well, Beau was still at the hospital when I fainted today, and seeing how I live at his aunt's and the fact I hadn't had lunch," she rambled on, then suddenly stopped. Why in the world was she babbling on about a man she wasn't even sure she liked? "Anyway, he took me to dinner."

"Really?" Gertie gave her father a knowing look. "That's a first."

"Why do you say that?" Edie glanced from one to the other, suddenly feeling like the odd woman out. "Surely the man has taken a woman out to dinner before."

"Probably but . . ."

"But what?"

"Gert, that was a long time ago." Mr. Stephens gave his daughter a stern look. "People say and do things when they're young, then change their minds once they've done some living."

"Maybe," Gertie replied.

Edie crossed her arms over her waist. "Would you please tell me what you're talking about?"

"Oh, it's just something Beau told me years ago." Gertie grinned at her, her dark eyes glittering with laughter. "So if you were with Beau, how'd you end up this far out of town?"

"Beau had some business he needed to take care of." Fire burned her cheeks. Before she knew it, the whole story spilled out. If she'd only kept her temper, she wouldn't be in this mess. "So I started walking home. I guess I must've taken a wrong turn because before I knew it, I was here."

"Beau must have gotten you pretty riled up for you to take off like that," Gertie said.

He hadn't, Edie realized, not really. If Mack hadn't showed up when he did, there was a very good chance she would have enjoyed the rest of the evening with Beau, not that she would admit it to anyone. "Well, that's neither here nor there. My problem now is getting home before Merrilee gets worried."

"I have a suggestion," Mr. Stephens said. "Why don't you come inside and set a spell, maybe have a bowl of my wife's pineapple pudding, and then I'll drive you home."

"I'm not sure that's a good idea."

Gertie stared at her. "So what do you suggest we do? Let you walk home alone in the dark?"

"I don't know." Edie shook her head. She couldn't walk another step.

But the thought of having Mr. Stephens drive her across town, drawing attention to him, maybe putting him in danger wasn't an option. She'd done enough for the Stephenses today by getting Gertie fired.

"I'll go with you." Gertie's hand on her arm drew Edie's gaze. Leave it to her friend to read her mind. "And we'll take the back roads."

Maybe, just maybe Gertie's plan might work. "I'd be happy to give you some of my gas rations."

The stern look Mr. Stephens gave her reminded her of her father, back in the days before the war. "Young lady, the Bible says we should minister to folks as if we were tending to the Lord himself. And you aren't just anyone, missy. You're my girl's friend."

Relief slid through her, and she took a deep breath. "Thank you so much."

"Come on in." Gertie nodded toward the front porch, leading Edie up the steps and into the house.

The living room was small in comparison to Merrilee's airy parlor, but comfortable. The palest of pale blue covered the walls while delicately stitched doilies added a touch of elegance to the chipped knick-knacks lining the end tables. Cushioned chairs in dark blues and greens made a half circle where guests could sit and enjoy the fire while listening to the radio, which dominated the far wall.

"Here, have a seat." Gertie motioned to an appealing rocking chair in the corner of the room. "Let me just tell Momma you're here."

Her friend disappeared down a hallway that must lead to the back of the house. Mr. Stephens closed the door then headed for an oversized chair resting in front of the fireplace.

Edie walked across the room, studying the framed black-and-white pictures placed lovingly across the mantel. Mr. Stephens and his wife on their wedding day, their faces pensive, their gazes staring off into their future together. Another showed Gertie, probably no more than twelve, her skinny legs and arms giving her a gangly look, like a newborn filly ready to test her legs.

Her eyes shifted to the next grainy photo. Three children, teenagers really, two boys and a slightly older Gertie. She and the boy standing next to her stared back at Edie with the same soulful dark eyes. Must be her brother. The wide smiles plastered on their faces competed with the sunshine of the day. But the other boy . . .

Edie focused on him. He was white, not the three or four shades of gray like Gertie and her brother, tall with pale eyes, probably blue or green. While he grinned as brightly as the Stephens children, there was something about him, a sadness that shrouded him like the shade trees casting shadows on the group. And a familiarity she couldn't shake.

She turned around to where Mr. Stephens had taken a seat, the top of his head barely visible over the newspaper he was holding. "Is this your son?"

"Bring it here and let me look at it."

Edie gingerly lifted the frame from its place on the mantel and carried it to Mr. Stephens. He held his hand out, drawing it close once he had it in his grasp. The playful teasing she had seen in his coffee-colored eyes faded, replaced by a shade of somber black as he studied the picture. "No, this is Gertie with George."

The man's fingers trailed across the glass, as if reaching out to touch his child. "George had just turned sixteen here."

"Is he in the service, too?"

"No." He shook his head slowly, his eyes

still glued to the photo. "He went missing not too long after this was taken."

"I'm so sorry." Edie rested her hand on the older man's shoulder, but that didn't feel like enough. What did someone say in a situation like this?

Mr. Stephens gave a little sigh and grinned. "I'd forgotten we had this picture. The kids had a good time that day."

"Gertie and George seemed like they might be laughing at something there."

"Even Beau looked happy." Mr. Stephens leaned closer to the picture. "Which wasn't always the case back then."

Edie's insides trembled. He couldn't be talking about the man she'd spent the better part of the evening trying not to think about, could he? "Beau Daniels?"

Mr. Stephens nodded. "He and George were like brothers. Just about killed my son when Beau ran off. Not too long after that, George went missing. He's been gone ever since."

CHAPTER SEVEN

The screen door smacked shut behind Beau, his mind wandering in every direction before always coming back to Edie. After Mack had left him on the street, Beau had walked around town, hoping to catch up with her, maybe even explain the sheriff's sudden need to talk to him. An hour of staring through every store window in town had turned up nothing so he gave up and headed home.

The light scent of newly bloomed crepe myrtle hung in the front hallway. He closed his eyes and drew in a deep breath. Did everything always smell this good at home, as if all the dust and dirt of this world had been washed away, leaving the tender blossoms clean and new?

Or was it that he'd forgotten everything but the death and decay that surrounded him at the prison camp?

"You're getting home mighty late." Merrilee walked down the hall toward him, wiping her hands with her apron.

"I'm sorry, Aunt Merri." He leaned down and kissed her on her cheek. "I spent the afternoon at the hospital, then Mack needed to talk to me. The evening kind of got away from me."

Merrilee smoothed the skirt of her apron over her dress. "Well, if you're hungry, there's a plate out in the kitchen for you."

He should have thought his aunt would hold dinner for him. "Oh, I'm sorry. We already ate supper in town."

One reddish-blond eyebrow spiked in an arch. "We?"

He didn't really want to get into the whole situation of Edie Michaels right now, then thought better of it. Maybe he should just tell his aunt what he'd found and get her take on the matter. "Can we talk for a minute?"

"Okay."

She led him into the parlor and motioned him to take a seat beside her on the couch. "Now, what's with all the mystery?"

Beau glanced over at the window. The blackout curtains he had tangled with the night before hung in neat lines, obstructing the glass. He looked back at his aunt. "How well do you know Edie Michaels?"

Leaning forward, Merrilee patted his knee, a smile playing along her lips. "I knew you two would hit it off."

"Aunt Merri."

"What?" Merrilee's smile faded slightly. "I can't dream of having a houseful of grand-nieces and -nephews to spoil and bake cookies for?"

"Maybe Maggie will help you out with that once she and Wesley get married." Laughing, Beau rested back against the cushions. "And who knows? Maybe you'll . . ." An uncomfortable silence filled the space between them. "I'm sorry, Merrilee. I didn't mean to . . ."

"It's okay." But the stark lines that creased the area around her mouth and between her eyes told Beau his comment had torn the scab off a deep cut in his aunt's heart. If her marriage had worked out, Merrilee might have enough kids to field a baseball team. Even now, at almost thirty, she had plenty of time to produce the family she longed for, if only she'd open her heart.

"Why do you want to know about Edie?"

Beau rubbed his hand across his chest, the folded paper safely inside his interior coat pocket. He couldn't burden her with the letter yet, not until he'd dug up more information on Edie, not until he was certain of her innocence. Or guilt, he reminded himself. "Just interested. Maggie said something about her being from the Detroit area."

"That's right. From my understanding, she still has family there, though I don't think she hears from them much."

"Why do you say that?"

Merrilee turned toward him, hitching one ankle under the other. "Why do you care?"

Because Edie's a threat. But that thought didn't sit well with him. What kind of woman gave her blood to a dying Negro soldier? No one Beau had ever known. He answered Merrilee the only way he could, with the truth. "No one should be alone."

Merrilee studied him for a moment, then nodded as if satisfied with his reply. "The reason I think she doesn't hear from her family much is that in the year she's been here, she hasn't gotten one letter from home."

There had to be a reasonable answer. Edie would stay in touch with her parents, at least. "Maybe she has a post office box."

"I asked her about it once, but she said her folks weren't much for writing letters. You could tell the situation bothered her." Merrilee glanced over at the mantel clock and huffed. "Not that the girl would have a lot of time to read them. Here it is almost nine o'clock and she's still not home from work."

A thread of concern knotted in his stomach. "I thought Edie was upstairs."

Merrilee shook her head. "No, but that's nothing unusual. Sometimes she goes back to the plant after she's done volunteering at the hospital, especially if she got a new project late in the day."

"But this late? The buses stopped running an hour ago."

"She likes to walk, says she needs this exercise after sitting at a desk all day long." Merrilee patted him on his arm. "I'm sure she's on her way home right now."

If that were true, he would have passed her on his way home. No, something had happened. Guilt brought Beau to his feet. "Can I borrow your car?"

"You're going out again?"

"Only for a little while." No use getting his aunt all riled up, at least not yet. Let him find Edie, and then the pair of them could blast him with both barrels blazing.

"Sure, but be careful, okay?"

Beau didn't wait. He hustled across the room and through the doorway, made a quick grab for the keys and headed out the front door.

The wood floors of the porch rattled as he bolted across the porch and down the stairs, almost tripping on the last step. As he rounded the front of the car, a set of lights, like twin fireflies, turned down the drive, growing brighter as they flew closer to the house. Beau lifted his hand over his brow and squinted. An older model car with two, maybe three people inside. He stepped back on the grass as the car pulled up alongside him and slowed to a stop.

Gertie pushed open the driver's side door and stepped out, pointing a playful finger at him. "I thought that was you."

Beau swallowed, his belly churning into a sickening knot as Mr. Stephens unfolded himself out of the backseat and stood next to the car. "Beau."

The Stephenses. George's family.

The reason he'd run away from his father all those years ago. "Gertie." Beau nodded toward the older man. "Mr. Stephens."

From the front seat of the car, Edie watched the different emotions play across Beau's face. Not sadness, though there were glimpses of it in the slight downturn of his mouth and around his eyes. But something else, a feeling she could almost touch with the tips of her fingers but not quite grasp, haunted his expression. The faint desire to put her arms around him and hold him close seared through her. Edie gasped. What was she thinking? She had just met the man.

But that didn't mean she didn't know Beau. He loved his aunt and cousins, even his scoundrel of a father. He'd worked hard to save lives on the battlefield and wanted to do the same here at home by being a doctor. He'd been friends with George and Gertie when others would have turned away.

Edie looked through the windshield at him. And he hadn't been arrested this evening like she'd thought he would.

"What you tryin' to do, catch bugs with that open mouth?" Gertie rested her forearms along the top of the car door and smiled. "You were the one all bent on getting home at a decent hour."

"Right." Edie pulled the handle up, then pushed on the door frame.

"What are y'all doing here, Gertie?" Beau's voice rumbled from nearby. "You know it's not safe for you to be on this side of town this time of the night."

"Couldn't help it. Had to return something that was lost."

Standing, Edie glanced over the roof of the car just in time to meet Beau's gaze. "Edie?"

Her heart pounded beneath her breast.

When did she get to be so silly about men, especially Beau Daniels? Shutting the door, Edie tested her legs, taking a couple of wobbly steps before stopping a few paces from him. Why didn't he back up a step, at least give her room to thank Gertie instead of standing so close, all wiry muscles and concern?

Edie moved, plastering her hip against the car. "Thank you so much for giving me a ride home, Mr. Stephens, Gertie. And tell Mrs. Stephens again how much I enjoyed her pudding."

"It's no trouble at all."

Beau glared down at her. If she didn't know any better, she'd think he was madder than a hornet's nest. But why should he be? He hadn't been the one lost in the middle of nowhere tonight. She straightened and looked at Mr. Stephens. "You know I'd be happy to give you some of my gas rations."

A deep, rich chuckle broke through the quiet of the night. "We've already talked about that, young lady."

Edie smiled. Even in the mess she was in, God had provided her with good friends. "You don't know how much I appreciate it."

"Thanks for bringing Ms. Michaels home." Beau held open the door of the car for Gertie. "But you'd better get a move on. Don't want any problems for you and your family."

Gertie walked around to the side of the car then stood at the open door. "Nothing we haven't dealt with before."

Beau rubbed his thumb across a puckered slice of skin near his knuckles. "Nothing we'd want to go through again."

Gertie gave a sad nod. "Night, y'all."

"Night." Edie waited until the taillights faded into pale pink in the pitch dark before heading for the porch.

"Where are you going?"

Edie stopped midstep at Beau's growl. What in tarnation did he have to be mad about? Dinner had been hours ago, and though she loved these shoes, she didn't like the blisters her hike out of town had caused. She turned toward him. "I don't know, Beau. Maybe I'll go to Atlanta. I was halfway there this evening."

Did his mouth twitch, almost as if he was holding back a smile? He pointed in the opposite direction. "Atlanta's that way."

Edie turned on her heel, a whisper of a smile playing on her lips. What was it about a man with a snappy sense of humor that always made her breath catch in her throat? "It's been a long day, and I just want to go to bed."

"So how did you meet up with the Stephenses tonight?"

If he was bent on hearing the whole story, she would tell it sitting down. Edie plopped into a nearby rocking chair and kicked off her shoes. "I got twisted around after I left the diner today and took the wrong road out of town. By the time I realized it, it was already getting dark. I ended up on the Stephenses' doorstep."

"Then why didn't you call?"

Edie glared up at him as he stood on the top step, leaning against a post, his arms crossed over his chest. "I thought you might be in jail tonight."

"Mack was just pulling your leg. He wants me to play ball for the police department when they go up against the bomber plant."

"I didn't know that. And the way he was acting, I just assumed . . ." She stopped. She'd been jumping to conclusions ever since she'd met this man. Time to examine the facts. "Mack seemed pretty serious for something as silly as a ball game."

"You don't know how serious he is about winning."

"And he can only win with you?"

"No, but he has a better chance of it." Strands of fiery gold shimmered in the pale moonlight when Beau chuckled. "Look, Mack and I have been friends since before both of us were old enough to use a razor, and sometimes his jokes just aren't that funny."

"No, they're not." With a tiny push, Edie set the chair to rocking. "I probably should have taken him up on his offer to have one of his deputies drive me home."

"I'm sure he would have liked that."

Was that a hint of jealousy in Beau's answer? And why did the thought make her feel like a bar of chocolate left out on the sidewalk in the middle of a heat wave? Well, she needed to stop this nonsense and stop it now. "Maybe next time, I'll take him up on it."

"Maybe next time, you won't have a reason to high-tail it out of there like that."

She gave a little snort of laughter. "Is that another way to say run away?"

He chuckled, a warm sound that caused a pleasant rumble down her spine. Beau pushed away from the railing and walked the short distance to the chair beside her. He lowered himself in the rocker, the wood moaning softly against the porch floor. "I'm sorry you felt like you couldn't call here. I'm sure Merrilee or Maggie would have been okay with picking you up."

"I know they would've, but that wasn't the problem." Edie put her weight on her forearm and leaned toward him. "Gertie and her family don't have a phone. Nobody in her neighborhood does."

This close, she could just make out the shadow of his brows furrowing together in a sharp line. "But it wouldn't take much to connect to the phone lines at the road."

So she hadn't missed the telephone poles. "Gertie's been trying for the last few months to get the phone company to string lines, but they told her it was too much work for a community that small."

"Sounds like somebody's just making up an excuse not to do the work."

That had been her first thought, too. Edie gave her rocking chair a hard push. "Well, that's just not right. What if something happened to one of those kids in the neighborhood? How would they get help?"

"I don't know." Beau rocked in a slow rhythm beside her. "At least they've got Gert to help them out if something does go wrong."

Edie jerked her chair to a halt. "But that's not enough. And what about Gertie? How is she going to find another job if no one can pick up the phone and call her?"

"I thought she worked at the hospital."

She put her hand over her mouth. Maybe the darkness had coaxed Gertie's problem out of her, or maybe it was the man beside her. Either way, she was sunk. "She got fired today."

The tempo of Beau's rocker slowed. "Does this have anything to do with you giving blood this afternoon?"

"I was the only match available. If this kid didn't get blood fast, he would have died."

"I know. I was there." He drew in a sharp breath then let it go. "Still, it wasn't a smart idea."

Smart? Maybe not, but they had been too busy saving the young man's life. "And I guess you would take Dr. Lovinggood's side?"

"No, in fact, I know he's wrong. I just wouldn't have gotten caught."

Now he was just being infuriating. "I didn't plan on passing out."

"But you did."

Edie curled back into the rocker. What did it matter who was right? Gertie had been punished by losing her job. "And now Gertie's out of work. Which makes it even more important to get those phone lines hung as soon as possible."

"You don't get it, do you?"

She glanced up to find Beau glaring at her.

Why did he look so stern? "What?"

The tension she heard in his voice suddenly made her nervous. "You can't help the Stephenses or their neighbors, Edie, and the sooner you realize it, the safer everyone will be."

"Safer?"

Beau gripped his fingers around the curved end of the rocker's arms. It wasn't Edie's fault she didn't understand the way things were around here. But someone needed to tell her, and it might as well be him.

"Do you have any idea how much danger Gert and her father put themselves in tonight, just driving you over here? Anybody sees them, the wrong person notices that they're out on this side of town after dark, and they could . . ." He swallowed, the words knotting in his throat. Edie needed only enough information to make her think, not to scare her. "There's a lot of people who wouldn't mind giving the Stephenses a hard time."

"I didn't know."

Pale moonlight revealed the pained look around her eyes, the slight tremble of her parted lips. He reached over and covered her hand with his. "I know."

"It's just not fair."

Beau nodded. When had life ever been fair? "Merrilee used to tell me that God didn't promise us that everything in life would be fair, only that He'd be with us when it wasn't."

"Sounds like something your aunt would say." Edie leaned her head back against the headrest. "It's just hard to live it sometimes."

The whisper of hopelessness in her voice touched something in him. It wasn't just the situation with the Stephenses that had Edie upset. No, only something more personal could cause the soul-wrenching pain he heard in her answer.

Without thinking, his thumb comforted the line of her knuckles, following the rise and fall of each delicate bone. She really was a dainty thing, and yet he sensed a strength in her that could match most men.

"Edwina?"

She lifted her head until her gaze met his, her eyes wide and luminous as if tears had gathered there but she had refused to let them fall. She drew in a shaky breath through parted lips, and Beau couldn't breathe. The crickets chirped a soft melody sweeter than any love song he had ever heard. He leaned toward her. Or had she met him halfway?

A muffled voice within the house drew him up short. What was he doing, holding Edie's hand like some besotted boy in the school yard? Protecting Merrilee and Claire had to be his first priority, and until he learned more about this beautiful German woman, she posed a possible threat.

Edie must have had second thoughts, too, for she reclaimed her hand and scooted back into her chair, as far away from him as she could. "Well, just because things have always been one way doesn't mean they can't change."

He blinked. "What are you talking about?"

The rocking chair swayed in a mesmerizing rhythm when Edie stood. "Gertie needs a job, Beau, and she's not going to get one if no one can reach her. And what if something horrible happens and those people need help? Someone has to do something."

An icy finger of dread slithered down his spine. "What are you saying?"

She gave him a determined smile, and he knew she had pushed whatever had passed between them just seconds ago from her mind. "I'm going down to the telephone company after work tomorrow to get them to run phone service into Gertie's neighborhood."

Had the woman not listened to a word he'd said? Forcing Ben Cantrell and those cronies at the phone company to string up lines down to the Stephenses was asking for trouble, and not just for Gertie and her family, but for Edie, too.

Beau glanced up at her. Well, if she intended to do this, she'd need some help.

He settled back against the chair, almost certain he'd lost what common sense he had.

"If that's your decision, I've got a business proposition for you."

"A business proposition?"

Edie grasped the back of the rocker, her bones turned to leaded weight, holding her in place. Her father had used those same words that morning he'd joined her in the kitchen two days after her college graduation. Companies weren't hiring with the economy still in shambles, much less considering a female architect. Why didn't she go and stay with her grandparents in Dusseldorf? Germany needed bright men and women to further Hitler's vision for Europe and throughout the world. Her talents would be greatly appreciated back home.

Only Germany wasn't her home, and never had been.

"Edie?"

"What's your proposition?" Her steady voice surprised her. Years of practice, of hiding the truth.

"I hear you're an architect."

Edie blinked. Not exactly the direction she'd thought this conversation would go, but then, what had she expected from Beau Daniels? "Yes, why?"

"I don't know if you've heard, but my father has a farm a few miles from here off Powder Springs Road."

That was news to her. "Then why was he freeloading on Merrilee before he got arrested?"

He shook his head. "Probably wanted to keep his eye on Merrilee to make sure he knew if she slipped up."

"Sounds like him." But what about his son? Was Beau here following through with his father's plans?

"Anyway, taxes are due and if they're not paid, he loses the house." Edie started to speak, but Beau's raised hand stopped her. "Now I know that would be poetic justice, but it's the only place my brothers think of as home."

"But not you?"

157

He didn't answer her but got right to his point. "With all the folks moving in the area to work at the plant, I thought I might be able to rent it out."

The idea had a lot of merit. "What does your dad think about this?"

Beau's low chuckle penetrated the quiet of the night. "I can only imagine. And I would appreciate it if you didn't mention it to anyone just yet."

"I still don't understand what this has to do with me being an architect?"

"Right," he answered, the chair rocking back and forth in a sluggish rhythm. "I just remember the living room floors sagging and some cracks in the kitchen walls. I want to make sure the place is safe."

Now she understood. "It could be something as simple as the foundation settling."

"Maybe, but I don't want to put someone in there, and then have the house fall down around them."

She nodded. Smart move. "And you want me to give you my opinion?"

"Yes, and in return, I'll do something for you."

A favor? "And what would that be?"

Beau stood. Suddenly the open-air porch felt smaller, more compact, as he walked the few steps it took to stand beside her.

The pleasant smell of soap and pure male scented the moist air around her, filling her lungs, making her long for . . . what? She tilted her head back to look up at him, but only gazed into the shadows of his face.

"I'll help you get Gertie her telephone."

She eyed him with suspicion. What had changed his mind so quickly? It had to be more than just fixing up an old house to rent out. "Why?"

"Why what?" he echoed.

Edie leaned a hip against the railing, knotting her arms in front of her. "Why the sudden change? Five minutes ago, you thought me helping the Stephenses was a bad idea."

"I still think it's not the most thought-out plan, but if you're determined to do this, you're going to need help."

Maybe, but then why the business proposition? "Why are you really renting out your father's house?"

He tensed beside her. "Because I have to hire a lawyer to defend him, and most of the ones I've heard from want quite a bit of money."

Edie sucked in a hard breath, the faint smell of smoke from the explosion James Daniels had set off with his moonshine still lingering in her memory. The man had been lucky no one had been killed. "I'm sorry,

Beau, but there is no way in this world I'm going to help your father get out of jail. I'll have to convince Mr. Cantrell to string those phone lines all by myself."

CHAPTER EIGHT

"But Mr. Cantrell, be reasonable."

Edie stared across the cherrywood desk at Ben Cantrell, owner and chairman of the Marietta Telephone and Telegraph Company, and knew her fifth request in two weeks was a lost cause.

"Ms. Michaels." The man stood, his long, lanky frame unfolding behind the desk until he towered over her. With his spindly arms and wire-rimmed glasses, he looked like one of the telephone poles his company erected along the roadsides. "I don't know if you've noticed, but there's a war going on. We just can't use up all of our resources on a community that's done quite well without phone service for many years. It would be unpatriotic."

What silliness! Edie leaned back, resting her elbows on the armrest of the leathered chair, her gloved hands tented in front of her. "Are you telling me that the phone company has stopped installing service for the duration of the war?"

Cantrell's face turned beet red, though from embarrassment or anger, she wasn't sure. "Why do you care, Ms. Michaels?"

Edie straightened. "Excuse me?"

"You've only been in Marietta for what, a little over a year? And that's because you have a job at the bomber plant, isn't it?"

So Cantrell had done a little digging, just like Beau said he would. Well, what did it matter how long she'd been in town? What mattered was getting those phone lines strung. "And the Stephenses have been a part of this community for many years, so what's your point?"

"The point is, it costs money to plant and wire telephone lines, funds this community doesn't have." He gave her a scathing glance. "I don't think the citizens of this town would appreciate an outsider coming in and telling us how to run our business."

Edie felt as if she'd been slapped. Never once in the time she had moved to Marietta had anyone ever treated her as — what had Cantrell called her — an outsider. The idea of giving up crossed her mind, but she couldn't. Gertie needed a phone to secure a new job.

She tipped her head back and looked at

Cantrell. "What kind of price tag are we looking at?"

If she thought her question would shock him, she was wrong. The figure he gave her almost made her gasp, but she refused to give him the satisfaction. Gertie's neighborhood would never be able to come up with that kind of cash. And while she had some savings, it wasn't nearly enough.

There had to be a way for her to bankroll the project. Beau's job offer floated through her mind. She couldn't take it, not if Beau intended to use the rent money to help in his father's defense. It would be like working for Merrilee's enemy. No, there had to be another way to get that much cash.

Edie stood and extended her hand to the man across the desk. "Well, thank you, Mr. Cantrell. I appreciate you taking the time to see me."

"Of course, Ms. Michaels." Rounding the corner of his desk, he shook her hand. "I'm just sorry I couldn't help you."

"Oh, but you did." Edie pulled her hand out of his grasp, schooling her features to remain neutral when confusion flashed across his face. "Now that I know how much the installation will be, I'll make sure to have a bank draft drawn up for that amount the next time I come by."

"Ms. Michaels . . ."

But Edie refused to give the man time to finish, grabbing her purse and turning toward the door. Three quick steps and Cantrell's door clicked shut behind her. She managed to hold herself together through the maze of offices until she finally reached the double glass doors.

Afternoon sunlight bathed the sidewalk with warmth, but Edie felt chilled to the bone. How was she going to come up with that much cash? She leaned back against the marble and closed her eyes.

"So how did it go?"

Beau! She'd managed to avoid the man for the most part these past two weeks since turning down his offer to inspect his father's house. Rising early for work and not coming home until the sun faded from the horizon had put some distance between them. Even Dr. Lovinggood had managed to help by assigning her to different patients when she was at the hospital.

But it hadn't meant she hadn't noticed him, bent over a patient, his focus solely on giving them the best possible health care. She'd seen the same kind of consideration in the way she treated Claire, always with respect despite her young age.

But she couldn't help him with James's

house. Could she?

Edie gave herself a mental shake. Of course not! She opened her eyes to see Beau walking toward her. Sometime between last night and this afternoon, he'd been to a barber, his thick auburn hair trimmed into a short style that made the angles of his face impossibly more masculine. The faint tang of his aftershave in her nose caused her stomach to do a pleasant flip.

She turned her head away. So she was attracted to the man. Who wouldn't be? But it wasn't the way he smiled at her that tugged at her heart. No, it was something else, something more — but until she was free from the scandal that had driven her away from home, from the kidnapping threats of the Bund, she couldn't think about the tug Beau seemed to have on her heart.

"So what did Ben say?"

She shook her head. "That it's going to take an arm and a leg to get those lines strung out to Gertie's."

He let out a low whistle at the figure she gave him. "What does he think you're going to do, rob a bank?"

She shrugged. "You know us outsiders. We're liable to do anything."

"He said that to you?" Beau let out a

shout of laughter. "At least he didn't call you a Yankee."

"But I'm from Michigan."

"You may think you're a Midwesterner, but anything north of the Mason-Dixon Line is Yankee country around here."

A Yankee German. A bubble of laughter caught in her throat. "Well, that's a new one."

His hand came to rest on her shoulder, and she glanced up. Humor crinkled the corners of his eyes and mouth, causing her heart to thunder a strange beat she'd never heard. Despite her disappointment with Mr. Cantrell, she couldn't help the laughter that had her grabbing her side, the pure freedom of the moment rushing through her, leaving her warm and relaxed for the first time in months.

"Come with me." Beau's hand at her shoulder slid down the length of her spine to the arch in her back, causing a pleasant tingle to zip along her nerve endings. With a gentle press of his fingers, he showed her to a nearby alley. "No sense giving everyone in town something to talk about."

Was that what he worried about, people talking about them? Grabbing her purse from under her arm, Edie took an uncertain step away from him. "Well, maybe the folks

166

around here ought to be talking. Maybe they ought to know that there are people who don't have the means to call for help if they need it."

"Hey, you don't have to convince me." He held his hands up in surrender. "I'm with you on this one."

"You are?" She shook her purse at him. "But you said . . ."

"I know what I said, and I still believe you need to consider the Stephenses' safety against this need for a phone." He dropped his hand to his side, leaving her with the vague sense of loneliness. "And I'm not just thinking about the Stephenses. There are folks around who wouldn't think twice about causing problems for you, too."

Edie's stomach fluttered. She worried so long over her safety, she'd never thought of someone else wanting to protect her, too. But Beau did, though she hadn't really been on her best behavior with him. So why do it? Was it because he was as drawn to her as she was to him?

She hoped not, for both of their sakes.

Edie clutched her purse between gloved fingers. "What am I going to do, Beau? I don't have near enough money in my accounts to pay Cantrell."

"You might if you'd reconsider helping

me with my dad's house."

Wrapping her arms around her waist, she shook her head. "No."

His eyebrows lifted high on his forehead. "What do you mean no?"

"I mean, I'm the one who started this. It's my responsibility." She rattled her brain for a better excuse. "You can't possibly swing it, not with your dad and the house."

"I'd rather give the money to the phone company than to defending my dad."

He probably meant it, but she knew he wouldn't. Beau cared too much, even for his father. "I'll find it, someway."

Beau didn't look too happy with her answer but he didn't argue. "Why don't you reconsider helping me out with my dad's house? I know you're not crazy about the thought of doing anything for him, but it would sure help me out."

Edie bit the tender flesh of her bottom lip. It wouldn't be a good idea to work so close to Beau, not when she longed to know him better, understand why he'd come back home after leaving all those years ago. Oh, she knew he wanted to take care of Merrilee and Claire — who wouldn't want to be around those two? But Edie couldn't shake that something else had brought him back to Marietta, some unfinished business Beau didn't even recognize yet.

Could she risk helping him? Edie gave him a quick glance. A long white coat hung open, hugging the muscles in his arms and chest, a stethoscope draped around his neck. Dr. Lovinggood had let it slip when she'd helped him suture Imogene Reynolds's cut hand that he was looking into scholarships to help Beau get to medical school but he needed his degree first. There would never be enough money with James Daniels's legal fees hanging over his head. And if anyone deserved to be a doctor, it was Beau.

"Whatever you can't cover, I'll pay you to work on the house."

Edie hated the thought of taking his money, but it was a job. A business venture. *Keep telling yourself that, and you might believe it eventually.*

"You've got yourself an architect." Edie held out her hand to him, not quite prepared for the shock of warmth that skirted up her arm when his fingers touched hers. She could ignore these feelings — she had to. For the Stephenses' sake.

For her own sake, as well.

CHAPTER NINE

No matter how slow Beau drove, Merrilee's old Ford rocked and swayed with the rain-induced craters in the old dirt road. A pine limb from an overhanging tree slapped the windshield with a soft thump.

"Oh!"

Beau glanced over at Edie and smiled at the look of shocked amusement on her face. "Are you enjoying this?"

"I'm sorry." Her soft laugher echoed through the cab of the truck when the next bump jolted her into the air slightly. "Just reminds me of riding a roller coaster."

"I've never been on one." But he'd heard of them. Like flinging yourself over the top of a cliff, one of his buddies had told him. Kind of how he felt every time he was with Edie.

He'd half expected her to throw his proposition — her expertise with his father's house in exchange for getting Gertie a phone — right back in his face. But she hadn't. Maybe the woman had listened to him and realized she might just need his help.

"Well, this is as close as I've been to one since Dad took Mom and me to this amusement park right outside of Chicago when I was ten." She grabbed the seat cushion, gripping as much of the tight fabric as she could in her fingers, her lips turned up, revealing even white teeth. "Dad was big on vacations. I think he always felt guilty over all the time he had to spend at the office, so he'd pick some place for us to go where he could give us his undivided attention."

That's how John had been, taking Beau fishing in a little pond he'd found or teaching him how to drive. James may have given him life, but John was the man whom he thought of as his father. "Sounds like you guys had fun."

"We did." Her voice held a hint of melancholy. "A long time ago."

He itched to reach for her hand, just to let her know everything would be okay. Instead, he glanced over at her and gave her a smile. "Once this war is over, you'll get to be with your family again."

But the brief gaze that met his held hurt, a bleakness, almost as if the sunlight shining from her face moments ago had never existed. What had caused this shift in Edie's relationship with her parents? She leaned her head against the side window, turning her attention back to the makeshift road.

Beau focused on the road again, too. "You know, I remember when my mom and dad bought this place. Dad sent me and my brothers to pick up rocks out in the fields."

"How old were you?"

"Eight? Nine?"

Out of the corner of his eye, he noticed her watching him. "That's hard work for such a little boy."

Maybe, but he hadn't known any other way. "We made a game of it. There's a pond on the back end of the property. We liked to skip stones across." He chuckled. "We'd spend all day looking for that perfect rock. You know, one that's smooth and flat that would skim across the water. Whoever got their rock to go the farthest won the game."

"I bet you won quite a bit," she said with a hint of a smile in her voice.

"Sometimes," Beau replied, not quite understanding this feeling drifting through his veins, warm and satisfying. "But usually, my brother Joe would win. He could make a rock skip across the surface of the water forever."

The truck lurched sideways on another bump, bouncing her against him. Instinctively, he put his arm around her, his hand clamped around her shoulder, bringing her flush against his side. Beau inclined his head just an inch or so, but it was enough to catch a whiff of her scent. Vanilla. She must touch the spice against the soft skin behind her ears, like the finest French perfume.

Edie pressed her hand to his chest and pushed away. "You may need to think about getting someone to level out this road before you rent out the house."

Had her hand trembled as she drew away? Or was that simply wishful thinking on his part? "We'll need to make a list."

She nodded, crowding the door on the far side of the seat. "How did you think our meeting with Mr. Cantrell went this morning?"

"All right." Beau gripped the steering wheel. They had caught Ben Cantrell heading out of his office this morning, and handed him a check to extend telephone service into the Negro community. But beneath Cantrell's graciousness, Beau had read the immovable truth. The man had no intention of giving authorization to string phone lines to Gertie's neighborhood, not any time soon.

"Cantrell's a hard sell, but I think that check may get him moving on the project."

Poor woman, she didn't know Ben Cantrell. But it didn't matter. Beau had made a deal with her, and he would see it through, even if it meant a private meeting with Ben to convince him.

He glanced out the window. Spring had come early. The water oaks, usually bare this time of the year, already bore buds of deep green, their skeletal limbs dressing in Easter finest. Pink and white flowers blossomed along the crooked branches of the dogwoods. Even the crepe myrtles were getting in on the act, the tiny buds seeming ready to burst with color. If he rolled down the window, he bet he could almost smell their heady floral scent.

"I'd forgotten how pretty it is out here."

"Wonder why your dad wanted Merrilee's house so much that he'd give up on this place?"

"Pride." Beau slowed the truck as they came up on the driveway. "Dad just always thought Grandpa owed him the house."

"That's a little presumptuous, don't you think?"

"Have you met my father? He figures everything in the Daniels family is his until someone tells him differently. Then he gets angry."

Edie chuckled. "You think that's why your grandfather didn't tell James he'd sold the house to John Davenport? He was afraid to?"

"Let's just say Dad came by his pride honestly," Beau answered, steering the truck onto a patch of gravel and dirt. "Grandpa couldn't tell anyone he'd run into money problems and had to sell the house. The only way he could save face was to leave it to Merrilee in his will."

"You think if he'd told your dad ahead of time, this mess would still have happened?"

"No doubt about it. Dad's always been mixed up in something — moonshine, gambling." Well, Beau could only hope this most recent mess would give his father a chance to make things right with the Lord.

The trees along the drive suddenly thinned out, revealing a small patch of barren land, save one or two scrawny azaleas his mother had planted before leaving. Beau brought the truck to a stop and looked out over the windshield. From the road, it hadn't looked so bad, but up close, the damage was evident. Paint peeled back from the outside walls, exposing gray unfinished boards to the elements. The front porch leaned to one side, and a mix of mortar, broken boards and rusty nails crumbled beneath it, leaving one narrow step that Beau would wager couldn't support a fly, much less a person. The shutters hung at odd angles, and the roof needed new shingles.

Beau fell back into his seat. Momma had been so proud of this place. It would have killed her to see how Dad had let this place go. But she'd left — everybody had except Dad. *God, how am I going to fix this place up? It's a dump.*

"It's not as bad as I thought it would be." Edie's words pierced through his thoughts.

Was she serious? "Are you looking at the same mess I am?"

"What is it Merrilee is always saying? Expect the worst, hope for the best and you'll usually get something in between." Her hand gently rested on his forearm, sending a shaft of warmth up his arm that burrowed into his chest. "So far, everything I see can be fixed with a little paint and some two-penny nails."

Was she right? Was this one mess his father had made that could be fixed? He pointed to the glove compartment. "There's some paper and a pencil in there. Could you please get them?"

Beau got out of the car, then after taking

one more glance toward the house, stepped around to help Edie out. Even with their visit to the phone company on the agenda, she'd shown up for breakfast this morning decked out in a pair of pale blue coveralls that gave just a hint at her feminine curves, the elastic gathers around her trim ankles offering the only evidence of her shapely legs. She'd pulled her chestnut hair back in a protective scarf, but on the trip here, a dark strand had come loose, curling around one flushed cheek.

Beau grimaced. He shouldn't have brought Edie here, to this place where the very walls spoke of mistreatment and neglect. Would she guess that his father took no better care of him and his brothers than he did this house?

She pocketed the paper and pencil. "Are you ready to go inside?"

No use putting off the inevitable, not that he thought Edie would let him. Beau nodded. "It might be easier to go in through the kitchen."

The back of the house looked as bleak and run-down as the front. Pulling a key out of his pocket, Beau jiggled it in the lock, his mouth a line of stubborn determination that Edie could handle, unlike the flicker of painful vulnerability that dulled his green eyes when they'd first driven up. No, the hurt she'd seen lodged deep in her chest, plunging through her like a penny nail in thick oak. Well, it wasn't Beau's fault his father acted like a cretin.

A soft click announced the lock slipping from the bolt. Beau pushed the door open. A thick wave of heat and stale air bore down on them, sucking the air right out of Edie's lungs.

"I'll get the windows."

She glanced over the room, mentally trying to map out a trail through the jungle of boxes, old newspapers and broken furniture. "We need to get a cross breeze going through here."

He gave her a stiff nod, then hurried across the floor, jumping over piles of scattered newspapers and old magazines. Beau pushed against the window frame, the metal hinges and glass panes crying out in protest against his brute strength. The heavy blanket of heat eased just a bit, the faded curtains lifting at the light breeze flowing through the house.

Beau drew in a shallow breath and coughed. "Sorry about that. Never thought to check this place out before now."

Was that because he'd never thought of

this place as his home? "Well, it's pretty obvious your dad hasn't been here in a while."

"It's a shame, too. This house used to be a showcase." Beau glanced around, his gaze perusing the rectangular room, as if making a schematic of where each chair, each pot and pan belonged. Piles of old clothes, cushions and other trash grazed the dingy ceiling, rounded out the room's corners. "Momma would die if she saw what Dad did to this place."

Edie glanced around, noting the handmade cabinets and engraved trim work that ran along the edge of pine hardwoods throughout the room. A little soap and water would turn the dirty walls back to a buttery yellow that would give the kitchen a homey feel any woman would want to come home to after a day at the bomber plant. A thick coat of dust covered the only exposed furniture top, a round kitchen table in the center of the room. Nothing that a little polish and elbow grease couldn't fix.

She flashed him an uncertain smile. "Have you found him a lawyer yet?"

"Everyone I've interviewed doesn't want to take his case." Beau grabbed an errant box and put it back in a short stack. "I guess they're afraid of losing the case, not that I blame them. Dad's been a loose cannon most of my life. I'm just surprised it took Mack this long to catch him at something."

"You don't mean that." Edie walked over to the dining room table, surveying the mountain of what looked like unopened mail. "Everyone wants to believe the best about their parents."

He laughed. "Unless those parents give you a reason not to trust them. Then you're either stupid or incredibly naive to think like that."

Edie should come back with something, some nonsense about believing the best in people, or mumbo jumbo like that. That's what he'd expect. But she couldn't, not when what he'd said was true. Instead she separated envelopes, shuffling them into distinct stacks.

Yes, she had problems, but whatever troubled Beau ran deeper, more painful than the embarrassment of a troublesome father. And for the life of her, she couldn't shake the need to know what troubled him. What could she do to help, to bring him comfort?

The name and address on the envelope brought her thoughts into focus. James Daniels couldn't be that cruel. "Beau?"

"What is it?"

Edie handed him an envelope yellowed with age. "You need to look at this."

Beau glanced over the letter, his brows furrowing into a stern line. One look at him told Edie she hadn't mistaken the familiar handwriting of her landlady, or the name of the addressee.

John Davenport.

"What would Merrilee be writing John Davenport?" Edie picked up another letter and studied it. "I thought she didn't even know where he was."

"She doesn't. The address she used is from more than ten years ago." Beau threw a letter on the table and grabbed another one. "My guess is that they've been here this whole time."

"I don't understand."

"Of course you don't. You're too nice for that." He grimaced. "I'm sorry. Didn't mean to take it out on you."

Edie nodded. At least he had the decency to apologize, but that was who she'd begun to realize he was, a stand-up kind of man. "Then tell me how did your dad get Merrilee's letters?"

"I don't know. More than likely promised to mail them, then brought them here." Beau started digging through the mess on the table, pushing paper off, letting them fall to the floor like heavy raindrops scattering across parched soil. "And if I were a gambling man, I'd bet the farm John's letters to her are somewhere in this mess, too."

"But what does that mean?"

"It means Dad's been jockeying for the homestead for more than ten years." Beau's fingers tightened around the letter in his hand. "And that he was willing to break up Merrilee's marriage to do it."

What James had done to Merrilee was much more than that! "He wanted her house that badly?" Her voice caught on her words, her throat thickening with tears. "Didn't he realize he wasn't just hurting Merrilee and John, but Claire, too?"

He glanced over at Edie before focusing his attention back on the growing pile of letters. "Dad's only concern is for himself."

Edie stared at him, a sharp ache settling in her chest at the tight pull of his lips and the lines that suddenly flared around the corners of his eyes. James might not care about his sister, but Beau did. He was hurting for Merrilee and John, and now for Claire. Without thinking, she laid her hand on his arm. "This isn't your fault."

He combed a hand through his hair, the thick auburn strands, an unruly mess that she found boyishly appealing. "Maybe if I'd stuck around, he wouldn't have had the chance to pull something like this."

"James would have found a way to keep them apart. You know that." Hard muscles bunched beneath her palm, causing a pleasant warmth to travel up her arm and pool in her chest. Edie swallowed past the sudden knot in her throat. "And he might have killed you, too."

"Death would be too permanent." Pressing his hands flat against the table, he dropped his chin to his chest. Beau shook his head. "He's only interested in the pain he can inflict."

Resisting the urge to touch him, Edie curled her fingers into a tight ball, her head beginning to ache, though from the thick layer of dust covering every piece of furniture or the confusion she felt, she wasn't sure. If being beat to within an inch of his life hadn't forced Beau into running, why had he left home? "What drove him to keep these letters from Merrilee?"

Beau shrugged one very broad shoulder. "Who knows? Could have been a fight over the house. Or maybe this was Dad's way of punishing her for getting married in the first place." His eyes met hers, the pale green darkening to a deep emerald that sparked with anger. "Dad always felt Merrilee married beneath her. He thought she'd shamed the family, settling with a sharecropper instead of marrying the son of one of Granddaddy's wealthy cronies."

"That's an antiquated way of thinking."

Beau looked at her, frowning. "Most of these people are still fighting the Civil War, and some, like my father, continue to live by the old traditions."

"But life changes."

He shook his head. "Not for some people."

Edie glared at the envelopes scattered across the table. Beau was right. His father was set in his ways, but surely her father could change, couldn't he? She focused on the address gracing the middle of the page. "These letters look old."

Beau nodded beside her. "Knowing Dad, he probably started stealing them after John bought the house."

Was he saying what she thought he was saying? "John Davenport might not know about Claire." Edie gave him a slight nod, regret clogging her throat. She'd just jumped to the conclusion that John Davenport had abandoned his daughter like her father had, but instead the man had possibly never known her. How sad! For John, for Merrilee who had welcomed everyone into her home as if they were members of the family. And most of all, for Claire. Someone needed to tell Claire the truth before the little girl uncovered it. "What are you going to do."

"I don't know." He shrugged, picking up the remaining envelopes, fanning them out in his hands to study them. "What would you do?"

"Me?"

"Yes." He glanced up from the letters. "You've been friends with Merrilee for over a year now. What do you think I should do with the letters?"

Edie thought for a moment. "I'm not sure. I just don't want to see her get hurt."

"Me, neither." Beau bundled the envelopes together and tied them together with a rubber band he'd found on the table. "We'll just have to pray on it and see what God wants to do."

Edie blinked. *Did he say "pray"?*

"Yes, even us reformed reprobates pray." He shot her a teasing grin that would have coaxed a laugh out of her if she hadn't felt like such a ninny. "Found it particularly came in handy when I was crouched down in a foxhole with the Germans bearing down on me."

Another swift judgment on her part. Edie wasn't sure how to rectify the situation, but she had to try. "You're right. Why don't we pray about it now?"

He held out his hand to her. "That's a great idea."

His fingers felt warm and callous against the tender skin of her palm. Masculine. Protective. "Go ahead."

He gave her a reassuring squeeze that sent a shaft of warmth up her arm, then bowed his head. Edie followed his lead, shutting her eyes. *Please, Lord, please give me some kind of answer this time. I want to help Merrilee and Claire.*

"Dear Father, Edie and I are coming to You today with a problem." Beau laid out his concerns about the letters and asked God to forgive James for stealing them. His hand tightened around hers as he spoke. "The truth is, we're not sure what to do about this situation. So if You could show us what the right thing to do by Merrilee, Claire and John is, we'd appreciate it. Lead us, guide us and forgive us, Lord. Amen."

She sniffed back the tears crowding her throat and nose. "That was a lovely prayer, Beau."

"I don't know about that. Only hope I didn't make a mess of it."

Why he told her that, she wasn't sure. But there was something endearing about his confession, an openness she hadn't expected from him. A tenderness she'd never felt toward any other person welled up inside her, frightening in a way, yet she couldn't stop it — nor did she want to.

She scolded her heart. Was this what it felt like to fall in love? But she couldn't. Love couldn't survive without trust. Until she told Beau the truth about how she came to the Bell, about how her parents had betrayed their country, nothing could come of these feelings taking root inside her. And she could never tell him, not if she hoped to remain hidden from her family, from the Nazi sympathizers her father had enlisted to ship her to Germany.

"You ready to give me your opinion on the rest of the place?"

Edie nodded, her pulse thundering against her eardrums when Beau pressed his hand to the small of her back, his fingers warm through the cotton material of her coveralls. She had to hold on to her heart. She didn't have any other choice.

CHAPTER TEN

Edie turned the page of the newspaper, scanning the various advertisements and articles. She toed off one high heel, then another, stretching out her feet, trying to get the blood flow back in her toes. They had been swamped in the emergency room all afternoon, but Dr. Lovinggood had forced her into taking a break. Didn't want another fainting episode on his hands.

Oh, here were the scores. Edie folded the paper, creasing it until she could hold it in one hand. She then grabbed her apple from the table, and leaning back in her chair, began to read.

"What's so interesting?"

Her heart did a little hiccup. She looked up over the top of the newspaper to see Beau, horribly handsome in his dark blue tie and white physician's coat. His long, purposeful strides covered the distance across the break room until only the table separated them.

Work on James Daniels's house was going slow. With all the garbage that needed to be cleaned out, they'd barely made a dent. But sitting on the floor, shifting through the piles of mail left unanswered for years, talking to Beau had become her favorite time of the day. Maybe because he could make her laugh with his stories of traveling the country with the Civil Conservation Corp. And they ended each day with a prayer, waiting for an answer about the letters James had stolen from Merrilee.

Beau's hand tipped the top of her paper. "Well, it's not the front page, and the society page only comes out once a week."

"It's the sports page." Edie grimaced against her automatic answer. All her life, Momma had warned her that boys didn't like a girl who took too much interest in baseball or building things. That fact had never bothered her much, not even in college.

So what would Beau Daniels think about her love of baseball?

Leaning forward, he glanced down at the paper between her fingers, then back up again, his lips twitching up at the corners in that familiar smile that did funny things to her midsection. "I didn't know you liked sports."

Heat climbed up the back of her neck. "I grew up listening to the Tigers play."

"A baseball fan, huh?" Beau pulled out the chair next to her and sat down. "Who's your favorite?"

"Charlie Gehringer. I mean, I know he lost his position to Billy Hitchcock but I'm hoping . . ." His bemused expression stopped her. "What?"

"It's not often you meet a woman who really knows her stuff about baseball." He nodded toward the paper on the table. "But there's no baseball because of the war."

"I'm following the local high school team. They've got a great leftie who got them to the playoffs."

"The Jones kid." Beau leaned back in his chair, crossing his arms over his chest, the cotton jacket pulling tight over solid muscle. "I heard about him."

"You follow the Indians?"

"My old high school. So how did they do yesterday?"

For the next several minutes, they talked baseball: the Indians' win over rival Marietta High, Beau's first practice with the police department. It still surprised her how easy he was to talk to, not just about sports, but about everything.

Everything except who she really was.

"Mack told me about the Jones kid, said it was the first time the Georgia Crackers scout had been to the school since we played."

Edie blinked. "You were a minor league prospect?"

His ruddy cheeks turned a deep red. Could he possibly be embarrassed? "Played first base with a three-ten batting average."

"No wonder Mack wanted you on their ball team." Sitting back in her chair, she pressed the unbroken skin of the apple to her upturned lips. "You're a ringer."

"Eat your apple." The sly smile he gave her made her heart quiver. "You need to keep your strength up."

Giving in to the smile, she took a small bite. Why had she worried Beau would rake her over the coals about baseball, about fainting spells? Maybe because her parents always had. "Have you been busy upstairs?"

"Swamped. We admitted a couple of patients this afternoon for observation." He stretched his long legs out beneath the table, and she wondered if his wound ached. "One's got a light case of polio, but the other took a turn about an hour ago. We're transferring her to Crawford Long as soon as the ambulance can get here."

He didn't have to tell her what that meant. An iron lung. "That's seven cases in the last couple of weeks. You'd think Dr. Loving-good would be in touch with the school board to cancel classes until the danger passed."

Beau shrugged. "Claire's already had a few polio days since I got back home. And most of the cases have been light so far."

"What about that patient you transferred downtown?"

"It's just one case, Edie." But the deepen-ing lines around his eyes and mouth told her that he was more concerned than his words let on.

"I just worry about the kids, you know."

His warm hand settled over hers. "I worry about Claire, too, but she'll be okay. I'm keeping my eye on her."

Edie nodded, her fingers tingling beneath his touch. She wasn't sure when she'd begun to trust him — perhaps when she'd heard him pray for guidance over Merrilee's letters, so humbly, with such earnest. A girl could learn a great deal about a man listen-ing to him converse with his Heavenly Fa-ther.

And what she'd learned of Beau Daniels broke her heart.

The door swung open, and one of the newer nurses from the surgical floor poked her head around the corner. "There you are, Beau. I've been looking all over for you."

The hint of familiarity in the woman's voice grated on Edie. The woman had something of a reputation with the staff, making eyes at the doctors, sometimes with the injured soldiers. Beau had to have enough sense to see the girl for what she was. A flirt.

Edie shifted slightly toward him. "We've been taking a break."

His warm hand tightened over Edie's, and her world shifted. Why did his touch bring so much comfort to her mixed-up life? Was it because out of everyone she'd met in Marietta, Beau seemed to be the one who might understand the mess her parents had made of things, recognize the guilt she felt?

He turned to the nurse. "What is it, Natalie?"

The woman's smile slipped a fraction. Maybe Beau hadn't been assuring her as much as using her to get this particular bloodhound off the scent. "Dr. Lovinggood needs you downstairs STAT."

"Tell him I'll be right there."

Natalie gave Beau a bright smile, but when she glanced at Edie, her expression turned frosty. With one last glance, she shut the door behind her.

Beau let go of her hand, a slight chill replacing the heat that had centered in her chest around her heart. Pushing back from the table, he stood, so tall she had to tilt her head back. She cleared her throat. "What do you think Lovinggood needs with you?"

"Probably wants me to help him with some procedure or something. He's been doing that a lot here lately."

"Only because he knows you ought to be thinking about medical school."

Edie wished the words back even as she said them. Beau gripped the back of his chair with both hands, the skin across his knuckles pulled tight across the bone. "I've got a lot going on with Dad, not to mention Merrilee and Claire. It may be years before I save up the money to go."

"Your aunt seems to be doing pretty good on her own."

"Well, I'm going to see that she does better."

Edie hurriedly stood. Why couldn't she leave well enough alone? But she couldn't. "It's like you're obsessed with making a good life for Merrilee, whether she wants you to or not."

"She deserves it."

"You're not to blame for what your father did to Merrilee." When he didn't answer, she continued. "God gave you a gift for helping sick people. Are you saying He was wrong when He did that?"

But she might as well have been talking to an empty room for all the notice Beau gave her. The door opened, and then he was gone.

The sharp clang of metal crashing against the tile floor met Beau as he stood in the entrance of the emergency room. Past the nurses's desk at the second bed to the left, Nurse Arnold plunged a needle into a brownish glass bottle and pulled back on the syringe. Dr. Lovinggood grabbed a surgical towel from a pile on the bed and packed it into a gaping wound in the man's side. Dark pools of blood puddled on the floor around the bed while the sheets were streaked in bright red.

"What happened?"

Edie. It figured she would follow him, would have continued their discussion if not for the scene playing out in front of them, but her words echoed in his head. God isn't wasteful. So why would the Lord give him this incredible talent for helping the sick if Beau would never be able to use it?

"I could use a little help over here."

"Yes, sir." He hurried over to the bed, aware of Edie trailing close behind him. Grabbing another towel, Beau folded it and pressed it into the wound.

Lovinggood straightened beside him. "We need to get him into surgery, but I want to get a couple of units of blood in him first."

"You don't have time to type and cross match. Do we have any dried plasma?"

"A couple of bottles in the pharmacy," the doctor replied. "But I don't have much experience with it."

Beau reached for another towel, but Edie was there, holding it ready for him, as if she knew what he planned to do next. He bunched the cloth up and folded it into the oozing wound. "On the battlefield, we found that plasma gave us a better chance of getting the wounded back to the field hospital alive."

Lovinggood eyed him before nodding to Nurse Arnold. "Could you call down to the pharmacy and have someone bring us up a bottle of plasma and a liter of saline?"

Apprehension flickered through him. The patient would be on his way to the morgue by the time the pharmacy filled Lovinggood's order.

"I'll go pick it up. It'll be faster that way."

He glanced at Edie over his shoulder. Had the woman read his mind? "Thank you."

"You're welcome."

Beau sat back on his heels, satisfaction thrumming through his veins. It had always been like this for him, this sense of purpose, of holding off death by rendering aid to the hurting. He had saved a life!

Maybe Edie was right. Maybe God had given him a gift, whether he deserved it or not. He could almost imagine what it would be like, spending his days solving the puzzle of a difficult diagnosis, comforting when all medical options had been expended. To come home content every night in your work.

But who would he share that contentment with?

Beau held the towels in place while Nurse Arnold adjusted the oxygen mask on the patient's face. Where had that thought come from? Probably from watching Maggie and Wesley together, two parts completing each other, reading each other's thoughts sometimes.

Just like Edie had read his.

"So how did this gentleman get stabbed in the first place?" Nurse Arnold's voice broke through Beau's musings.

"All we know is that a fight broke out at a

gas station down on Roswell Road because someone wasn't crazy about his name." Lovinggood didn't look up from the chart in his hand. "And I'm betting it wasn't his first time in a fight."

Beau grabbed another towel. The bleeding had slowed, but he didn't want to take any chances. "Why would you say that?"

The doctor lifted his gaze from the documents. "His name is Joseph Schmitt."

German American, just like Edie.

Beau held the towel tight to the wound, stemming the flow of blood. He'd been so worried about protecting Merrilee and Claire, but he hadn't given any thought to who would protect Edie Michaels.

CHAPTER ELEVEN

The old church looked so much smaller than Beau remembered. Stained-glass windows reliving the scenes of Jesus's ministry lined both sides of the sanctuary, the bright reds and blues casting a vivid kaleidoscope across the wooden pews. It was early still, but a few people had beat him to the church. Most he didn't recognize, but those he did came by to shake his hand and welcome him home.

Pastor Hubert Williams walked up the aisle, his suit coat flung over his arm, his white shirtsleeves rolled up as if he'd been preaching for a full hour already. He was grayer, a bit shorter and still just as friendly as Beau remembered, stopping to talk to each person.

"Preacher?" Beau called out.

The man turned and studied him for a moment before recognition dawned in the gray eyes staring over the top of wire-framed glasses. "Beau?"

Beau led with his hand. "Yes, sir."

The preacher clasped his hand and pulled Beau into a bear hug. "I heard you were back, son. I bet Merrilee is beside herself."

"I don't know about that, but I'm enjoying being home." Beau shifted back, glancing toward the door as another couple walked into the sanctuary. "Can I talk to you for just a minute?"

Williams glanced down at his wristwatch, nodding. "We've got a little time before the service starts. Would you like to go back to my office?"

"No, this will only take a second." Beau sat down. Now that he had the pastor's attention, he wasn't exactly sure how to start this conversation; he only knew that it had to be done.

The pastor took the seat beside him. "What can I do for you, Beau?"

"That's the thing — you've already done it." The pastor's puzzled look prompted Beau to continue. "I need to thank you. All those years ago, when I sat in the back row trying to ignore the preaching, it somehow managed to get through to me anyway."

"Well, I'm glad to hear that, son." Williams clapped him on the shoulder. "Merrilee's been praying for you for years."

And his aunt's prayers had been the only thing that helped him survive during his year in Moosberg. One day, when he was ready to share the details, he'd thank Merrilee.

The two men talked for a few more minutes before Preacher Williams stood up to go. "I want to thank you, Beau. This morning, I had some trouble dragging myself out of bed. But hearing how God's been working in your life, it's put a fire in my belly today."

"I'm looking forward to listening to you, Preacher. It's been too long."

As the pastor walked away, Beau stretched his arms out along the back of the pew. It had been a long time since he'd been here, not regularly since his mother ran out on their family when he was ten. Well, that would change now that he was back home. He needed accountability and encouragement in growing his new faith.

He sensed Edie's presence before he saw her, a kind of awareness he heard the other guys in his platoon talk about but had never actually experienced himself. Shifting in his seat, he watched her, noting how people reacted to her with a level of respect and affection usually reserved for natives. Her blue dress accentuated her feminine form, the skirt flaring slightly below her knees. Her wide-brimmed hat slanted, hiding her face, leaving only a pair of bloodred lips in view.

And in her gloved hands, she held a Bible. From his vantage point, Beau could see the cracked leather cover looked as if it had been opened and read many times over the years.

"Cousin Beau!" Claire walked along the edge of the pew and sat down, curling up into his side.

Something wasn't right. Claire usually bounced through life, faster than this lethargic pace. And was it just him, or did the little girl look a bit peaked around the eyes? "You're awfully quiet this morning."

"Momma says we're supposed to be quiet in church." She stared up at him with wide-eyed innocence. "If we're not, we won't be able to hear God talking to us."

"That's right, sweetheart," Edie said, sliding in beside Claire. "It's very important that we sit quietly and listen to the Lord."

"Momma says He talks in a still, small voice."

"Your momma's right." Beau dropped his arm around Claire's tiny shoulders and drew her close. And what was the Lord going to tell him about this morning? He glanced over the child's head to where Edie sat. "Good morning."

"Good morning." A light flush of color infused her cheeks as she lowered her gaze to her gloves. She undid a tiny seed pearl button along the heel of her hand, then gently tugged at each finger until the glove slipped off her hand.

When did removing a glove become so utterly feminine? He stared at the pulpit. Edie Michaels made him think too much. Between the conversation in the break room and the German-American patient that followed, Beau's mind had bounced around like a ball made of rubber.

"Where's your mother?" Beau asked Claire as she straightened her dress.

"She had an emergency meeting of the church's ladies auxiliary. Dr. Lovinggood asked to address them this morning about a dire situation," Edie answered, setting her Bible carefully on her lap.

The polio outbreak, probably. Over the last week, they'd seen several new cases of the virus in the emergency room. Most cases had been mild, not even necessitating a hospital stay. But the threat of an epidemic still existed.

"Then how did y'all get here?" He'd walked the three miles so his aunt would have the truck to get to church.

"Ms. Edie drove us. Momma got a ride with Annabelle Smith's mother to the meeting," Claire answered, snuggling under his arm.

The tinkling of piano keys signaled the beginning of the service, thankfully. Claire pressed against his side, providing a natural barrier between him and Edie. But he couldn't help noticing the soft tremble of her voice as they sang, or the way her fingers knew instantly where to turn when the pastor read out the Bible verse.

Beau fumbled with his own Bible before finally closing it, turning his attention to Pastor Williams as he gave the message from the Bible. He settled back into the pew, the peace he always found in learning from the sermon flowing through him. It had been the same at the prison camp, this sense of calm joy that surpassed anything he'd ever known.

Claire clung to his side, listening intently, her strawberry-blond head pillowed on his chest. Two pale pink patches blossomed across her cheeks and nose. Is this what it felt like to love unconditionally? He'd read about it in the Bible, but never having experienced it, he wasn't sure it existed for everyone.

"Does she look flushed to you?"

Beau glanced over to find Edie staring down at Claire with concerned eyes. It was one of the first things he noticed about her, the way she mothered Claire. That and her protective nature. Edie had turned out to be a lovely surprise, unaware of her beauty, kind with a sweet nature.

Very different from the woman who'd come after him with a poker.

He brushed his hand across Claire's forehead. "She's a little warm, but it's kind of hot in here."

She handed him a replica of the paper fan most of the congregation were waving like flags on Flag Day. Did the woman think he wasn't capable of caring for his cousin? "Thank you."

Before he knew it, the choir director had the congregation stand for the invitation. Edie sang with a gentle sort of reverence that tugged at him, while Claire's childish voice added sweetness to the blend of sounds.

After the last note died, Beau glanced down at the upturned face of his little cousin. "I guess your mother's still busy with the meeting. How would you like to spend the day with me?"

"Really?" the little girl squealed.

"Excuse me, but Merrilee asked me to

watch Claire this afternoon." Edie wrapped an arm around the child's slight shoulders. "She said something about math homework."

Beau frowned at Edie. Did the woman really think he couldn't handle a ten-year-old child? "I'm sure Aunt Merri wouldn't mind if I took her off for a little while. I'll have her back in plenty of time to do her schoolwork."

"What are you going to do?"

Claire's face glowed when she stared up at him. "Yeah, Beau. What are we going to do?"

Do? He'd never really thought about it. It wasn't like he'd had a lot of experience entertaining little girls before. What did they like to do for fun?

"Maybe we could go home, and I could make the two of you a picnic while you change out of your good clothes."

"Maybe Kolb Farm? I've always wanted to go there," Claire blurted out.

A picnic? He would have never thought something so simple would make his little cousin so excited. He stole a look at Edie. She didn't look as if this change of events bothered her much, but there was something in the way she held herself, a stiffness that spoke of loneliness that pulled at him.

"Would you like to go with us, Edie?"

"Oh, yes, Ms. Edie! You have to go with us!" Claire swayed from one foot to the other.

"I thought I'd go in to the office today," Edie said.

Why would she go into work on a Sunday? Was it because she had B-29 plans that needed configuring, or something more sinister? The idea didn't sit well with him. "Why don't you come along, at least for a little while? Then when I take Claire home to do her homework, I can drop you off at the plant."

"Well," Edie started, looking a bit uncomfortable.

"That's perfect, Ms. Edie. Oh, please come with us."

Any reservations she might have had were forgotten in her smile. "You've talked me into it."

Claire commanded the conversation the entire walk to the old truck, talking about the kite she hoped to fly today and some of the rooms she wanted to visit at Kolb Farm. Beau couldn't help but notice that Edie listened with great interest, almost with a pride reserved for a close family member, like a cousin or an aunt.

As they approached the truck, Edie

handed him the keys, their fingers brushing slightly, sending a thrill of excitement through the pit of his stomach. There were worse things than sharing a picnic with a lovely woman, even a German one. Beau opened the passenger-side door and waited until Claire scooted to the middle of the bench seat before turning to Edie.

"Beau?" She stared into the bed of the truck.

Beau glanced over the metal siding. There, with his dark eyes wide with adventure and fear, lay a young Negro boy.

"Do you have enough room, Claire Bear?"

"Yes, ma'am." She looked up at Edie with innocent eyes. "Why is that boy sitting in the back of the truck?"

Edie glanced back at the little boy huddled in the bed of the truck, then at Beau. "I'm not sure. Why didn't Ernie sit up here with us? There's plenty of room."

Beau glanced right, then left before pulling out on the dirt road that led west out of Marietta Square. "My guess is he doesn't want to take a chance of anyone seeing him with us."

"Why would Gertie pull this kind of stunt?" She glanced through the window again at the child. He didn't seem to mind riding in the back of the truck. In fact, from the wide smile that spread across the lower part of his face, she got the feeling he was enjoying himself.

"You heard him. She wanted to make sure we'd come to the neighborhood lunch today." Beau glanced over his shoulder. "Probably safer for him to be in the back if he happens to be seen by the wrong sort of people."

"I don't understand this." She stared out the window, the newly plowed fields and blooming trees flying by, though not too fast. Beau obviously didn't want to chance injuring the boy. "Why is it always the bullies who control how everyone else behaves?"

He didn't answer, though his fingers tightened around the steering wheel. *Stupid question, Edie.* If anyone knew what living with a bully of a man was like, it was Beau. And yet, he wasn't the least bit like his father. She stole a glance at him. How she wished life had been easier for him, but then he wouldn't be the man he was today.

A man whom she had grown to care for very much.

Beau's next comment broke through her thoughts. "Truth is, I think Ernie's a bit nervous. He's more than likely going to be in trouble when he gets home."

She hadn't thought of that. "Gertie talked him into this. And little boys lose track of time." Edie nuzzled Claire's hair. "I know little girls do."

"What would cause a young lady like yourself to lose track of the clock?"

The light teasing in his voice brought a smile to her lips. "Stickball."

Claire gasped. "Girls don't play stickball!"

His laughter rumbled throughout the cab of the truck, surrounding her like a heartbeat, made her stomach do a pleasant little tumble. "Some girls do, brat. In fact, I wouldn't mind seeing Ms. Edie play."

"Maybe you will," she teased. "I still play when the weather is good."

Beau glanced out the window, then back at her. "Maybe Ernie can get a few of his friends together and we could play this afternoon."

"You think so, Cousin Beau?" Claire's eyes danced with excitement at the possibility. "Could I learn how to play?"

He laughed again, but this time she joined him.

Bumping down the dirt road toward the Stephenses' house, the conversation shifted to everyday things: the latest movie at the Strand, the announcement that Bob Hope was coming to the bomber plant to sell war bonds, the new batch of soldiers admitted to the hospital. For those few minutes, Edie forgot about the situation with her parents, enjoying the comfortable rhythm of their chat. By the time they pulled up in front of the Stephenses' home, Beau had talked her into an evening at the movies, though she'd admitted to herself, it hadn't taken much convincing.

As she sat waiting, watching Beau walk around the front of the truck to her door, she was struck again by how handsome he was. Oh, the jeans and button-up shirt he wore now reminded her of the boy he must have been, ready for a day of playing in the sunshine.

A vast difference from the devastatingly attractive man who'd sat next to her at church this morning. The dark suit and tie had fit him to perfection, but it was his expression, as if each point taught from the scriptures was precious. It had confirmed everything she'd learned about Beau in the past weeks — that he wasn't as much of a troublemaker as he thought himself to be, but the brunt of his father's misguided anger.

Who, despite the odds, had grown into a kind and decent man. Why did the thought of an evening with Beau Daniels make her feel all bubbly inside, floating away like a balloon that had broken free, dancing on wispy clouds, reaching for the heavens?

She didn't have time to ponder the question. The door opened and Beau held his hand out to her. "Ready for some of the best cooking you'll ever have in your life?"

A playful gleam danced in her eyes. "Are you saying Merrilee's not the best cook in town?"

"And get myself in trouble? Oh, no, I know the hand that feeds me." Her fingers slid across his palm, sending a pleasant tingle up her arm that left her breathless. "But these women give her a run for their money."

Beau closed the door while Edie stepped away, busying her shaking hands by brushing at the creases in her pants. Was she the only one left discombobulated by this attraction, or did Beau feel it, too? Her cheeks went warm at the thought.

"Thanks for the ride, mister." Ernie vaulted over the side of the truck and ran.

"I guess he was in a hurry," Beau said.

"Can I go, too?" Claire eyed a group of young girls swinging a long jump rope.

The two adults exchanged glances before Edie answered. "Yes you may, but stay close.

No wandering off into the woods, you understand?"

"Yes, ma'am," Claire tossed over her shoulder, skipping away.

Beau leaned back against the frame of the truck, his gaze traveling down the line of clapboard houses ending with a field shaded on one side by a large magnolia tree. "First time I came out here, there weren't more than a couple of houses on this road."

She leaned back beside him, the heated metal of the truck stinging her skin through her cotton shirt. "When was that?"

"About a year after I met George."

"You must have been good friends. The Stephenses have a photograph of the three of you on their mantel. You were at the lake."

"Sawyer Lake. We were teaching Gertie how to swim." Beau snorted, his hands stretching and flexing at his sides. "That was the night I left town. Wasn't too long after that that I heard George ran off."

She turned; her shoulder pressed against the glass window. "Did he ever talk to you about leaving before you left?"

"He wanted to join the army when he got out of school, but he shouldn't have left like he did." Looping one ankle over the other, Beau crossed his arms over his chest as if to protect his heart. "I had to leave home. If

I'd stuck around, people might have been hurt."

People? As if Beau were talking about someone other than himself. Had James Daniels's threats against others sent Beau packing all those years ago with the hope that in leaving home, he could prevent others from his father's wrath?

"George should have stuck around, at least made sure Gertie was okay." He took a deep breath, then let it go. "If I had stuck around, he might not have felt the need to run away. Then he would have had the life he was supposed to have."

How could she argue with such twisted logic? But she had to try. "I think you're taking too much credit for George's decision."

"You don't understand."

But she wanted to.

"He made the decision to leave his home, not you."

Dropping his arms to his side, Beau scrubbed the back of his neck with one hand. "But Dad told me he'd kill him if I hung out with him anymore."

So that's why Beau ran away, to protect his friend. Sounded like something the Beau she was getting to know would do. "It was still George's choice."

He didn't look completely convinced. "I'll think about it."

Well, it was a start in the right direction. Once he went through all the facts as a man, not a boy of sixteen dealing with a tyrannical father, he'd realize the truth — that he wasn't to blame for his father's actions.

Then why couldn't she believe that about her own situation?

Edie pushed away from the truck, grabbing him by the shirtsleeve, and tugged at him. "Now, come on. It's rude to keep the Stephenses and everybody waiting when they've gone to all this trouble planning a party for us."

He tilted his head to the side, his cockeyed smile causing her heart to stumble against her ribs. "You just want a piece of whatever dessert Mrs. Stephens made."

"I bet I'm not the only one."

Just as she was about to drop her grasp on his shirt, Beau snagged her hand, threading his fingers between hers. Her breath caught as he gave her a wide smile. "I'm glad I've got you on my side."

Edie nodded, unable to speak past the lump in her throat. She was in trouble here, in real peril of losing her heart to this man. Well, she just couldn't let that happen. Returning his smile, she squeezed his fingers. "Come on then. Let's go have some fun."

CHAPTER TWELVE

"Now make sure you get lots of that smoked pork. We've got plenty more where that came from."

Beau nodded, his mouth full of Mrs. Anderson's potato salad. Some of the best cooks in the entire county lived in this neighborhood, and they all seemed to be determined to fatten him up, not that Merrilee's cooking hadn't added a few pounds to his frame. A year ago, the most food he'd see in a day consisted of a forkful of spam and a small block of chocolate, if he was lucky.

He glanced across the makeshift tables, shuffling through the crowd until finally finding Edie. She stood under the shade of a water oak, talking with a small group of young women her age, a few he barely recognized from years ago. She pumped a cardboard fan in one hand, but the other flitted about like a butterfly floating aimlessly·on the air. His arm still tingled under his shirtsleeve where she had touched him today.

Beau took a sip of tea, then wiped his mouth with his napkin. Nothing had gone according to his plan with this woman. He was supposed to be finding out if she posed a threat to his family, if she was using Merrilee's house to pass information about the B-29 to the Germans.

The problem was, he liked her more than he wanted to admit. But how could he stop himself? Something about her tugged at him, drawing him to her in a way that intrigued him. Kind and smart, there was a genuineness about her that made him want to be a better person. Her warm rich laughter echoed through the underbrush around the trees, causing a pleasant tug on his heart.

He liked her, but that was it. So what was it about her that made him open up, talk about the past when he'd kept it locked away inside all these years? He wasn't sure, only that she made it easy, not judging him for his mistakes, pointing out things he'd never thought of before.

Did Edie truly believe he wasn't at fault for George leaving? Was it really his friend's choice?

"Penny for your thoughts."

Beau glanced up to find Gertie standing beside him. "Just a penny?"

"I'd give you a nickel, but I've got my vast fortune tied up in war bonds." The woman flopped down on the bench beside him.

"The neighborhood really outdid themselves with this fine spread y'all laid out today." Beau forked another bite of potato salad into his mouth. "Even though your method for getting us here was a little suspect."

"Maybe, but we had to make sure the two of you came. How else are we going to show our appreciation for the work you've done getting us telephone service?" She stretched her long legs out under the makeshift table, cradling her hands in her lap. "I mean, who would have believed it, the Stephenses getting a telephone?"

He motioned toward Edie. "That's who you should be thanking. She's the one who wouldn't leave Ben Cantrell alone about stringing the lines."

"The way Edie tells it, you're the one who strong-armed Ben into actually doing something about it."

A few heated discussions with the man wouldn't intimidate the telephone company into action. Edie had helped Ben to change his mind. The woman had a way of making a man think — including him. "Have you heard anything from George?"

Her sigh tore through him. "Not since a couple of days after you left."

"What happened?"

She shrugged one shoulder. "Who knows? George always wanted to be on his own ever since I can recall. Remember when he tried to sign up for the navy and Daddy wouldn't give his permission?"

"I didn't know that."

"Oh, yeah. You know what I think?" Gertie asked, crossing one leg over the other. "I think that George couldn't stand the thought of you being gone, and decided it was time to start his life, too."

The happy shrieks of children playing faded into the background. So Edie had been wrong. George leaving *was* his fault. Maybe he hadn't encouraged his friend to leave home, but he'd talked about it enough, figured running was his only way out of the continuous battles, the constant beatings. Why would George leave a fine home with good parents if not for him and his stupid advice? "I'm so sorry, Gertie."

"What have you got to be sorry about?"

Beau hesitated for a moment. "I'm the one who talked about leaving all the time."

"And with good reason," Gertie whispered. "We all worried you'd come up dead one day. So when you left, every single one of us was thankful you were out of that situation." Beau followed Gertie's gaze over to where her parents sat, Mr. Stephens talking to a young man holding a baseball bat while Mrs. Stephens sat huddled with some ladies rolling bandages. "Particularly Mom and Dad. Look, I'm telling you here and now that you could have stuck around till the cows came home, and George would've still found an excuse to go."

Maybe Edie was right, maybe it wasn't his fault his friend left town. He waited for relief to flood his body with a lightness, but instead he couldn't figure out how he felt. "How's the job search going?"

"Slow. I'm thinking about joining the army nurse corp if nothing pans out in a couple of weeks."

Gertie on the front lines when the hospital needed help at home. "Why don't I talk to Dr. Lovinggood, see if I can change his mind and get you reinstated?"

"That man can be hardheaded."

Maybe, but an influx of patients and a shortage of nurses was running the staff ragged. Beau blotted a napkin to his mouth. "Oh, I think he'll come around."

She hesitated. "That might not set too

well with him, you nosing into the workings of his hospital."

"Maybe not, but hiring you back would be the right thing to do for the patients and the staff."

Her caramel cheeks flushed a bright pink. "You always were a sweet talker, weren't you? So tell me." Gertie tilted her head toward Edie and the other young women. "What's going on between you and Edie?"

"Nothing." He snorted. And he aimed to keep it that way.

"That's not what it looked like when you came walking down the road a little while ago, holding her hand." Her voice held a hint of laughter.

He'd forgotten about that. "The drive has a lot of washed-out areas that sneak up on you. I didn't want to risk Edie falling and hurting herself."

"She looks like she can stand pretty well on her own." Gertie's lips twitched. "Unless you don't mind holding her hand."

"You're still a pest, Gertie, you know that?" Beau scrubbed a hand over his face. He had liked the feeling of Edie's hand in his, the delicate feel of her palm against his making him feel extremely male. It made him want more, to know everything about her, to earn her trust enough for her to share her secrets. And yes, to share a kiss or two. But to ask more of her meant revealing himself, and he wasn't sure he could do that. Or could he? "It's complicated."

A low-pitched humph brought his head around. "Why is it people are always making things harder than they have to be?"

Gertie would see it that way. She'd always been loved and wanted by her mom and dad. "You couldn't understand."

"What's there to understand?" She glared at him like he was one egg short of a dozen. "Do you realize you look at Edie like she's the Christmas display over at Saul's Mercantile? And she watches you the same way when she doesn't think anyone is looking. What in blue blazes is complicated about that?"

His eyes shifted to where Edie sat shaded under a large water oak. A gentle smile had settled over her face as she bent over a small bundle of cotton and uncoordinated limbs. She pursed her lips as if to coo at the infant, sending a tiny set of arms and legs flailing into a jerky dance. His pulse thundered in his veins, every nerve ending in his body popping and hissing as if an electric switch had suddenly been thrown.

But Gertie didn't know the entire story. The letter Edie had dropped, the German writing. He wanted to hear her side of the story, needed to confirm that everything his heart was telling him, about Edie's compassion, her selflessness toward others, her loyalty, was true.

But would Edie be able to forgive him once she learned the truth of his deception?

"Tell me another story!"

Beau looked up at Claire, the thin pieces of pink yarn keeping her pigtails in place flying behind her as she ran into the dining room like a tattered flag in a brisk wind. The look of adoration in her pale green eyes as she climbed up in his lap made his breath catch in his throat. He'd only known his baby cousin a little over two months, and his heart was already wound tight around her stubby little finger.

Beau smothered the chuckle rising up in his throat and struggled to put on his most serious face. "Didn't anyone tell you it's polite to say hello first?"

"Oh." Her pale red eyebrows scrunched together, then she smiled. "Hello." She glanced around. "Where's Ms. Edie?"

"At work." It was natural his cousin thought he'd know where the beautiful brunette was. In the last few weeks, he and Edie had spent most evenings together, either at the hospital or on the front porch, planning out the details for the work on his dad's house.

Or at least, that's how it was supposed to be. Then he'd come across her in the hospital's break room, skimming the sports page for his old high school's baseball scores, and his determination to keep her at arm's length evaporated. She had got him thinking about what a man like him should expect out of life, especially with the mistakes he'd made.

But then, why would the Lord waste the incredible gift of healing people on him, unless Beau intended to use it?

He touched the tip of Claire's nose. "What have you been doing today?"

"Momma dropped me off at Katie Lawson's house on her way to Uncle Jeb's." The words rushed out of her like Sweetwater Creek after a spring rain. "Me and Kate decided to collect old tires and stuff for the rubber drive so we can get our Red Feather badge. Her dad has all this junk out back."

"And you girls thought what better place to start than the Lawsons' garage," Beau replied, pulling the loose yarn from one lopsided pigtail. He studied the girl from head to toe. "Did you get Mr. Lawson's permission before going through his things?"

Claire's smile dimmed. "Kate's dad is in the Pacific, but Mrs. Lawson said it was okay."

"Then that's okay. Just as long as you got permission." Beau handed her back the piece of yarn, then cupped the child's face in his hands and studied her, angling her head this way and that. "You know what you need? A water hose and a cake of soap."

Claire's lips twitched. "You're funny."

"And you're filthy as a little piglet. Are you going to my ball game like that?"

"No!" Her childish giggle made him laugh out loud, enjoying the simple pleasure of his younger cousin's company. Merrilee had done a good job of raising her daughter into a sweet little girl.

John would adore her. *If he knew.* The letters he and Edie had found weighed on him more with each passing day. He'd prayed for an answer.

And still nothing.

"Beau?"

He cleared his throat and focused his attention back on Claire. "What is it, pumpkin?"

"I was just thinking," the young girl replied, her usual happy-go-lucky voice suddenly serious. "If I had anything of my dad's, I don't think I could just give it away, not even for the war."

Beau's heart lurched in his chest. "But you do have something of your dad's. You and your momma have this place."

Claire tilted her head back and looked up at Beau. "Daddy must love us a lot to buy us this house."

"Of course he does." He brushed a kiss across her forehead. "What has your mom said about it?"

"That's the thing. Every time I ask about Daddy, Momma gets all sad-looking, like I've hurt her feelings or something. I think Momma misses him."

"You do?" He'd thought that was a possibility, but he wasn't good with situations like that. Maybe he'd ask Edie.

Claire snuggled against Beau's shoulder. "Do you think Daddy loves me?"

The fear threaded through Claire's voice twisted in his gut. What had his father been up to, keeping Merrilee's letters from John? But it didn't take much thought for Beau to figure it out. Plain and simple greed.

Had Dad known Merrilee was expecting a child? Had he thought about the price Claire would pay, growing up without her father? And what about John, never getting the chance to know his own flesh and blood?

Beau cradled Claire close to his chest. "I think your dad loves you very much."

"Really?" She looked up at him with such longing in her eyes, a knot formed in his throat. "Then why hasn't he ever come to see me?"

Her innocent question plunged through Beau's heart like a knife, ripping it to pieces. He glanced toward the door. If only Edie was home. She had a way with Claire, a manner he'd seen repeated with the children at the hospital, a calm truthfulness that soothed a child's unease without bruising feelings.

Was that what Claire needed, honesty? Beau gathered her little body close, resting his cheek on a pillow of reddish-blond curls. "Well, he can't come home right now, sweetheart. You see, your daddy is so good at building things that the navy asked him to train other men to build roads and bridges. He's over in the Pacific right now, doing just that."

"John is in the Pacific?"

They both turned their heads toward the doorway. Merrilee leaned against the door frame, her hands fisted into the apron she was wearing. Tiny lines worried the area around her eyes and mouth while sadness cast long shadows across her pale green eyes. Was Claire right? Did Merrilee still have feelings for her former husband?

"Claire, I've got your bathwater running."

"But Momma . . ."

"No buts, young lady. Get on upstairs."

"Yes, ma'am." Claire snuggled into Beau's side, her warm body flush against his. "I'm so glad you're here. You'll tell me everything I want to know about Daddy."

"If you want to go to the game and see Beau play . . ."

"Yes, ma'am." The young girl's expression fell as she scooted off Beau's lap onto the floor.

Merrilee placed her hand on Claire's tiny shoulder as she started to walk past her. "Maybe Beau can tell you another story if you do an extra special job cleaning those dirty nails."

"Really?" Claire answered, then turned back to Beau. "Could you tell me about how my daddy built that big old dam on the Colorado River?"

Would he ever get enough of his cousin's smile? "You mean Hoover Dam? I think your daddy had some help on that particular one."

Claire's eyebrows furrowed together. "Why?"

Beau gave Claire a loving swat on her

backside. The joy John was missing, watching his daughter grow up. "Go take your bath, brat."

The young girl giggled, skipping off, then flashed a bright smile at her mother before bounding up the stairwell, stumbling once or twice but always bouncing back up like a punching bag. Claire wanted anything she could find out about her father, and there wasn't much Beau could do about it. Not yet, at least.

Merrilee walked across the room and pulled together the blackout curtains. "I would've thought you'd be on your way to the ball field."

"Not yet." The truth was he'd been hoping to catch Edie, maybe talk to her about her letter. Beau watched his aunt work her way around the room. It was beginning to look like there were a lot of things he needed to come clean about, starting with his uncle. "I should have told you about John being overseas."

"Why?"

Her reply threw him for a long second. "I don't know. Maybe because you might want to know. For Claire's sake."

"Oh, I didn't think about that, Beau. If something should happen to him . . ." Her voice drifted off, a shadow falling across her face for the briefest of moments before she gave him a tentative smile. "Claire's been curious about her father lately. And goodness knows, I don't have any new stories to tell her."

Her voice trailed off, as if that fact bothered her more than she cared to admit. Beau watched his aunt move from one window to the next, her movements purposeful as usual but with a slight hesitation. Maybe the munchkin had made the right diagnosis. Maybe his aunt missed John Davenport more than she'd let on.

Smoothing her apron, she walked over and dropped down into the chair beside him. "Do you keep in touch with him much?"

Stretching out his arms in front of him, he laced his fingers together in a steeple. "It's been a while since I've gotten anything from him."

"He never was one for writing."

Her little snort of a sad chuckle drew his attention. What would Merrilee say to the dozen letters — letters she'd written for John — that he had stashed in his dresser upstairs? Would she welcome them? Or had he found them too late to repair his aunt's life?

"I ran into Hessie Cantrell at the grocery store today."

Ben Cantrell's wife? From the tone of her voice, Beau knew he wasn't going to like this. "How is Ms. Hessie?"

"She's fine, maybe a bit rattled." She hesitated. "Did you know that Edie paid Ben to put phone lines into the Stephenses neighborhood?"

If Merrilee worried about her lovely boarder, he could calm her fears. "Ms. Hessie left out the part that I went with Edie to make the request."

"Why would you let her do that?"

Beau stared at his aunt. Merrilee couldn't mean what her question implied, could she? "You don't think the Stephenses deserve to have a phone?"

"Of course I do. Even if the phone is the most confounded irritating thing, it's good to have around in case of an emergency." She gave him a silly frown. "I should smack you for asking me such a question."

"Then why are you so concerned that . . ."

"I'm worried about Edie. You know as well as I do how some folks around here are about . . . folks like the Stephenses."

"You mean Negroes."

Merrilee's face paled beneath a sprinkle of brown freckles. "Everybody seems keen on dividing folks up into groups so we know who to hate. Whites, Negroes, Japs." She swallowed. "Germans."

Beau blinked. He'd been going on the assumption that Edie had kept her German heritage from Merrilee. But as he stared into his aunt's face, he knew the truth. "You know Edie's German."

Merrilee pressed a finger to her lips and glanced toward the door. When she was satisfied they were alone, she turned back to Beau. "I was told in confidence."

"Edie?"

She nodded. "Yes, then Major Evans. He wanted me to know in case I had a problem with it."

It bothered him that the military was involved. Or was it the slightest twinge of jealousy? "Why is the major so interested in her?"

She gave him a gentle smack on his arm. "I don't know if you noticed, but our Edie is a very talented architect. So much so, Bell considers her essential personnel."

Beau blinked. *Essential personnel!* "But she was Abner Ellerbee's secretary."

Merrilee gave him a proud smile. "Only until her security clearance went through."

Thus, Edie's recent promotion to the drafting department. She wasn't just an ally — the United States felt her necessary in the fight for freedom.

"What I'm surprised at is how you know about her background." Merrilee gave him a knowing smile. "But then, the two of you have been spending a lot of time together. She probably feels she can trust you."

Beau swallowed against the hard knot in his throat. He'd only held on to Edie's letter until he could learn the truth about her. At least that's what he'd told himself. But he'd known she was no more of a spy than he was, ever since that day at the hospital when she'd passed out giving blood to a Negro soldier.

I'm no better than my father.

The truth slammed through him. And he'd been trying to do better, be the man God wanted him to be for his family. For Merrilee and Claire.

Maybe, one day, for someone like Edie Michaels.

It mattered that he correct this wrong he'd done her. Not just because he'd been stupid in keeping her letter, but because he'd completely misjudged her without even knowing her. And what he knew of Edie, he liked. A lot.

If we confess our sins, He is faithful.

God may have forgiven him, but what about Edie? Could he make her understand why he had kept her letter? Probably not, but he had to try. "Has Edie come in yet? I know she had to work late."

"Not yet." Merrilee glanced up at the mantel clock. "In fact, I'm expecting her any time now. Why?"

"I think I'll go and walk her home." Beau pushed back the chair and stood, not sure what he would say to Edie when he met up with her. But he would apologize. Give her back her letter. And start rebuilding the trust she'd placed in him. Let the Lord handle it.

Then why couldn't he shake this feeling of dread? That if Edie couldn't find it in her heart to forgive him, he would have lost something infinitely precious?

Merrilee gave him a motherly smile. "That's very nice of you, sweetheart."

Beau walked out of the dining room and headed up the stairs. No, not nice. Necessary. It was time he corrected the wrong his father had done to Merrilee. Even if nothing came of his aunt's letters to John, Beau would have absolution.

And what about Edie? He'd been suspicious of her since the very first, when she'd almost taken a swing at him with the fireplace poker. Maybe she would have knocked some sense in his thick skull. Even if it meant never being forgiven, the hurt of los-

ing her friendship — and the hope of
something more — just might kill him.

CHAPTER THIRTEEN

Gravel crunched beneath Edie's feet as she turned down the road toward Merrilee's. Shards of dull light danced in and out of the shadows of the tall oaks lining the drive, the muffled sounds of Bing Crosby crooning in the distance from the radio in the parlor. Edie smiled.

Almost home.

It had been a good day. Not only had Major Evans come by to personally thank her for her slight modifications on the latest B-29 plans, she'd gotten a message from Gertie. Construction on the phone lines in her neighborhood would start in the next week or two.

She quickened her pace. She couldn't wait to get home and share the news with Beau.

It had been a little more than a week since they'd started the repairs on James's house, not that they had made much of a dent in the growing to-do list. They'd fix one thing, only to find two more problems that needed work. Most nights, they'd sneak in long after the house had quieted down for the evening, only to be met by Merrilee with two plates of food, warm from the oven.

Edie smiled to herself. Those late dinners had become the best part of her day, sitting in Merrilee's kitchen, talking baseball and school and life after the war.

"Edwina Michaels?"

She jerked around. Had she been so deep in her thoughts about Beau that she hadn't heard the man sneak up behind her? A quick glance around the moonlit drive revealed the shadows of two more men standing at the edge of the tree line.

"The Bund?"

The words escaped Edie's throat before she could call them back, her nose burning at the nauseating smell of animal excrement that clung to the man's clothes as he took a step toward her. "You're causing problems around here, woman, and we don't like it."

Here? Then these weren't the men her parents sent to take her to Berlin. She tried to draw in a breath, but coughed instead. "What exactly is it that you don't like?"

"Quite a few folks around town have noticed that you've taken a shine to . . ." He struggled with the words, almost seeming to choke on them before finally spitting them out. "That Stephens girl."

Edie's hands fisted in disgust by her side. "Why can't I be friends with whom I want?"

"Not when she's a . . ."

Before the profanity had barely left his lips, her bare palm connected with his cheek.

He snatched her up by the waist and drew her flush against him, his stench robbing her of what little breath she had left. A sharp pain ran through her shoulder when he twisted her arm behind her back. "Who do you think you are, asking Ben Cantrell to string phone lines out there? Making those people think they deserve a telephone?" He pressed her hand in between her shoulder blades. "We don't cotton to folks like you, sticking your nose where it don't belong."

Edie closed her eyes. She'd scream if she could, but the words wouldn't come. *Lord, help me! Please!*

"Let her go!" The familiar voice punctuated each word with a terrifying fierceness.

Edie gasped a lungful of putrid air. *Beau!*

"You stay out of this, Beau Daniels." The man's hold relaxed, but he still held her close. "This has nothing to do with you."

"I beg to differ. You're trespassing on my aunt's property and harassing one of her boarders." Beau took a step toward them. "Most folks around here wouldn't blink twice if I shot you first and asked questions later. Got to worry about spies and all, being this close to the bomber plant."

The man tightened his grip, then pushed her away. Edie fell back, hitting the hard ground, pain stinging like tiny pinpricks along the tender skin of her palms and her right ankle.

She'd figured the man would run, but instead he just stood there, staring at Beau. "She's sticking her nose where it don't belong, bothering Ben Cantrell for one."

Beau chuckled. "I wouldn't mind having Ben's job then. Must be hard, being harassed by a beautiful woman like Ms. Michaels."

Beau thought she was beautiful? The night air did nothing to cool the heat flaming her cheeks. Well, she refused to just sit there like a bump on a log. "Gertie Stephens and all those people need to have a way to call for help if they need it."

"Those people don't need any help," the man bit out, his arms waving wildly, casting frightening shadows against the pale canvas of gravel. He swung around to Beau. "And you'd be doing her a favor if you'd remind her of that."

Those people. Edie bristled. Wonder what this guy would say if he knew how many of "those" people were fighting and dying over in Europe or the Pacific? And what for? To come home to *this?*

"Are you making threats, Bobby Ray?"

"Nothing you hadn't said before yourself, Beau." The man barked out a harsh laugh that clanged through Edie, off-key. "You and I both know how things are around here. Accidents happen. And it would be a crying shame if something happened to such a pretty little thing like Ms. Michaels."

Before Edie could blink, Beau pounced, grabbing the man by the collar, dragging him along the moon-drenched path before throwing him up against a tree like a rag doll. The man squirmed to catch his balance, but a hard shove from Beau stopped him dead.

Gathering up the man's shirt front in his fisted hand, Beau stared down at him until they were at eye level. "You come near Edie again, and I'll kill you."

"You're not going to be able to take us all out, Beau. I'm not the only one around here who doesn't appreciate that woman nosing in where she has no right." He pointed an accusing finger at her. "Helping those n—"

"Get out of here!" Beau roared, then

241

pushed away from the man. "Before I change my mind."

Bobby Ray fell over on all fours, and crawled away from them. "You're going to regret this." He pulled himself up and disappeared into the inky darkness.

The world went still around her, as if waiting for the next burst of poisonous words to spew from that disgusting man. Only the sound of gravel shifting close by brought her head up.

Beau kneeled down beside her, his arm going around her, making her feel safe for the first time since the ordeal began. "Are you okay?"

Nodding, Edie stretched her hands, prickles of pain scattering across both palms. "Just scratched up a bit."

He took her hands in his and turned them palms up. Dark ribbons of blood spread into tiny tributaries across her pale flesh. "We need to get you cleaned up. Maybe put some iodine on those scrapes."

She came out of the fog she'd been in, suddenly worried for her landlady. Edie shook her head. "I don't want Merrilee to know about this."

"There's a first-aid kit in the kitchen."

"Okay." Before she could figure out how to stand without doing further damage to her hands, Beau put his free arm under her knees and lifted her to his chest. She raised her gaze to his and her breath caught, the clean scent of his aftershave teasing her nose. She stiffened. "I can walk, you know."

"This way will be a lot faster."

"What about your knee?"

Beau's lip quirked up in a half smile. "Are you worried about me?"

"It's just that I've already fallen once today." She looped her arm around his neck, bringing him closer still. "Don't want to do it again."

His low chuckle rumbled against her side, causing her to tremble. "And here I was, thinking you had finally changed your mind about me."

"No." The word left a bitter taste in her mouth. When had she changed her mind about Beau? Was it working alongside him at his father's house, or was it sooner — maybe when she'd regained consciousness after giving blood and looked up to find him watching her with a mixture of concern and gentleness? "Well, maybe a little."

"I'll take it." He smiled down at her, his breath warm against her cheek, his eyes dark with sparks of silver from the moonlight.

Edie's heart melted a little. She'd just been spooked, that was all, thinking the

Bund had finally found her, were going to whisk her away. These feelings for Beau were just nerves strained from the attack, nothing more, not when she couldn't tell him the truth, that her parents believed in Hitler's doctrine, that their one desire was for her to follow them back home to Germany. Would he believe she'd chosen to stay and fight for Old Glory? Or would he think the worst of her?

Beau hurried across the yard, weaving in and out of the oak trees' shadows like an infantry man dodging enemy fire. Behind them, the static of the radio cut through the silence until finally settling on a station. The faint scent of freshly cut grass and Beau's aftershave caused an interesting sort of dizziness that only seemed to worsen when she dropped her head to his shoulder.

A rush of warmth flooded through her when he opened the door to the kitchen. A large stone building in the far corner of the yard, Edie had thought it inconvenient when she first moved in, but now it felt like a haven. Or was that just the feel of Beau's arms around her?

That thought spooked her. "You can let me down now."

He looked at her then. Moonlight filtering in through the window over the sink carved deep lines of concern across his forehead and around his eyes. "Are you sure?"

Her head bobbed up and down. "Yes."

Beau set her on her feet gently, his arm still encircling her, steadying her as she touched the floor. With something akin to reluctance, she pushed out of his embrace and headed for the sink. Beside her, she heard the scratch of a match, then light from the kerosene lantern filled the room.

"Let's see how bad your hands are."

"I can take care of this myself, you know."

Beau grabbed a dish towel from a drawer and folded it in two, laying it on the countertop in front of her. "I have no doubt you could. But what if you've got some gravel or a sliver of wood embedded in your palms? It'll be kind of hard working a pair of tweezers with an injured hand."

The man had a point. Edie unfolded her fingers and laid her hands, palms up, on the towel. "Just be careful, okay?"

The cockeyed grin he gave her made her stomach flip. "As gentle as a kiss."

For the next several moments, Beau worked quietly on her hands, his movements steady and purposeful as he picked tiny pieces of gravel from the tender flesh and placed them in the towel. Edie drew in a deep breath and relaxed. A girl could get used to this feeling of being taken care of, as if Beau considered her a precious treasure whose price was far above jewels.

Beau lifted his head, his eyes meeting hers. "I think I've got everything. All we need to do now is get you cleaned up."

Where had the air in her lungs gone? And how had she ended up so close to him, almost able to touch noses? She jerked her head back. "I can do that."

"Here." Was that a flash of disappointment in his eyes as he led her to the sink? Or merely hopeful thinking on her part?

When Beau turned on the faucet, tepid water sluiced over her skin. Beau stood close by, his fingers rubbing tender circles against her palms. She couldn't fall in love, not until this war was over and the danger of her parents' betrayal didn't hold power over her anymore.

Turning the water off, Beau handed her a clean towel. "Go and sit down at the table, and I'll get us some coffee."

"Thank you." Edie blotted the water off her hands gently. With her few scratches, she should be as good as new in a couple of days. Pulling a chair out, she plopped down. "And not just for cleaning me up. I don't know what I would have done if you hadn't showed up when you did."

"It was nothing." He placed a mug in front of her, a ribbon of moisture coiling out of the cup in a perfect cloud. "But I do have a question for you."

She wrapped her fingers around the cup, her scratches stinging a bit before the warmth relaxed the muscles of her hands. "What's that?"

"What is the Bund?" Her heart slammed against her chest. Every avenue of escape suddenly evaporated like the steam from her coffee cup as he continued. "And why did you think they were after you?"

Edie's fingers tensed around the coffee cup. Made her look guilty as sin. What on earth had she gotten herself into? Beau grimaced. "I can't help you if you don't tell me what's going on."

"You can't help me." Her sad little sigh tugged at his protective nature. "Nobody can."

Didn't she know he would do anything to keep her safe, even at the risk of his own life? The thought startled him. Yes, he wanted to protect her, but she had to be honest with him. "Try me."

He could see the struggle going on inside her, the tug-of-war that played out on her expressive face until finally, she slammed her eyes shut and let out a defeated sigh that tore a hole through him. "I don't know where to start."

Maybe his confession about her letter would make it easier for her to talk. Leaning on one hip, Beau reached into his back pocket and pulled out the folded paper. "I know you're German. I found this on the floor the night I came in through the front window."

Edie unfolded it. "Part of Grandmama's letter. I must have dropped it that first night when you climbed in through the window." She rested her forehead in the palm of her hand. "I've been so busy, I didn't even notice it was missing."

"I'm sorry, Edie. I should have returned it to you that next morning, but I didn't. I wasn't sure what to make of it." Beau hesitated a second. "Are you mad?"

"I guess I should be, but no." Pressing both palms over her eyes, she shook her head. "You were just looking out for Merrilee and Claire."

Beau wasn't sure he deserved complete absolution from this woman, but if she was willing to give it, he'd grab it with both hands. "So talk to me."

Edie swallowed, her throat moving in awkward little waves. "My parents came

over after the Great War to find work for
Daddy. He was a banker, and there weren't
very many opportunities for him back in
Germany at the time."

"And you?"

"I was born a couple of years after they
settled outside of Detroit. An all-American
girl." She scoffed.

"So what happened with your parents?"

"Nothing for a while. They just went
about living their lives." Her shoulders
caved in slightly. "Then when I was about
eleven, the bank failed and Daddy lost his
job. But it was more than that. He was different. Lost. As if everything inside him died
the day they nailed the bank's doors shut."

Beau nodded. He'd seen those men while
traveling the country with the Civil Conservation Corp. The vacant look in their eyes,
the gnawing fear, not just in men but in
their wives, their children. The idea of Edie
— smart, beautiful Edie — being one of
them twisted his gut. "How did your family
get by?"

"Daddy was good with his hands so he
picked up some jobs repairing stuff — you
know, toasters and things. Momma took in
mending. We managed."

"And you?"

She chuckled softly. "A little bit of everything. Daddy called me his Jackie of all trades. But I hated it, Beau." She closed her eyes, as if shutting out the memories. "When the university offered me a full scholarship, I thought it was my way out."

He could see her thinking that. Reaching toward her, Beau settled his hand over her forearm, his fingers wrapping around the delicate bones and soft skin. "There's no shame in that."

She dropped her chin to her chest. "I should have stayed at home."

He pushed a loose curl behind her ear. "Now why would you say that?"

Edie drew in a shaky breath and met his gaze again. "That's where the Bund comes in. Like I said, Daddy changed after the bank shut down. He felt like this country had let him down. So he joined this political group. At first, I thought it might be the best thing for him. You know, working toward changes that would ensure anyone who wanted to work could find a job. But then I started hearing things about them."

The hairs on the back of Beau's neck stood razor sharp. "What kinds of things?"

Her face went pale in the dim light of the lantern. "That the leadership of this group had gone to Munich and had an audience with Hitler himself. That they were harassing Jewish businesses in Detroit. I thought it was rumors. I mean, how can that kind of thing be happening here in the United States?" Edie drew in a shaky breath. "So when the Bund came to campus, I went to go hear them out.

"Listening to them speak, I realized the truth." Edie bowed her head, the light catching the glitter of tears shimmering on her cheeks. "My father was a Nazi."

What this woman had gone through. Standing, he gently pulled her into his arms, cradling her head in his hand, whispering a kiss against her hair. He sensed there was more, but he wouldn't rush her like he might have done in the past. She had been held captive, not by barbed wire or loaded guns, but by a child's love for her father, a man who had betrayed her trust.

Minutes later, she lay heavy against him, her tears spent. Beau tightened his arms around her. "I'm so sorry, Edwina."

"I tried to talk to Daddy right after I graduated," she whispered, her voice shaky. "Bell Bomber had just approached me about working for them, but I hadn't really made up my mind." She swallowed. "Daddy wasn't too happy to hear about the job offer."

"What happened?"

"He started spouting the Bund's propaganda. That if I was a good German, I would go to Hamburg and stay with my uncle's family while I took my place in the local artillery plant fight." A little sob escaped her lips. "The thought of what Hitler and his regime are doing to Germany, well, to most of Europe just makes me sick. And if I can help stop him in any way . . ."

"I believe you." He leaned his cheek against the silky softness of her hair. Her delicate hands curled around his neck, drawing him close, clutching for strength, robbing his lungs of air. He stroked the long line of her spine, taking in each delicate curve before gently putting some distance between them.

When she stared up at him, her eyes wide and luminous, Beau had to fight the urge to kiss her. Edie needed protection, not another complication. But in order to keep her safe, he had to know the whole story. And she still hadn't told him why these men were after her. "Sweetheart, why did you think it was the Bund attacking you tonight?"

Edie sniffed. "When I refused to go to Hamburg, Daddy thought my job would be a good opportunity to secure information the Germans could use in fighting the Allies." Her voice broke, as if each word inflicted a fresh wound on her heart. "It also wouldn't have hurt Dad in getting a better post once he and Mom returned to Germany. Even after I refused, he told them I would do it."

Despicable. It was the only word that came close to describing what Mr. Michaels had done. A tight ball twisted in Beau's gut. The Germans would do anything to win this war.

Including kidnapping Edie.

"Does Major Evans know about this?" Beau asked.

She nodded. "He's in charge of securing clearance for essential personnel. Why would it matter?"

Beau didn't know whether to shake her or kiss some sense into her. It did matter. *Edie* mattered. And the major would understand that better than anyone. "Evans could provide you with protection."

"No, Beau." She lifted her chin in a determined angle. "I won't put anyone else at risk."

"But you need . . ."

Edie dropped her chin to her chest, her hair forming a dark curtain of silk. "If Major Evans did put a detail on me, it would just draw attention to me. It may even help the

Bund find me quicker."

Beau grimaced. The last thing Edie needed was more attention, not with her work at the plant and her scheme to get phone lines into Gertie's neighborhood. But that didn't negate the fact she still needed a guardian, someone who could shield her from the watchful eyes of the Germans. A seed of an idea took root. "What about a chaperone?"

The hint of a smile she gave him as she stepped back tugged at his heart. "You make me sound like a teenage girl going off to her first formal."

The image of a younger Edie, dressed from head to toe in satin and lace, danced through his thoughts. Bet the boys were lined up at her front door that night. Beau shook the jealous pangs away. "I just think it might be a good idea if you weren't walking home alone late at night."

"But my job requires long hours, and the bus stops running at seven." Edie paced across the room, then stopped and stared at him. "As much as I agree with you, I refuse to let fear keep me from doing my job."

Another option, a better one, came to mind. "Then why don't I meet you at the plant and walk you home every night."

"You?"

Was that a brief flash of pleasure that crossed her face? For some reason, the thought pleased him. "Why not? It's on my way home from the hospital, and if you have to stay late, you can get a note to me quicker than sending a messenger to Merrilee's."

She bit her lower lip in that adorable way she did whenever she had to make a decision. "I don't know. That's a lot to ask of you."

"Not really, if you think about it. We're both going the same way," he said, crossing the room to stand in front of her. "I figure on the evenings you get off early, we could head out to Dad's house, maybe get a little work done. If that's okay with you."

An emotion he couldn't quite read flickered in her blue-green eyes. Pleasure? Relief? "Of course."

"So I'll meet you at the front gate tomorrow afternoon?"

Edie hesitated for a moment then gave him a slight nod. "Yes."

"Good." Beau released the breath he'd been holding. Edie would be safe. He would make sure of that.

God willing.

Beau walked over to the back door of his dad's house and held it open for Edie. "I bet that the barn and the fields are worse than the house was."

"For all I know, your daddy used that part of the farm for his business. We may walk into a barn with all the tools shined to a high gloss." She gave him an encouraging smile as she walked past him, the scent of fresh air and cookies causing his heart to do a funny little flip.

"He didn't bother to clean his stuff when he was working the fields." Beau laughed, shutting the door behind them. It had been two weeks since he'd confronted the band of hoodlums accosting Edie in Merrilee's drive. Two weeks of waiting outside the front gates of the bomber plant, scanning the crowds of workers before getting a glimpse of her, her expression tentative in those first few days.

But in the past week, he'd noticed a change. She looked for him, too, her gaze scanning the area outside the chained link fence until she found him, her lips curving into a welcoming smile that always drew an answering one from him.

Beau caught up with her in the backyard, matching her stride for stride. "What made you decide to become an architect?"

She shot him a quick glance. "That's kind of out of the blue."

Beau wasn't sure, only that it suddenly seemed important to know everything he could about this woman. "I know you got a scholarship but what made you go into architecture?"

Edie hesitated, her steps slowing until she stopped right outside the barn door. When she turned to him, there was a faraway look in her eyes. "I guess it was my dad. When I was little, he'd come home from the bank and go out to his shop and tinker with stuff. One time, when Mom and I had gone shopping, Daddy tore apart her toaster." Her voice held a trace of laughter. "He had wires and springs tossed all over the kitchen table, grease everywhere. I thought Mom would kill him. While I watched him put it back together, I wondered what it would be like to design things, particularly buildings."

"If your dad was so good at fixing things, then how did he end up a banker?"

"I don't know. He didn't talk about it much. But from what I got from Grandma's letters, Grandpa put a lot of pressure on him to go into banking. Guess he thought Dad would be able to find a good position once the Great War ended." The spark that had lit up her eyes just moments before dulled. "Grandpa couldn't have known how difficult it would be to get a job after the war so my parents left Hamburg and came to the States to find a better life."

Yet the Michaelses had turned their backs on the life this country had offered. Beau pushed a thick curl that had escaped from her snood behind her ear, brushing the silky skin of her earlobe before dropping his hand. How hard it must be for Edie, to be betrayed by her parents.

"I pray for them, you know," she whispered, almost like an afterthought. "That one day, they'll realize their mistake. It's the only thing I can do."

The truth hit him like a truckload of bricks. Despite what they had done, what they still threatened to do, Edie loved her parents. The question spilled out of him before he could stop it. "Why?"

She lifted her hand, cupping his cheek against her palm, the frozen wall around his heart melting into a warmth that flooded through him. "If God can love us despite our mistakes, shouldn't we be willing to do the same for everyone else?"

"But your parents . . ." *My captors. Dad.*

"All of us mess up, Beau, but does that mean we should stop loving everybody who makes a mistake?" She dropped her hand to her side. "This world would be a pretty lonely place then, wouldn't it?"

Beau wasn't sure how to react, Edie's words echoing inside his heart. Had his life been that lonely existence she described because he couldn't forgive his father? He wanted his father to seek God, but why should he when Beau refused to mirror God's love by forgiving him?

Grabbing her hand in his, Beau took off toward the barn. "We're going to take a break."

"A break?" Her cotton jumper swished out a rapid beat as her steps moved to keep up with his. "We just got here."

"I know. But between work and this house, neither one of us has had a day off in a while. I don't know if you know this or not, Edie, but fun is good for the soul."

"It depends on what kind of fun we're talking about here." She slammed to a halt beside him, her eyes twinkled with mischief while her lips twitched with laughter.

He turned to face her, leaning toward her until he could feel the warmth of her breath against his face. Beau noticed little things like the tiny lines around her mouth and eyes that deepened when she smiled or the perfect curve of her mouth.

But that was just all window dressing. Inside, where it mattered, Edie was equally beautiful. Unselfishly giving of her time and her talents to help people no one else would give a second glance to. Protective of those she loved, ready to do battle like she had the night Beau had snuck in the front window. And now forgiving of the very people who should have never betrayed her trust: her parents.

Why did she even bother with him? But he knew why. The job of repairing his father's house had provided a way for her to accomplish the impossible — get phone lines strung for the Stephenses' neighborhood. She probably wouldn't give him the time of day in other circumstances. Beau's stomach sunk.

But right now, Edie was here, smiling up at him. He would make it a good day for the both of them. "I thought I'd show you Sawyer Lake, maybe do a little fishing."

If possible, her smile spread even wider. "I've never been fishing before. Don't you have to mess with earthworms?"

He nodded. "If you'd like, I'll bait your hook."

"No, if I'm going to do this, I want to learn to do it right."

Her reaction didn't surprise him in the least. In fact, he half expected her to offer to bait his lines, just for the practice. Beau started toward the barn again. "Dad always kept a stash of fishing poles just inside the barn door along with his tackle box and fishing line."

"And the worms?"

"I'll get a shovel, too." Beau smiled. *This,* he thought opening the barn door for her, *is going to be a good day.*

Sawyer Lake was everything Edie had thought it would be from the grainy images of Beau, George and Gertie on the Stephenses' mantel. Nestled in a batch of hundred-year-old water oaks, the shaded banks provided a welcome reprieve from the heat of the mid afternoon sun.

"Over here." Beau pointed to a slab of flat granite, close enough to the lake to drop their line in the glassy water but large enough to accommodate them both.

Anchoring the fishing poles against the corner of the stone, Beau laid down the tackle box then grabbed the horse blanket he'd found in the barn. He folded it in half and draped it over the granite. He cupped her elbow in the palm of his hand. "For you, ma'am."

"Thank you." A shiver that had nothing to do with the temperature ran up her spine. "This is a beautiful spot." Edie set their lunch basket down beside her. "So is this the infamous lake where you and your brother used to have those rock-skipping contests you've told me about?"

A look of surprised pleasure flashed across his features. "I can't believe you remembered that."

"Why wouldn't I?" Edie settled herself on the blanket. "It sounded like fun."

"Wait a minute," Beau said, stretching out beside her. "Are you telling me you've never skipped rocks across a lake before?"

Was the air getting thicker or did her lungs refuse to function properly whenever this man was nearby? Edie shrugged. "The only lake my parents ever took me to was Lake Michigan and that's not exactly the best place to learn how to skip rocks."

"Then we'll need to take care of that." Beau lifted one of the fishing poles and angled it between his knees.

Edie leaned back to get a good look at him. "Exactly what do you mean?"

"You're a college girl, Edie." He gave her a wicked wink. "I'm sure you can figure it out."

She looked out over the glassy waters. "But won't we scare the fish away?"

"Not if we wait until after we're finished fishing." He handed her a pole already baited with a nice juicy earthworm. "If that's okay with you."

"That would be great." The warm wood of the fishing pole settled against her palms and she relaxed. What was it about this man that made her want to play hooky, to forget all her problems for the day and find joy in the simple things like casting a line or skimming a rock across a lake? It had been so long since she had taken time to enjoy the life God had given her. Maybe this once, she could forget about all her problems and just be.

She cast a quick glance toward the man next to her. Who better to spend her time with than Beau?

They settled in, dropping their lines in the water, talking as they fished. It didn't take long to realize that Beau had done a great deal of living in his twenty-six years, traveling the country with the Civil Conservation Corp, then the world with the army. There was an easiness between them, an openness Edie had never felt for anyone else, not even her grandmother.

For the next hour, they talked baseball — high school and major leagues — agreeing to disagree on the Tigers versus the Cubs. But their conversation didn't stop there, talking on a range of topics from how to win the war to who was the best Stooge:

Curly, Moe or Larry?

"I usually have a nibble by now." Beau grabbed another earthworm, and pinned him on the end of the hook.

"They seem to be stealing all our bait."

He had a nice laugh, she realized, faint ripples of pleasure stealing across her chest. "Maybe they're smarter than we are today."

She joined him with a soft chuckle of her own. "Do you use that excuse a lot?"

His shoulder brushing against hers, Beau tilted his head toward her as if sharing a state secret. "Only when I come home empty-handed which is most of the time."

"Then why fish?"

He looked at her then, the silver sparks in his eyes dancing with laughter. "Because I live in the hope."

Edie stared off into the water. When was the last time she'd lived in hope, for the present, for the future? Months? Years? There had been little hope in her household — at least not since she was a little girl.

She slid a quiet glance at Beau. From what he'd shared with her about his home life, Beau had no reason to hope, and yet he did. About fishing. About Merrilee and Claire. Even about his medical career.

Laying their fishing poles to the side, Beau stood and extended his hands to her. "Time for a rock-throwing lesson before it gets too late."

Edie glanced up, noticing the sun peeking over the top of the trees on the opposite side of the lake. Where had the day gone? She brushed her hands together then took his hands. On her way up, her foot gave way beneath her and she felt herself begin to tumble toward the water.

Strong hands lifted her and Edie found herself pressed against the hard muscular plane of Beau's broad chest. "Are you okay?"

"A little shaky." But she wasn't sure if it was from the fall or being held in Beau's wonderful embrace.

"Then take a little time. We're not in a hurry." He tightened his arms around her, his cheek coming to rest on top of her head.

She snuggled deeper into his embrace, filling her lungs with his scent, tracing the line of his spine beneath her fingertips. She had not planned for these feelings Beau brought out in her, this tenderness that only he seemed to tap from deep within her. If only she could tell him, but she couldn't. She couldn't put him in danger.

Not if she truly loved him.

CHAPTER FOURTEEN

"Right down the middle, Mack."

Beau crouched down, stretching his fingers inside his baseball mitt, the leather crackling after years in the back of his closet.

"See if you can catch my fastball." Mack glared over the top of his glove, his eyes shifting from home plate to first base. With a high kick of his leg, he reared back and slung the ball at Beau.

The ball landed in Beau's glove with a pop. "Not bad for a sheriff."

Mack glowered at him. "I could give Dizzy Dean a run for his money."

Beau laughed. There had been so many things he'd taken for granted in the life he'd led since leaving here. The crack of the bat, the dusting of chalk that got between his fingers whenever he held the bat in his hands, the roar from the bleachers. He glanced up toward the bleachers where Edie sat with his cousin Maggie.

Or the thrill of a beautiful woman coming to see you play.

Beau tipped his head back, the warmth from the sunlight dancing across his face, coaxing a smile out of him.

Thank you, Lord, for giving me this moment, and every moment, Father. And thank You for bringing Edie into my life. In Christ's name.

"Well, are you going to hang on to that ball all day or what?" Mack called out.

Lowering his gaze, Beau walked over, palming the ball in his mitt. When he reached Mack, he dropped the ball in his outstretched glove. "You're as ready as you'll ever be."

"I hope so. These bomber boys are tough."

"That's what I've heard," Beau answered, removing his glove. He'd been surprised to find it among the clutter in his old room, not that he'd found anything else of his. When he'd asked Merrilee about it, she told him how his dad had thrown out most of his possessions after Beau had left, right down to the curtains hanging in his bedroom window. He slapped his glove against his thigh. Guess the old man must have missed this one.

"I drove by your dad's house the other day. It's coming along on the outside."

"I'm happy with it." And he was. Instead

of barren tracts of weeds and red clay around the front of the house, staggered rows of azaleas and box hollies had been planted under the large picture window in the dining room while a large hydrangea bush bloomed beneath the window of his old bedroom.

And it had all been Edie's doing.

"So how's the work going inside? Was it bad?" Mack tossed the ball in the air then caught it.

Beau shook his head. "Once we cleared out most of the mess, there wasn't as much repair work to do as we'd thought."

"That's good. So you'll be able to get it rented out soon."

"Well, there's still some painting that needs to be done, and little odds and ends to do. But it should be ready soon."

Truth was, the more time he and Edie spent working on the house, the more he thought about living there himself. Which was nuts. Not one decent memory of his childhood came to mind when he took the time to think about it, only images from the last few weeks. Edie glancing up over a pile of newspapers, her eyes wide with interest and intelligence. Edie wielding a paintbrush, splashing different colors on the living room walls then standing back, chewing on her thumbnail before finally asking him to choose. Edie bowing her head to pray, her words reaching out to God. Prayers for Merrilee and Claire, for the Stephenses, for her parents.

For him.

She only wants my protection, not my heart.

Beau slowed to a stop. It might be for the best. He wasn't sure how to give Edie the kind of love she rightfully deserved. But he could protect her. "I don't know if you've heard, but Edie's working with Mr. Cantrell to string phone lines into Gertie Stephens's neighborhood."

When Mack turned, it was the lawman standing before him. "I'd heard some rumors. Is it true she paid to have the work done?" He stepped alongside of Beau, his voice a rumble of a whisper. "You know how Cantrell feels about Negroes. If he has his way, he'll stall Edie until the cows come home."

"That's why I've been at the phone company every day since the check was cashed."

Mack's eyebrows knitted together. "What's got you so concerned about the Stephenses all of a sudden?"

Beau could have said for Edie's sake. At least, that was part of the truth. "Do you remember Gertie's brother, George?"

"Big guy, six-two, six-three. Had a few little scrapes with the law, mainly kid stuff." He crossed his arms over his chest. "Didn't he run away years ago?"

"Yeah." No need to tell Mack it had been ten years ago, almost the same night he'd left Marietta. The lawman might start asking questions. "George was a good friend of mine."

"I didn't know that."

Not too many people had. It had been too dangerous. "Anyway, the Stephenses are good people, and with Gertie needing a job now, I figured I would help."

Mack scowled. "There's folks out there who aren't going to be too happy about this."

"I know." Beau turned to face the outfield, looking for some degree of privacy. "We had some visitors a couple of weeks ago." Beau filled the sheriff in on the details without mentioning Edie's parents or their connection to the German Bund.

Mack blew out an impatient sigh. "Maybe it's best Cantrell's taking his time stringing those lines. Edie might lose interest if she sees how long it's taking."

Clearly the sheriff didn't know Edie at all. "Gertie told Edie yesterday that the phone company was going to be at her house next

270

week to install her telephone."

"I bet Edie was over the moon at the news."

"She was." Beau couldn't help the smile he felt tugging at the corners of his mouth, remember the look of sheer joy on Edie's face when she'd told him the news.

"Keep an eye on her, Beau." Mack squinted into the sun. "You and I both know folks are likely to do anything when they hear about this."

Beau eyed his friend. "I figured you'd want to protect her seeing how you want to court her."

It felt like a lifetime before Mack finally shook his head. "No, I've thought about it, and I don't think Edie's the right woman for me."

Had the man lost his mind? "Edie Michaels is everything a man would want in a . . ." He glanced over to find Mack staring at him with a wide smile on his face. "What's got you grinning like a possum?"

"You want to know why I decided against courting Edie?"

Beau fell silent. Sure, he wanted to know what had changed the sheriff's mind about wooing Edie, though just the thought of them together made a sick knot form in his gut.

Mack leaned toward him. "I've seen the way the two of you look at each other."

"It's not like that." At least, not on her end. But what would Beau know about love? It's not like he'd ever seen much of an example of it between his father and mother, or between his parents and himself. So what if he found it charming the way she nibbled on the tip of her pencil when working on a problem? Or the endearing way she cuddled with Claire as they read together on the couch every night? And he'd admit he fought a ferocious battle every time an errant strand of her chestnut hair broke free from her snood. How he wanted to feel the soft curl against his fingertips as he pushed it back behind her ear.

Very much afraid that he wouldn't stop until he'd tilted her head back and brushed his mouth against hers.

But what if Beau was like his father, incapable of real love?

"Hey," Mack called out, coming up beside him. "If I said anything out of line . . ."

"It's okay," Beau answered. "And you're right. I need to watch out for her. With her living in the boardinghouse, her presence could put the whole household in danger."

Mack nodded. "Merrilee's had enough excitement with your dad's doings to last a while. Have you found a lawyer yet?"

"Interviewed a few from Atlanta. I've got to finish the house before I have enough money for a retainer, and that's going to be at least a couple of months."

"I'm sorry to hear it's taking so long."

Beau was startled to realize he wasn't. The longer it took to repair the house, the more time he got to spend with . . . He frowned. "How's the old man doing?"

"You should come by and see for yourself."

"I've been busy." Or had he filled his days up to the brim to keep from making a trip to the county jail?

Mack gave him a friendly smack on the back. "You know, you're not like him, Beau."

Beau glared at him. "I know that."

"Do you?" Mack answered. "I'm not sure about that, but I do know one thing. If you don't face your dad, you're going to regret it for the rest of your life."

Beau stared into the outfield. Was Mack right? Would he regret not facing the man who had caused him so much pain? Oh, he'd thought about such a meeting, but in his imagination, things had ended with his fist firmly planted in the center of his father's face. Beau gritted his teeth, waiting for the roar of anger to race out of control through his veins, but it never came. For now, it was best to leave things between him and his father as they were.

"Just think on it, will ya?"

Beau smacked his glove with his curled-up fist. "I'm praying on it, too."

"Anything that can get you on your knees is a blessing," Mack threw over his shoulder as he walked toward the dugout.

Was that true? Beau followed him as far as the infield. Was he supposed to feel blessed by his time in a prison camp? But if he hadn't been captured, he would have never made his decision for the Lord, never known the meaning of true freedom through God.

In all things, give thanks.

Thank You, Lord, for all You've done for me and all You have planned for me now and in the future. Beau lifted his head, catching a quick look toward the bleachers before centering his attention on one woman on the far side of the first base line.

Edie.

Warmth flowed through him, an awareness he'd tried hard to fight but lost. She gave him a shy smile that robbed him of his breath, making him feel like he had just taken a line drive to the ribs. Then she took her place next to Maggie.

"I can't even count the number of men that woman's turned down an invitation to come to our game with. Well, at least we know how to get her here now." Mack threw his arm around Beau's shoulder. "We'll just make sure you're on the guest list."

"Just play ball, okay?" Beau strolled over to his position at first base, taking one last look in the stands, a smile playing on his lips. So Edie had never been to a ball game with Mack. Though he knew it shouldn't, that knowledge satisfied a primitive part of his masculine pride.

Beau crouched down, waiting for Mack to throw the ball to the first hitter. At least the game would keep Edie occupied and away from the danger of her phone-line project. At the crack of the bat, Beau charged toward first and caught the ball just as the batter crossed the base.

As he stepped on the bag, Beau couldn't help looking toward the stands. Standing, Edie clapped, her bright smile lighting up his heart like the stars lit up the night sky. He didn't deserve her friendship, but she had given it to him freely.

Then why did he suddenly want so much more?

■ ■ ■ ■

Edie tightened her fingers around the wooden boards, barely able to keep herself from flying out of her seat in the bleachers. It was the top of the ninth, and the Bombers had a one-run lead, but not for long if the runners on first and third had anything to say about it.

"I wonder who's up next?" Maggie asked from her perch beside her.

"I'm not sure." Edie watched the dugout, then softly gasped as Beau stepped out into the batting circle.

Maggie gave her a knowing look then turned her attention back to the field. "I have a feeling this game is about to get interesting."

"I'd just settle for a base hit," Edie replied, watching as Beau took a few swings. The man cut a handsome figure in his ball cap and rolled-up jeans. The muscles in his arms clenched and flexed as he tested the weight of two bats before finally settling on one.

"With his knee, I'm thinking the only way he's going to get around those bases is a home run!"

Good gracious, his knee! She'd plumb forgot about it until Maggie mentioned it!

Edie held her breath, watching for a limp or any weakness in his legs as Beau stepped into the batter's box. He glanced back at the stands, his gaze roaming the numbers of people before finally coming to rest on her. He didn't smile, only looked at her, and with a wink turned and faced the pitcher, bringing the bat to his shoulder.

A nervousness she'd never felt for anyone else welled up inside her. Edie drew in a deep breath. She'd realized in recent days she only wanted the best for Beau.

Even if it meant walking away from him.

Edie shut her eyes against the thought. She should have come up with an excuse when Beau had asked her to the game. Overtime in the drafting room. Extra shift at the hospital. Plague. It would have been easier on her heart. But the thought of Beau being right outside her window had tugged at her, pulling her away from her desk and out into the afternoon sunshine.

It'd felt like forever since she'd told Beau about her father and the danger she faced from the Bund. Her heart fluttered at the memory of being held in his strong embrace, her senses filled with the smell of aftershave and Beau. She hadn't felt so safe since before the war, before her father had turned against all she held dear. Beau hadn't run at the truth of her life. Instead he was standing by her, offering her shelter, a place to hide beneath his watchful eye.

In that moment, despite all her precautions, she'd fallen in love with him.

"Strike one!"

Maggie's hand came to rest on her arm. "Are you okay?"

Edie nodded, her head bobbing up and down. Who was she trying to convince, Maggie or herself? "Of course I am. I'm just a little bit caught up in the game, that's all."

"Are you sure? You just went a bit pale there for a second."

"It's nothing. Probably just the heat."

But Maggie had never been one to be swayed from her objective. "Are you sure?"

Edie hesitated. This woman had been her friend through thick and thin, had been with her when Edie couldn't keep the secret surrounding her family anymore, though she didn't share the danger she faced from the Bund. "I told Beau about my father."

Maggie leaned toward her, glancing around, lowering her voice so that no one heard their conversation. "What did he say?"

"Nothing much," Edie answered in a whisper. "Mainly, he listened."

"Really."

Why did Maggie sound so surprised? "To

be honest, he was more upset when I asked him to help me convince Mr. Cantrell to string phone lines out to Gertie's house."

"Well, that I can understand. He just wanted to make sure you stayed safe."

Edie glanced down at the man at home plate. A few weeks ago, she wouldn't have agreed with Maggie, but now, knowing how it felt to be in Beau's arms, to know the comfort of his protective nature, she knew it to be true. "I know."

Maggie turned her attention back to the game. "You're in love with him."

Edie's heart slammed against her chest. "Excuse me?"

"You heard me." Still watching the game, Maggie grabbed her hand and gave it a squeeze. "You love Beau, and I think it's wonderful."

Edie mashed her lips together. What would Maggie think if the Bund caught up with her and Beau, in his need to protect her, ended up hurt, or worse? She refused to let her thoughts go there, just the idea of such a thing twisting like a spike through her heart.

"Strike two!"

The floorboards swayed beneath Edie's feet as Maggie jumped up beside her. "Come on, Beau! Knock it out of the park!"

"Sweetheart," Wesley called out from his place at third base. "Isn't it part of the engagement agreement that you cheer for your fiancé's team?"

Her friend's face broke out into a smile. "Someone has to keep up the morale of our local policemen after you blasted that triple a couple of innings ago."

The crowd broke into laughter around Edie, and after a few seconds, she couldn't help but join in. That was what was so neat about the town of Marietta, the feeling of community she'd picked up since the moment she'd crossed into the city's limits. Of neighbors enjoying each other's company, of being there for one another in good times and in bad. Oh, it had its problems — every town did, but it was easy to overlook them because Marietta was home.

POP!

The crack of the ball against wood drew Edie's attention to the field. Beau had dropped his bat, his eyes riveted to the chain-link fence in center field as he made a slow trot down the first base line. Edie looked up, searching the cloudless sky before finally catching sight of the ball as it sailed into a nest of oaks beyond the metal barrier.

The wooden bleachers dipped and swayed

like waves on Lake Michigan as people around her jumped up and down, the air exploding in a roar of appreciation. Beau rounded third, glancing up at the stands until his eyes locked with hers. Edie's heart beat against her ribs in a wild rhythm, her mouth suddenly dry as the faint white cloud of chalk floating along the third base line. Then, as though he thought better of it, Beau lowered his gaze toward home plate.

She loved him. Despite trying her best to keep her heart safe, he'd snuck around her barriers, protecting her when most people would have abandoned her, earning her trust. Edie smiled to herself. Beau even shared her love of baseball.

"You want a pop?"

"Huh?" Edie blinked, glancing over at her friend.

"A soda. Water, something cold to drink." Maggie pumped the paper fan she'd brought from home, the image of Jesus standing at the door waving back and forth. "It's hot enough to fry bacon on the sidewalk — that is, if bacon wasn't being rationed. All I can say is heaven help us in August."

The next player hit a fly ball to the right fielder for the last out of the inning. Edie stood. "You want anything else at the concession stand?"

Her friend's auburn hair bounced in red-gold waves against the stark white of her shirt as she shook her head. "I can go with you."

"And possibly miss Wesley's next at bat?" She shook her head. "Not on your life."

"Well, no." Maggie grimaced. "I hate putting you out like that."

After all the kindnesses Maggie and her family had done for her in the past year, nothing they could have ever asked would have been too much for Edie. "It's settled. I'll be right back."

Edie gingerly stepped around the two teenage girls sitting directly in front of them, zigzagging her way down, the wood boards beneath her giving a little with each step. Late stragglers, probably workers just clocking out of their shift, watched from the end of the bleachers, putting the cares of the war aside for the moment to enjoy a baseball game.

With everything that has breath, praise the Lord!

Edie frowned as she fell into line behind two men she recognized from the plant floor. Had she been so busy worrying about what the future might hold, she'd forgotten to praise God for what He was doing in her life now? Hadn't the Lord taken care of all her needs, given her professional opportunities once thought impossible for women? And what about her friends? He'd blessed her with them, too.

Her gaze slid to first base where Beau stood. Could she praise God for a love that would in all likelihood leave her heartbroken for the rest of her life?

"Did you hear the government is opening another one of those prisoner-of-war camps up at Fort Oglethorpe?" The sharp-toned question from the man behind Edie sliced through her haze of emotions.

"How many does that make in the state now? Four? Five?" another lower voice behind her replied. "Who are they aiming at putting in this one?"

"Stinkin' Germans." The man spit out as if the word left a bad taste in his mouth.

Edie's stomach clenched into a tight ball. *Please make them stop, Lord. Why do they have to drag the war up here, when I'm happy and laughing and so in love with that wonderful man guarding first base, it almost hurts?*

But the men didn't stop. "Personally, I think FDR ought to load up the whole lot of them and keep 'em locked up just like they're doing to the Japs out west. It would sure make it a whole lot easier to keep track of them. You just never know with those people."

Those people. The words twisted around Edie's heart, knotting into a tangled ball of raw pain. How she hated those words and all the ugliness they implied, as if being German or Japanese or Negro somehow made you less of a person!

What about Beau? He'd fought long and hard against getting Cantrell and his cronies at the phone company to string lines out to Gertie's place. Had it been out of concern for her and the Stephenses' safety or was he really like the man who tried to attack her, only stopping her with kindness rather than a fist?

Edie sucked in a breath of fresh air, but tasted salt instead.

Am I just one of "those people" to You, Lord?

A hand came to rest between her shoulder blades, and she glanced over. The man who had been standing behind her, the one saying all those horrible things, looked at her through concerned eyes. "Are you okay, miss?"

She stretched forward, anything to flee his touch. What if he knew the truth, that she was German-American, that her father had defected to the Nazis? Would he be so quick to run to her aid then? "I'm fine, thank you."

"Are you sure?"

She nodded, unsure of her voice as a knot climbed up her throat. Maggie would have to forgive her for not getting her drink. Spinning on her heels, Edie fled.

CHAPTER FIFTEEN

"Time!" Beau called out as he jogged to the pitching mound.

Mack met him with an irritated glance. "I'm one out away from striking out the side and you're calling time? What gives?"

"Something's up." Beau pointed out Edie's retreating form as she disappeared into the tree line. If he hurried, he'd catch her in no time. "I need someone to replace me."

"She sure is taking off in a hurry. What do you think happened?"

"I don't know." Beau yanked off his glove and shoved it under his arm, his fingers curling into his fist at his side, heat running up the back of his neck. "But she looked pretty upset when that guy over at the concession stand started talking to her."

Mack put a hand to Beau's shoulder. "Now, don't go getting yourself all worked up. I wouldn't want to be forced to arrest you over a simple misunderstanding."

Beau nodded. "You're right. It's just Edie's not one to get upset over nothing."

"Go after her." Mack grabbed the mitt under Beau's arm and tossed it to the ground. "I'll have a little talk with that fellow after we wrap this game up, okay?"

"I'd appreciate it."

Within minutes, he was deep in the forest, the noise of the crowd fading in the distance behind him, the rapid thrumming in his heart the only sound in his ears. His T-shirt clung to his damp skin, warm moisture so thick that even with the heavy umbrella of new leaves, you'd have to cut the air with a razor-sharp knife. A patch of blue sky to his right drew Beau's gaze to a grove of storm-twisted pines carpeting the forest's floor.

There, on a fallen log in the center of the clearing, sat Edie.

"Are you okay?" He came up beside her slowly. No sense startling her.

"Fine."

Liar. The log dipped slightly beneath him when he sat down. He reached into his jeans pocket for a clean handkerchief and handed it to her.

She took it from him. "Thank you."

"Where are you going in such a hurry?"

"Home."

Beau smiled. He liked that Edie thought of Merrilee's place as home. Gave him hope she might stick around after this war was over. "Didn't you like the game?"

She swung around toward him then. Tears gleamed in her blue-green eyes but refused to fall, as if by sheer willpower. "Of course I loved the game. I haven't had that much fun in years."

He slid closer. "Then what made you take off before the final out?"

The smile she gave him didn't quite reach her eyes. "I don't know. I mean, I ducked out of work early to go so I figured I'd go home, get something to eat and maybe come back for a while this evening."

So that was how she was going to play this, by keeping him in the dark. He wanted Edie's trust more than his next breath, but he couldn't force it. She'd make the decision when she was ready. "Well then, do you mind if I sit with you?"

"The game's already over?"

"Almost," he replied, stretching his right leg out in front of him. "Figured I'd already knocked in the winning runs, no need to keep hotdogging it at first. So I pulled myself out. You know, needed to give someone else the opportunity to play."

Edie lowered her head, but not before he

caught her lips twitching. Good, he'd hoped to coax one of those beautiful smiles out of her. "You're very sure of yourself, aren't you, Mr. Daniels?"

"Sometimes, like on the ball field or at the hospital. But I'm still trying to figure most things out," he answered. Now why had he told her that? Maybe because it was the first time he'd admitted it to himself. From the look on her face, she didn't believe him, either. "It's true. Growing up the way I did, there was never anything to have a lot of faith in."

"You had Merrilee, didn't you?"

He shook his head. "Dad didn't take us up to the big house much when we were younger. I don't know if me and my brothers were too rambunctious for our grandfather or Dad just didn't want to mess with us. I didn't get to know Merrilee until she married John." One side of his mouth tipped up in a smile. "She was probably one of the first people I ever learned to depend on."

"And now?"

He looked at her over his shoulder, studying the fine lines gathered around the corners of her eyes and around her mouth. "I've learned that no matter how much people let you down, the Lord never will."

"Maybe that's true for you and for Merrilee and most folks," she whispered, worrying her lower lip with her teeth. "But not for everyone."

Maybe they were finally getting to the heart of what happened back at the concession stand. "Where did you get that idea from?"

"I shouldn't have let the man bother me so much, but he just kept saying things." She filled him in about the prisoner-of-war camp opening up at Fort Oglethorpe, and the men's position on Germans in general. His heart contracted into a painful knot. No wonder she ran. "I can't help the choices my parents made. All I can do is give my all to help this country claim victory over that mad man over there. But it's never going to be enough, is it? Some people are always going to think I'm the enemy simply because I'm German."

Beau grimaced. Hadn't he done the same thing, judging her based on an old letter from her grandmother, thought her guilty based on — what? His only experience with Germans? He knew better than anyone what it was like growing up in the shadow of evil, to have people wonder if he'd go down the same rotten path as his dad. And Edie had done nothing to deserve this kind of censure, save being born.

Lord, forgive me. Help me to always see people for who they are. And give me the right words to comfort Edie.

"You know, when I was a kid, my momma always made us go to Sunday school. I didn't like wearing a tie and the shoes always hurt my feet, but I liked the music. There was this one song I always remembered. 'Red and yellow, black and white, they are precious in His sight, Jesus loves the little children of the world.' "

Edie gave him a watery smile. "That was one of my favorites."

"I didn't know what it meant," he replied, warmth flooding his cheeks. "But when I landed with my platoon over in Africa, and I looked around at the people from all over the world, working together to secure our freedom, that song came back to me for the first time in years. I realized the Lord didn't want us to pick and choose who we would love. He wanted us to love like He loved."

"Even the enemy?" Edie whispered.

Beau reached down and took her hand, entwining his fingers with hers, the soft peaks and valleys of her palm a perfect fit against his own. She tilted her head back until her eyes met his, and he was lost.

So this was love.

He didn't have a chance, not from the moment she aimed that fire poker at his head, doing her best to protect those she loved the most. Beau had been falling ever since.

"Beau?"

She was waiting for an answer. A long strand of silky curls had made a break out of her bindings, instead caressing the delicate skin of her jaw. With his free hand, he fingered the unruly curls back behind the shell of her ear. She wasn't breathing now, but hanging by the thinnest of threads for his answer.

Beau leaned his forehead against hers. "Especially the enemy, Edwina."

He could tell from the play of emotions on her face that she wanted so much to believe him, to grab hold of his words and cling to them for dear life.

But then she leaned away from him slightly, the warmth of their contact suddenly replaced by a cool emptiness that sent a chill through Beau's heart. "We ought to be getting back."

"Sure." Beau stood, then turned, holding her hand while gently wrapping his arm around her waist to help her down. As soon as her saddle shoes touched earth, she scooted away from him.

Beau followed behind her. So she planned

to simply sweep her uncomfortable feelings under the rug. Didn't she know that one day, when she threw back the carpet, her problems would still be there, growing larger over time? But she needed to make the decision to deal with them for herself.

For some odd reason, his father came to mind. Maybe he was something of a coward, not wanting to talk to James. But he feared Mack would be right. Beau would regret not speaking to his father, if only to offer forgiveness.

"How's your knee holding up?"

Beau looked over at her. She really was a sweet woman, just the kind of girl who could make a man give serious thought to marriage. But not him. This talk had convinced him Edie already had a tough row to hoe without adding his own brand of troubles. What would she want with a man like him, someone with sins of their own making — not to mention a father heading for prison and an absent mother? She deserved a man like Mack. Yet something about that idea stuck in his craw.

He cleared his throat. "Got a little nervous rounding second that last time, but it's feeling pretty good."

Was that a sigh of relief he heard? "I'm glad."

Beau smiled, the thought of Edie worrying about him sending a slice of warmth
across his chest. "I think all that work we've
been doing out on the farm is rebuilding
some of the strength I lost when I got
injured."

"You know, I haven't thought about that,
but you're probably right." She paused for a
second. "Can I ask you something? Just
something I've been wondering about for a
while now."

He leaned in close, enjoying the faint
fragrance of vanilla that lingered in the air
around her. "Sweetheart, you can ask me
anything."

Her face clouded with uncertainty. "It's
just that a lot of guys have been injured like
you, and most times get sent right back to
the front." She paused, the muscles in her
throat a delicate ripple when she swallowed.
"I figure your wound must have been worse
than you let on to Merrilee. If it is, she
needs to know. Merrilee worries about you."

Beau's mouth pulled into a tight line. "If
you want to know why I'm not back on the
line, don't hide behind Merrilee. All you
have to do is ask."

"I'm sorry. It just seemed . . . wrong to
pry."

Well, if Edie wanted to know what had

happened, he would tell her the truth, or as much as he could without going into too much detail. He glanced around, trying to find a place for them to stop for a while, somewhere out of the early evening sunlight that danced across the forest floor, playing peekaboo with the newly bloomed shoots. Just up ahead stood a massive water oak, its flouncing spring green leaves a perfect umbrella to rest and talk under.

"Look, if you don't want to talk about this . . ."

"No, it's just that this is going to take a while." Sliding his hand up the length of her forearm, he took her elbow. The soft contour of her arm pressed against his fingertips, sending little shocks of awareness through his hand and up his arm. He led her over some downed limbs, steadying her as she stepped across the thin branches until they reached the tree. Once he was sure she was comfortable, he turned to her. "So what is it you'd like to know?"

"What happened?"

He glanced out over the wooded area, trying to put his scattered memories of that time into some semblance of order. "There was a bridge right outside of Tunis that we were ordered to take, but there were too many of them." He snorted out a humorless chuckle. "We were like ducks on a pond, just there for the picking. By the time we got the order to retreat, my squadron was surrounded. We were forced to surrender."

"You were a . . . prisoner?"

He nodded. "In Italy at first, but once our boys got them on the run, the Italians shipped us north. I ended up in a prison camp near Moosberg."

"But that's in . . ."

Had she heard of Moosberg? Beau studied her for a moment. The color in her cheeks had faded to an alabaster cream, her blue-green eyes deepening to match the churning seas just off the African coast. She bit into her lip until he feared she would draw blood.

He dropped his gaze to their clasped hands. When had his fingers sought out and entwined with hers again? "You familiar with the village?"

"I believe Grandma still has a sister living there."

He hadn't considered that she might still have family back in Germany. How painful that must be for her, the thought of people she loved right there on the front line?

He snuck a glance at her. The tension in her face had softened a bit. The lines that had creased her forehead and around her eyes were fading, her lips slightly parted as if waiting for his next question.

Or a kiss.

Beau cleared his throat. "Not much left to tell. It wasn't a picnic, but we had the Geneva Convention to protect us and Red Cross rations to feed us, so it wasn't as bad as it was for some."

"What happened to the men who didn't have that protection?"

He met her gaze and held it for a long moment. No way on earth was he going to tell her what the Germans had done to the Russians, to those unprotected by the bullheadedness of their leaders. The nightmares that followed his time in the prison camp didn't visit him as often anymore, but in the recess of his soul, he still heard the unearthly screams of terror from the Russian side of the camp.

"How come Merrilee never talked about you being missing?"

"I didn't put her down as a contact. I didn't want her worrying about me if something did happen."

"Does Merrilee know?"

He shook his head. "No, I haven't told a soul about my time there."

Until now.

Beau studied her. Why had he told her?

After all, he'd decided it wouldn't be right to burden anyone with his time in Moosberg, so he swore to himself that he wouldn't burden anyone with it, ever. But Edie didn't view his imprisonment as anything but what it was, a consequence of war. He felt free to talk without needing prodding. Edie was so easy to talk to — asking questions, yes, but never expecting more than he was ready to give. She understood without making him go into every detail.

"Beau?"

"Hmm?"

She bent her head forward, her hair cascading into a dark curtain across her face. "How did you feel about the Lord then, when you were in that . . . camp?"

His heart shifted slightly inside him. Could a man fall more in love than he already was? Before today, he would have doubted it, calling it silly mush, but he knew he'd never stop falling for this woman all the days of his life.

But she needed comforting, not love just now. Reaching out, Beau gently outlined the silhouette of her face, the skin beneath his fingertips warm, the weight of her hair a soft mass of curls against his hand. He pushed the strands back, tracing the shell of her ear as he secured her hair into place.

Edie glanced up at him then, her wary eyes studying him. Yes, she was searching, much like he had been during his time at Moosberg. Railing at the Lord, wondering why the God he'd been told about in Sunday school would forsake him in his need, only to discover He'd been there with him all the time.

Beau leaned back against the trunk of the oak, gathering her close. He'd be honest with her, even if she didn't believe him. "The thing is, I didn't lose my faith in the Lord then. That's where I found it for the very first time."

The evening air hummed a soft tune, but Edie's mind was a muddle as she walked beside Beau up the dirt driveway to Merrilee's. He'd dodged bullets, running along the front lines, nursing the wounded, only to get shot and left for dead. But would death have been a better alternative to the horrors the Nazis inflicted on their prisoners? The night birds rustled in the trees overhead, their mournful song echoing in the high branches.

I didn't lose my faith there, Edie. It's where I found it.

Edie sucked in a deep breath of moist air. She had faith in the Lord, maybe not the kind Beau had and maybe not as strong as his, but a faith nevertheless. But what she'd been calling faith wasn't enough now, not now that she'd seen what God had worked through Beau.

Lord, I don't want to be worried by what others say about me anymore. I just want what Beau has, an absolute faith in You.

"You're being mighty quiet over there." His deep rumble held a hint of concern.

She smiled to herself. Another thing she loved about this man. He didn't let her ponder on problems too long. "Just enjoying the night, that's all."

"Me, too." He grasped her hand in his.

A tiny part of her thrilled at his touch. But as much as she loved him, Edie knew this feeling couldn't lead to anything more. Beau was a war hero, albeit a silent one who had suffered at the hands of the Nazis, but one all the same. She didn't doubt he felt something for her, but would it be enough? Or would he, in the years to come, look at her with a special brand of hatred reserved for her people?

Best to cut and run now, before her heart broke even more. Edie walked up the first two steps. "Thank you for walking me home."

"My pleasure."

One memory. That's all she wanted right

now, something to hang on to when she remembered Beau in the months and years to come. She turned toward him, stumbling a bit when she realized only a breath parted them. The stairs had erased the distance between them, so close their noses almost touched.

"Edwina."

Her name sounded soft and melodic as each syllable slid from his lips. No silly nickname for this moment, this memory. She leaned toward him slightly, unsure what to do next.

But Beau knew. Grasping her around her waist, he bent his head toward her cheek, but when she turned, his lips brushed against the corner of her mouth. He leaned back, just far enough for her to see his green eyes deepen to a dark shade of emerald, the silver sparks that had seemed so dull just minutes ago firing back into life. She barely registered his arms wrap around her, tightening as he bent his head again, this time his lips closing firmly on her mouth.

Edie tilted her head back, her hands reaching up, grasping the soft cotton of his shirt, anchoring herself against him. He knew all her secrets, all the sordid details of her life, and yet he was here, holding her close, making her feel cared for in a way she'd never felt before.

Beau broke the kiss, resting his forehead against hers. "I guess most gentlemen would apologize, but I can't. Not when I've been wanting to kiss you since that very first night you held that poker to my head."

A smile curved her lips. "Good, because I have no intentions of apologizing for kissing you back."

His laugher rumbled beneath the palms of her hands, his lips brushing a kiss against her forehead. "I like a woman who knows her mind."

It was time to let go, before she began believing all the lovely little things he would say. Pressing her hands against the sinewy wall of his chest, she stepped back, staring at him for just a moment, remembering the small details of his face — the tiny scar on his chin, the way his cheeks exploded with color when he was angry, the way his lips felt against hers. She turned then. Halfway upstairs, the screen door opened and Merrilee came rushing out.

"Oh, thank goodness, you're home." Merrilee hurried toward Edie, her face masked in worry. "I wasn't sure what I was going to do if you didn't show up soon."

"What is it, Aunt Merri?" Beau asked somewhere behind her.

Merrilee glanced at Beau, then turned all her attention on Edie. "It's your mother, darling. She's upstairs in your room."

CHAPTER SIXTEEN

Edie blinked. Her mother here? But the last time she'd seen her parents, they were within days of leaving for Hamburg. What was her mother doing all the way here from Detroit? Had her father changed his mind about going back to Germany to take his place in Hitler's army?

"I took a tray up to her a little while ago, but she said something about lying down for a while." Glancing back into the house, Merrilee lowered her voice. "She said she'd been living at the train station for the last few nights."

Confusion clouded Edie's mind. What was going on? Had her prayers, at least for her mother, been answered? Or was this some sort of trap laid by the powers in the Bund? "Thank you, Merrilee. I certainly appreciate everything you've done."

As she moved toward the screen door, Beau's fingers tightened around her elbow, his voice low, his body warm and protective behind her. "You're not seriously thinking about going up there to talk with her alone, are you?"

He'd be disappointed in her, but this was her mother. She had to find out what was going on. "I have to find out why she's here, Beau."

He leaned closer until she could almost feel his lips touching the soft flesh of her ear. "And what if it's a setup? The Bund could be using her as bait."

Edie tilted her head to the side to look at him. His eyes had darkened to a stormy sea green, churning with anger and something else that she couldn't put a name to. Vulnerability? Her breath caught in her lungs. Beau wasn't worried about himself or his family. No, he feared for *her.*

Edie turned to him, cupping his face between her hands, his day-old stubble a pleasant roughness against her soft palms. He responded by circling her waist with his hands, drawing her flush to him as if to shield her from the harsh realities that might come.

What if this was the last time she was in his arms, feeling his heart thundering between her fingertips, safe in the knowledge that whatever she faced, Beau would be there, going to battle just for her?

A battle that might even now be waiting in her room. Edie cleared her throat. "I can't just leave her up there in my room, Beau."

"Then let me go with you."

"Why, so you can talk to her?" Dropping her arms to her side, Edie stepped back. "I'm not even sure she'll open up to me, let alone someone she doesn't know." She shook her head. "I have to do this alone, and pray that maybe Mom has had a change of heart."

He released a sharp sigh. "I don't like the situation she's put you in one bit."

"I don't, either." Edie reached for the door handle and pulled it open. "But the only way to deal with this mess is to get all the facts. Then we'll know how to make a step-by-step plan to handle it."

"Just like an architect. Always making blueprints."

At least Beau was back to teasing her. Edie gave him a slight smile. "It's what I do best."

"Just be careful, sweetheart," Merrilee said from behind Beau.

She'd forgotten all about Merrilee! "Yes, ma'am."

The climb up the steps to her room seemed to drag on forever, or maybe it was just Edie's feet as she slowly made her way up the stairwell. The hall outside her room stood empty, not unusual for this time of evening, but still, Edie couldn't help but hope someone would walk by. But no one did.

The metal doorknob felt cool beneath her touch. *Lord, whatever happens, please give me the right words to say. Please keep me safe. In Your Son's name.* Turning the handle, Edie pushed open the door.

Hilda Michaels stood at the window, her thin frame even more fragile now than when Edie had left home three years ago. The dark hair Edie had inherited from her mother was threaded with strands of pearl white now and pulled tight into a severe bun at the nape of her slender neck.

A tight lump formed in Edie's throat. "Mom?"

Her mother turned then, taking a halted step before finally breaking into a quick pace. Edie barely had time to shut the door before her mother's arms came around her, holding her close. Unable to help herself, Edie buried her face in her mother's neck. Rosewater, like always. For the briefest of seconds, she felt at peace.

"I'm so sorry, dearest."

The words held a million meanings, none

of which Edie could decipher at the moment. Maybe she should have let Beau come upstairs with her, if only as emotional support. No, this was her problem and she needed to handle it.

Stepping back from her mother, Edie straightened, clasping her hands into a tight ball at the base of her spine. "What are you doing here?"

"I had to come." The muscles in her throat twitched as if she had problems forming the words. "The officials came through our old neighborhood. They took possession of the house."

"No!" The word exploded from Edie. Why, she wasn't sure. What she couldn't understand was why her mother would care? "Wasn't it the plan to leave the house and everything in it?"

"That may have been your father's plan, but not mine." Her mom shook her head, her body trembling, the foundations of the life she once knew weakened and crumbling. "Never mine!"

There was more to this mess than Edie had ever dreamed. Silently, she led her mother to a grouping of two chairs facing the dormant fireplace. Once Hilda was comfortable, Edie sat on the edge of the other chair, facing her mother. "What were you doing living in our house?"

"I couldn't leave our home." Her mother gave her a weak nod. "When we first saw that place, it was a mess, but your father and I, we worked hard fixing it up, making it a home." She paused for a moment, looking off as if into the faded past. "We started our lives there, a happy life in a new country that we loved. And then we had you." Tears gathered in Edie's throat at the look of pure love her mother gave her. "We thought God had given us a great gift."

Edie nodded. Growing up, she'd never doubted her parents' love for her. But now, her father's betrayal had left her uncertain. Could she trust their love?

"But then your father lost his job." Sable lashes fell quickly over her eyes, but not before Edie saw the pain, the disappointment there. "He went out every morning trying to find a position, and most days didn't come home until late into the evening, but there was nothing. Just so many people needing a job and not finding one."

"He lost hope," Edie whispered.

Her mother nodded, her hair shimmering like white gold in the lantern light. "I tried to tell him it wasn't just us, that the whole country was having a hard time, but he wouldn't hear of it. He remembered how it was in Germany after the Great War and felt those people in Washington had let everyone down. It wasn't long after that he met Fritz Kuhn."

"I don't remember a Mr. Kuhn from the old neighborhood."

"He fought with your uncle Fredrick at Lorraine during the Great War. Mr. Kuhn came by the house to pay his respects."

For a man who had died some twenty years before? "What did they talk about?"

"The war mainly." Her mother paused. "I don't know. But before Kuhn left, he offered to send your father for training at a camp in Wisconsin, and told him if he did well, there would be a position waiting for him in the *Gau*."

Edie fell back into the chair and closed her eyes. How had she missed this? Had she been so absorbed in her new life at college that she hadn't bothered to see the trouble brewing until it was bearing down on her, and the only way out was to run away? Was it possible that her father had only good intentions of taking care of his family when he was led astray? "Oh, Mother, I'm so sorry."

She covered Edie's hand with her own. "It's not your fault, dearest. It's your father's," she admitted, the slight accent reminding Edie of the German neighborhood she'd grown up in. "And mine. I knew what your father was doing, and yet I never stopped him. He used their money to put food on our table, and I never once said a word."

Lifting her eyelids, Edie stared at her mother, squeezing her fingers gently. "Where's Dad now?"

Hilda drew in a sharp breath, her mouth a taunt line. "I don't know. I haven't seen him in almost three months."

Three months? "But he told me three years ago you were leaving for Hamburg within days. He said there was a position for him waiting there."

"Well, all I know is he wasn't with me when they came and took our home."

Edie studied the woman beside her with new eyes. In all her twenty-three years, she'd never heard her mother speak as she had in these last few moments, of the pain of the last ten years. Mother had always left the politics to Daddy, like most women of her day. But had this war given her a voice, one that spoke against the Bund and the evil they propagated?

The silence finally got to be too much for Edie. "I always loved that old neighborhood.

Do you remember how Mrs. Schmitt would hand out chocolate chip cookies to the kids after we'd been playing stickball all day long?"

"Yes, I remember." Her mom chuckled softly. "I gave her the recipe."

Mom always was the best cook. Well, right up there with Merrilee. "I can't imagine the Schmitts not living there anymore."

"They're still there."

A throbbing started behind Edie's eyes. "But, Mom, you said the officials came into the neighborhood and cleared everyone out."

"You must have misunderstood, Edwina. No one else on our street was removed from their homes."

The pounding in her head intensified. "Are you saying we were the only ones evicted from our house?"

Her slight nod troubled Edie. This whole situation didn't make sense. She'd been honest with the folks at Bell, telling them right from the start about her father's activities. The government would have never given her security clearance if she hadn't. Major Evans had even offered a security detail if she ever felt in danger from the Bund.

So if the government already knew the

truth, who had thrown her mother out of their home?

The answer punched her in the gut with the force of a baseball bat swinging for the outfield. Her father might not know where Edie was, but what better way to find out the truth than to take her mother's home and hope she'd lead them to Edie. But how?

"Mom, how did you know where to look for me?"

"A couple of months ago, I got a letter from an old friend now living here in Atlanta. She mentioned she saw you leaving the USO one night."

Drat! Edie's one night out in months had blown her cover. "Did you ever show the letter to Daddy?"

Hilda shook her head. "Your father lost interest in anything important to me soon after he found his new buddies."

Thank goodness — at least her father didn't know where she was hiding. Walking over to the closet, Edie pulled open the doors and tugged at the suitcase hidden there. "Mom, I've got to get out of here."

"But why?" Hilda's eyebrows furrowed into a single perfect line. "Your landlady said it was okay for me to stay here with you."

Edie pondered the deal for a moment.

Maybe it wouldn't be such a bad idea for her mother to stay at Merrilee's. "Then stay, Mom. But I can't. It's too dangerous for everyone."

"And how are you going to explain this to your friends?"

Good question. But she already knew the answer. She'd have to slip out without saying goodbye. That way if the Bund came looking for her, Merrilee could be honest and say she didn't know where Edie was.

And Beau? What would he say when he learned that she had put Merrilee and Claire in danger? Would all the tenderness he'd shown her earlier tonight fall to the wayside? She had to warn him, had to share the enormity of the situation with him. Because even if nothing ever came of the love she felt for him, she had too much respect for him to just sneak out of his life like most everyone else did. Not when she'd seen the echoes of those heartaches branded on his soul like scars of war.

The leather handle of the suitcase cracked against her palm as she tossed it on the bed. Broken, just like her heart. Edie snapped the metal fasteners open. "Mom, no matter what you do, I have to get out of here tonight."

Sitting at the kitchen table, Beau topped

off his glass, shoving the Bible he'd been reading to the side. He'd come out here to the kitchen looking for something harder than milk to chase the worry from his mind, but found Merrilee's Bible instead. Beau smiled to himself. Much better than a hangover.

Where was Edie? He glanced at the clock on the sill over the sink. It'd been a whole hour now — an hour! He'd come close to marching up the stairs and pounding on her door, demanding to know she was all right, but Merrilee had talked him out of it. But his aunt didn't know the danger Edie faced from her parents.

So what had brought Hilda Michaels to Marietta now?

The door swung open, and Beau looked up to find Edie standing in the brick archway. "I thought you'd be in the parlor."

It was the way she hung at the door, as if she were looking for a quick escape, that bothered him. "I was, but when you didn't come down after a few minutes, Merrilee sent me out here to get a glass of milk." He didn't tell her his aunt had thought it would calm him down. Nodding to the empty place at the table beside him, he pulled out the chair. "Care to join me?"

"Maybe for a minute."

315

Beau lifted his glass to his lips and took a sip. A minute wasn't nearly long enough, not with this woman. "How's your mother doing?"

Edie padded across the room, collecting a cup before sitting down next to him. "I don't think she knows what's hit her."

Not exactly the answer he'd expected. "What do you mean?"

She reached for the blue-stenciled pitcher in the center of the table. "She's homeless, Beau. Someone came a few days ago with papers and told her to get out. They took everything. The house, the furniture. All Mom's got are the clothes she managed to pack before they threw her out."

"Was she behind on her payments?" But if it was the bank, wouldn't they let her keep her furniture? Suddenly, he remembered a newspaper article from months ago about plans to confiscate German-American properties near the coastal cities, much like what was done to the Japanese in the days following Pearl Harbor. But he'd heard nothing about that since. And why Edie's house? "You think it's the government taking the house because of what your dad's been up to."

"I think that's what these people want

Mom to believe." Edie slumped back in her chair.

Beau scowled. No more of this beating around the bush. Turning toward her, he captured her chin between his fingers and tilted her head up until he could look her square in the eyes. "Talk to me."

Sable eyelashes fluttered down against her pale cheek, but not before he glimpsed a flash of pain. "It was my father, Beau. And his cronies with the Bund. They threw Mother out of her house."

"Why do you think that?"

She opened her eyes. "Everyone in my old neighborhood was German, Beau, yet we were the only ones thrown out of our house. Why would the government take possession of our home and leave everyone else alone? Particularly since I warned them about my father's activities."

It made sense, all of it. "And you think the Bund put your mom out so that she could lead them to you?"

She gave him a quick nod. "After I left, Dad wasn't allowed to take his position in Hamburg as he'd planned. Mom and Dad have been here in the states the whole time I've been with Bell."

"Where's your dad now?"

"Your guess is as good as mine. According

to Mom, he left three months ago and she hasn't seen him since."

Beau grimaced. So the man could be anywhere. Why hadn't the government brought these people to justice yet? True, the country's resources were being stretched by the war, but this group lived right on our doorstep, threatening this nation from the inside out. Threatening Edie. "And you think your father's still after you after all this time?"

"If he wants to cement his position in the *Gau* Midwest, then yes, it's a strong possibility."

A certainty, more like it. Anger burst through his veins, making him grit his teeth before he said something he'd regret. If Edie's father ever came snooping around here, he'd plant a fist in the older man's face for what he'd put his daughter through. And Mrs. Michaels? Silly woman, didn't she think to use the good sense God had given her, instead of putting her daughter, a woman who had already faced so much, in harm's way? Or was that her plan? To expose Edie, have her kidnapped, then turn her daughter in to her superiors for whatever prize they dangled like a toy in front of Mrs. Michaels's face?

"I don't need you to get angry, Beau."

He'd never been able to hide his temper, not with his auburn hair and fair skin, but he had a feeling Edie would be able to read him anyway. "I'm sorry. But it just burns me up thinking about what she's done."

"I know. I'm upset, too, but I also think she didn't do this on purpose."

Beau leaned back, crossing his arms over his chest. "Why do you say that?"

"Look, Mom's always been more of a homebody, always taking care of us or helping out around our neighborhood. She's never been much on politics. She's always let Daddy be the one to tell her who to vote for." Her eyes grew wide and her mouth turned up into an incredulous smile. "But when she learned the full scope of what Daddy was into, she stood up to him."

Beau wasn't so easily won over. "Are you sure she's just not telling you what she knows you want to hear?"

Lantern light shimmered along the golden highlights of her dark hair when she shook her head. "I might have thought that if we were still at home, but she didn't sugarcoat the problem like she would have in the past. She's being honest, not just with me but with herself."

Beau nodded. The jury was still out on Mrs. Michaels for now. He blinked as the realization hit him. "You're not safe here."

Dropping her chin down, she stared at the wooden surface of the table, as if looking for an answer there. "No, and neither is anyone else living here while I'm still here. I have to leave, the sooner the better for everyone involved."

Not everyone. The thought of looking across the dinner table and not seeing Edie, or sharing the night sky with her on the porch swing, tore a hole through him. But that was beside the point. Edie needed him and he intended to do whatever he could to help her. "Knowing you like I do, I bet you've got a plan."

Her cheeks turned a delicate shade of pink, as if the fact he knew her so well pleased her. "I always figured if worse came to worst, I could bunk down at the plant. Major Evans even gave me the okay when I told him what was going on." Edie leaned her head back, a cascade of silky brown curls falling around her shoulders, her eyes staring up at the ceiling. "But I can't do that now, not with my mother here."

"Why not let her stay with Merrilee? No one would even know she's still here, and after a while, those men looking for you would realize they've run into a dead end."

And Edie would be safe. Everyone in town

knew you couldn't get inside the plant without an identification card complete with a photograph, so the possibility the thugs after Edie could breach security was slim to none. Once inside the gates of the bomber plant, Major Evans would protect her. That was all that mattered to Beau.

"I don't think these guys are the give in and give up types."

He hated to ask this next question, but if it kept her safe, that was all that mattered. "Do you have any college friends who could take you in for a little while?"

"No. They're either in the service or working at one of the automotive plants that's been converted for military usage. So I'm stuck."

"Don't say that." Beau knew Edie was just telling the truth. Of all the times not to have an escape plan. Now he desperately needed one to save this incredible woman. He needed time to analyze these feelings she'd brought out in him, tenderness and hope.

And love.

"Beau," she whispered, her hand closing over his, her fingers grasping his, tightening into a snug knot. "Would you please pray for me?"

He covered their hands with his free one. No way was he letting her go, not now, maybe not ever. He watched her bow her head, then followed suit. *Father, You know the plans You have for Edie, good plans that will bring You glory and honor. Keep her safe.* Beau started to lift his head, then lowered it again, remembered something Edie had once told him. *And, Lord, help her parents. They've made some bad decisions, but who of us hasn't? Lead them in the way You'd want them to go. In Jesus's name, Amen.*

Edie's tremulous smile greeted him as he lifted his head. "I know how hard that was, praying for my parents, but I appreciate it."

Beau nodded. Truth be told, it hadn't been that difficult. In fact, in the moments since raising those words up to heaven, the exasperation he'd felt for the Michaelses had eased a bit. "Maybe I'll have to give that a try with my dad."

Edie had barely registered a smile when a knock at the kitchen door put him on alert. One glance at the clock above the stove told him it was too late for visitors, and Merrilee would have called out, then bustled inside.

Beau leaned close to Edie, keeping his voice low so that only she could hear. "Did your mother think she'd been followed?"

She shook her head, her eyes wide and watchful, her teeth nibbling at her bottom lip, reminding him how soft and warm and sweet her kiss tasted. "No. In fact, she ended up on a couple of bus routes before she finally figured out how to get here."

"Good. Maybe whoever is out there will take the hint and go away."

A rap on the door came a second later. "Beau Daniels, your aunt told me you were out here, puffed up about some such nonsense. Now let me in."

"Gertie!" Before he could stop her, Edie had pushed back her chair and stood.

He stopped her before she got any farther, grasping her elbow. "You can't just go around opening doors anymore, understand?"

The pink glow in her cheeks faded, her vivid blue-green eyes paling to a translucent aquamarine. "I understand."

"Okay." Releasing her arm, Beau pushed back from the table, a tension coiling through his body, his muscles tightening, preparing for the fight. He'd seen the look Edie had given him before, in the faces of his fellow inmates at Moosberg, imprisoned in a world with no color, no life.

The walk to the door only consisted of four or five steps, but it felt like forever. Whatever happened, Edie had to be safe. When he held the doorknob, he glanced back at her one more time. Her dainty shoulders squared, she lifted her chin just a tad, a familiar move she made when she wanted to prove her point. With a brief nod, she straightened, her spine a ribbon of steel.

With a quick prayer, Beau turned the knob.

CHAPTER SEVENTEEN

Edie's lungs stung from the breath she'd been holding for what felt like forever. She gripped her hands together in a knot at the base of her spine to keep them from trembling. She would go with the Germans if they caught her. It was the only option that kept Beau and his family out of harm's way.

Beau cracked open the door a few inches. "Are you alone, Gert?"

Something in his voice must have alerted her friend because she gave a nervous nod. "Why wouldn't I be?"

"Come in." He held the door open.

Gert removed the black scarf from around her head and looked at Edie. "What in the blue blazes is going on here? Come here to talk to you two, and what do I get? Left sitting on the doorstep like a cat put out for the night?"

Edie stared at Gert's outraged expression, a hint of a chuckle rising up in her throat.

Before she knew it, she doubled over at the waist, laughter bubbling up, erasing the tension of the past few hours, even if just for a moment.

A low chortle from the doorway made her lift her head. Beau had joined her, his eyes dancing with merriment, the troubled lines that had been plaguing his features suddenly softened. This was the Beau she'd carry with her in memory in the lonely months and years to come.

The thought sobered her, and she caught her breath. "I'm sorry, Gert. It's just been an interesting afternoon around here."

Her friend leaned into one hip, perching her fist at the dip at her waist. "Well, if I had known I was that funny, I would have put in for a radio job with Burns and Allen."

Edie bit back a new round of giggles, motioning to a chair. "What are you doing here anyway?"

Walking to the cabinets, Beau opened the door and grabbed a clean cup. "It's kind of late for you to be on this side of town."

Gertie gave them a smug look. "When the only good time for a woman like me to be on this side of town is to clean somebody's house or cook their meals, I figured I'd take the chance."

Wonder what had her friend in high spirits

tonight? "So tell us what brings you here."

"Well," she started, her dark eyes gleaming with excitement, "the telephone company came out today and started digging out to plant the poles. It's really happening."

"That's wonderful!" Edie leaned over and pulled her friend into a hug. Only she wouldn't be around to see Cantrell fulfill his promise, wouldn't see the sunlight glisten against copper wires, wouldn't be in the room to see the wide-eyed delight when Gert heard the operator on her own telephone for the first time.

She glanced over her friend's shoulder. Beau knew it, too, the lines plowed out around his mouth and eyes, though not as deep.

Releasing Gert, Edie shifted back in her chair. "I'm so happy for you."

"Me, too, Gertie," Beau added.

Gertie shifted her gaze between them, then reclined back in her chair, folding her arms over her waist. "What's going on here? You two look like I just kicked your pet dog."

No sense lying to Gertie. She'd know soon enough about her mother arriving, that Edie had moved out of the boardinghouse in a hurry, taking off for parts unknown. Maybe the ugly truth about her father would remain hidden. She stole a look at Beau. His lips tightened into a sharp line, but he gave her a grudging nod.

Edie turned to face her friend. "Truth is, I'm leaving town tonight and I won't be coming back."

Gertie turned to Beau. "When did this happen?"

"This evening," Beau answered, his eyes wandering back to Edie's face. "We've tried to figure out a way to keep her here, but nothing has panned out so far."

"Is Bell transferring you?"

"In fact, I'm going to quit my job." Edie shrugged at the quizzical look Gertie gave her. "It may upset Mr. Ellerbee for a while, but I've been working hard. I deserve to live the life of leisure for a bit."

One dark eyebrow shot up in surprise. Several seconds passed in awkward silence before Gertie spoke again. "You almost had me there. Until you started squalling about giving up your job. So why don't you tell me the truth?"

"Fine, but it can't go beyond this room."

"Beau!"

Gertie gave them a sharp nod. "Done."

Edie glared at him. "Why drag her into this mess?"

"Because she might have an answer that we haven't thought of yet."

Edie blinked. Maybe Beau had a point. Maybe having someone look at her situation from another angle might yield a solution to her problem. "Okay."

For the next several minutes, Beau explained the situation to Gertie, looking to Edie to fill in the gaps he might have missed. Her friend's expression never changed, as if Beau was reading her the society column out of the newspaper instead of a devious plot to steal plans for the B-29 bomber by kidnapping Edie and forcing her to Germany.

"I tried to talk her into camping out at the plant, but she won't listen. She's worried about her mother."

His scowl irked her until she realized that before a few hours ago, she'd thought, much like Beau did, that her mom had betrayed her like her dad had. She was stepping out on faith believing her mother, wasn't she? "Mom wouldn't be safe here. Neither would anyone else."

Beau tensed, as if what she'd said had in some way insulted him. Well, he'd have to get over it. She'd rather have him angry than dead.

"I think you're wrong, Edie," Gertie said.

"If your mother is here and doesn't know where you are, she wouldn't be able to tell anyone because she wouldn't know."

Both Gertie and Beau were beginning to make sense. "Then I could just stay at the plant."

"Why not come stay with us for a while?" Gertie gave her an encouraging smile. "We've got the extra room, and you wouldn't have to worry about getting to work because Dad drives the bus route for the plant. It would be like you hiding in plain sight."

Edie shook her head. "It's like jumping out of the frying pan into the fire. I won't put you and your family in danger just to hide from my father."

"Think about it, Edwina," Beau said, covering her hands with his. "This might just be the answer we've been praying for."

How could that be, when instead of Merrilee and Claire, Gertie and her family would be in danger? The man she loved would never value one person's life above another's, but in this case, it sounded like that was exactly what Beau was suggesting. Edie swallowed against the lump forming in her throat. "It sounds like you're trading Gertie's family's safety for your own."

"It's not like that, Edie," Gertie answered

before Beau had the chance. "All Beau is saying is that no one in their right mind is going to come looking for a white woman in a Negro community."

But Edie wasn't so sure. The only thing she knew was that she had to leave here, tonight if possible. If keeping his promise to John to watch out for Merrilee held so much importance that he'd put other lives at stake, she couldn't stay.

Because staying would break her heart that much more.

Walking into the parlor a few hours later, Beau headed for the sideboard and the coffeepot waiting there. Everyone in the house had retired upstairs hours ago, except Edie, who spent the majority of the evening packing. It had taken a promise from him to see that the rest of Edie's possessions made it to the Stephenses later, after he knew she was safe. He turned over a clean mug and reached for the pot.

"You want to pour me a cup, too?"

Beau looked over his shoulder to see Merrilee walking toward him. "Sure. Cream and sugar?"

"Yes, please."

The coffeepot clinking against the porcelain filled the silence around them. He doctored her coffee, then held it out for her.

"Thank you." She took the cup, blowing at the little swirls of steam rising from the liquid. "So did Edie get off okay?"

"As far as I know. Her mother wasn't too happy when Edie decided she should stay here for now, but we thought it was best if Mrs. Michaels didn't know where Edie was going."

"So Mrs. Michaels is staying in Edie's old room."

Beau hated the sound of that statement, as if Edie were never coming home. "Just until the danger has passed. But what about you? What's got you up this late at night?"

"Ever since Annabelle Smith came down with polio, Claire's been having night-mares." She lifted her cup to her lips and drew in a long sip. "You know, for all the fussing those two girls do, I think they really like each other."

Bowing his head, Beau chuckled. "Kids."

"I don't know. Seems to me the adults around here are just as bad." She reached for the bottle of milk in front of him and splashed a drop into her cup. "When she first started at the plant, Maggie and Wesley were constantly butting heads over one thing or another. But now, one doesn't speak before the other one is finishing their thought."

"I've noticed."

Merrilee wrapped her hands around her cup. "So how do you like Mrs. Michaels?"

So that's what Merrilee was up to, digging for clues as to why Edie had to leave. "I'm not a fan."

His aunt walked over to the sofa and sank into the cushions. "I can imagine you're angry with her, leaving Edie with that pack of snakes her husband deals with. It must be devastating to know that you almost let your husband sacrifice your daughter to the enemy, all for the sake of prestige and power."

The coffee scalded a fiery trail down his throat. "You knew about that?"

"There's not much that goes on in the house that I don't know about, Beau." Merrilee reclined back against the sofa. "I figured she must have had a falling-out with her parents. She never got any mail from home. A couple of weeks after she moved in, I got a visit from Major Evans. He told me about Edie's father and his political involvements in strictest confidence."

Merrilee knew? "Then why did you let her stay?"

"Why wouldn't I? She's a wonderful girl." Merrilee took a sip from her cup. "Are you suggesting that I should have thrown her out?"

The denial came to his lips, but he couldn't speak. Isn't that exactly what he'd thought when he'd first discovered Edie's letter? Now he only wondered how he ever could have thought such things about her. "That's what most people would have done."

Her gaze fell to the table, but not before he recognized a flash of pain. "I've had some experience at dealing with someone I love who hasn't always made the right choices, and I thought I could help her."

Sounded like something his aunt would do. "Aunt Merri, this is different."

"Is it?" With a feminine snort, she leaned her head back against the headrest. "You know, I used to think the sun and the stars rose with your daddy." Merrilee laughed. "One day, he came down the third grade hall just to make sure I had milk money. I was so thrilled. I told everyone about my big brother and how he took care of me."

His father, kind to Merrilee? This was a side of his father he'd never heard about. "What happened?"

"I don't know. For a long time, I thought it was me, that I must have done something to make him hate me."

"No," he reassured her. "I know you. All you've ever done is love Dad despite his meanness."

Merrilee flashed him a sad smile. "Well, that's the reason I decided this was the best place for Edie. I see a lot of that same guilt and pain that I used to carry reflected in her."

Beau sank down beside her on the couch. "I'm glad you let her stay here. And I think you're right. She does feel a lot of guilt over what her father is doing. I just wish I could figure out a way to help her let go of that feeling."

Merrilee smiled at him over the rim of her coffee cup. "It sounds like Edie has become very important to you."

"I . . . care about her." The words sounded so bland, nothing like the colorful woman he'd come to know so well over the last few weeks. Then what exactly did he feel for Edie? Beau frowned. "But I don't understand her at times."

"That's nothing new under the sun." She laughed, setting her cup on the coffee table then leaned back again. "I haven't met a man yet who's figured out women."

"It's not that, it's just —" He took one last sip of his coffee then set his cup down. "Even now, after everything her parents have done to her, she still seems to love them."

"Of course she does, sweetheart."

Beau plowed his fingers through his hair, his hand settling at the base of his skull. "Why? They've hunted her down like she's some mangy dog, put her life in danger, and for what? So they can dance at the same parties in Hamburg with Hitler?"

"Love can't be turned off and on like a light switch. Just because someone makes a bad choice doesn't mean that love goes away."

"Someone hurts you bad enough, and it can."

Merrilee lowered her chin to her chest. "You're not talking about the Michaelses now, are you?"

"I just don't understand how Edie can still love them."

"Because you think you don't love your father."

Beau's head snapped around. "I haven't cared about him since the night I left ten years ago."

"And yet you're fixing up his house to get the money for his defense lawyers. You've talked about this being his chance to know the Lord." She tilted her head to the side, her lips pulled into a knowing smile. "That sounds to me like you care."

There may be a sucker born every minute, but he wasn't going to be one. "No use putting the cost of Dad's lawyer on the backs of struggling citizens."

"True, but at the same time, why are you going all the way to Atlanta to secure the best defense lawyer money can buy?"

He scoffed at her question, even as he wondered if there wasn't a nugget of truth to what she said. Why was he doing all this for his father? "Don't read too much into this."

"As long as you consider the possibility that you might actually care about what happens to your father. It's okay for you to love him, Beau." She gave him a friendly shove. "In fact, it's in the Bible."

"I know. The Ten Commandments. I remember."

"I was thinking about the book as a whole." She gave him an indulgent smile. "Let me ask you something. Do you think I love Claire?"

Beau scrubbed the bottom half of his face. "What has that got to do with me and Dad?"

"Just answer the question."

"Anyone with eyes in their head can see you love Claire very much."

"But Claire disobeys me. She plays in her Sunday dress or hounds you about her father, but I choose to love her despite those mistakes. That's the way God loves us. He knows we're going to mess up and He hates when we do it, but He chooses to love us anyway."

Just like Edie chose to love her mother.

Merrilee pressed her lips against his cheek, then stood. "You'll figure things out, sweetheart. Just pray on it."

He watched her pick up the cups and cross over to the sideboard. Is that what he'd done, considered his father the enemy for so long that he didn't realize he had a choice — to forgive his father and love him despite everything?

CHAPTER EIGHTEEN

"Edie?"

Edie's eyelids fluttered open. Pale sunlight playing peekaboo with the blackout curtains formed unfamiliar shadows around the modest room, and for a terse second, fear pulsed through her. She quickly glanced around the room, looking for a fast exit and found Gertie instead, standing in the doorway leading to the kitchen. The Stephenses' house.

Her heart rate settled into a slower pattern. "What time is it?"

"Almost five." Wrapping the edges of her bathrobe around her, Gertie walked over and sat down in the chair beside her. "What are you doing sleeping out here?"

She sighed, her eyes on fire from lack of rest. "I couldn't get my mind to stop spinning long enough to go to sleep." Truth was, she'd spent the last few hours trying to pray, but the words wouldn't come, her thoughts jangled and messy.

Her life had become a prison, existing only inside the gates of the bomber plant or the Stephenses' home. Not for the first time, she thought of Beau, of what he had endured. How had he managed to grow his faith while enduring incarceration by the Nazis? But she knew what his answer would be.

Prayer.

Are you listening, Lord? Do you hear me at all?

"You haven't slept a full night in almost a week now. Are you sure it's not the bed?"

Edie had taken over Gertie's brother's room since her mother's arrival five days ago. While it was clean and reasonably comfortable, it wasn't her room back at Merrilee's. It wasn't home. "It's fine."

"Why don't you send Daddy with a note for Mr. Ellerbee and tell him you'll come in later so you can get a little nap in?"

She shook her head. At least when she was at work, guards could provide protection. Here, the people in the neighborhood were sitting ducks, out in the open, ready to be picked off the pond.

"I'd better get up and get moving. I don't want to throw your dad's bus schedule off by being late." Moving to the edge of the cushions, Edie arched her back, the muscles around her shoulder blades throbbing in time with her heart. "What are you doing up so early?"

"I've got a meeting with Dr. Lovinggood this morning. He wants to talk to me about coming back to work."

"Are you sure you want to work for him again?"

Gertie slouched back in her chair. "I haven't exactly been getting job offers, and Momma starts to cry every time I mention the army nurse corp. I've got to make a living so I haven't got much of a choice. I'm just thankful Beau talked Lovinggood into giving me a second chance."

Beau. He was as much her home as the four walls of the room Merrilee rented out to her. She missed their talks, missed sitting out on the front porch, rocking beside him in a rocking chair, listening to the crickets sing in the soft shadows of the evening.

But she knew what it felt like to be in his shoes, to be held captive by the enemy — maybe not physically, but mentally. Could Beau look past her family, past her German heritage and love her for who she was, a woman who loved him very much?

Could he ever forgive her for the danger she put his family in?

"How is Beau?"

"He's fine. Seems to have his mind on other things lately, but other than that, okay."

Edie nodded. Of course he was preoccupied, probably thinking about how to protect Merrilee and Claire if the German Bund showed up at the boardinghouse. Men who were after her for what little information about the B-29 she could give them.

She should have never moved into Merrilee's. Sure, she'd tried to be as honest as she could without drawing attention to herself. But now the people she cared about most were in danger, and the fault of that situation lay solely at her feet.

Edie leaned back against the headrest and closed her eyes. There was nothing she could do to make things right, nothing but pray. *Lord, forgive me for stepping around the truth and putting the people I love the most in the world in harm's way. Please, hide us in Your protection. Keep us safe.*

Now, time to get the day started. Edie stood, holding on to the armrest when her knees wobbled beneath her. "If we're going to make it to work on time, I'd better start the coffee."

"I'll whip up a pan of biscuits." Gertie

raised the lantern, throwing a dim light across the living room, throwing shadows against the couple of chairs and end tables. "If we've still got some bacon, I'll fry some up."

Together, they walked quietly down the hall. Edie pushed the door open with her shoulder, holding it for Gertie. "I'll go get us some water."

"You sure you know how to use the pump?"

Edie could understand why Gertie had concerns. The old water pump at the end of their yard had given Edie fits the first couple of days she was there. Edie scooped up the empty bucket sitting on top of the stove. "Not really, but the pump's easier to work than getting a good fire burning in that stove."

"You don't have to tell me. How Momma cooks on this thing, I'll never know." Gertie grabbed two coffee cups from the dish drain and headed back to the refrigerator while Edie walked to the back door. She was halfway across the room when a low knock rattled the glass window of the door.

The two women exchanged looks. "Who could be here this early in the morning?" Gertie asked.

Edie stepped around the table. Heart

hammering against her rib cage, she cracked open the door. A shard of light fell across the threshold and she threw the door completely open. "Ernie?"

"I'm sorry to be bothering you so early in the morning, Ms. Edie." The little boy wrung his hands together, his shirttail hanging at an awkward angle from the waist of his jeans, as if he didn't have time to tuck it into his pants properly. "Momma says I need to get Ms. Gertie."

"Well, she's here." Edie moved to the side. "Why don't you come inside and get warmed up. Then you can tell us what's going on."

"There ain't no time, Ms. Edie. Just told me to come and get Ms. Gertie."

Something was horribly wrong, though what, she couldn't fathom. She glanced over her shoulder as Gertie came up behind her. "You have a visitor."

"What is it, Ernie?"

He glanced back and forth between the two women, his dark eyes filled with fear and worry. "It's Bea. She woke up this morning, burning up like she was on fire. Momma's been working on her the last hour or so, but she can't get the fever to break. She said you had to come."

"Go tell your momma that I'll be there

just as soon as I throw on some clothes."

"Yes, ma'am." The little boy barely waited for an answer before disappearing into the shadows of the early morning light.

Gertie hurried over to the cabinets next to the kitchen window and pulled back the sunny yellow curtain covers. Bottles of various sizes and shapes lined the shelf.

"What are you looking for?" Edie asked.

"Rubbing alcohol." Gertie read the label of one bottle before setting it on the counter. "If Bea is as feverish as Ernie said, I might need to rub her in alcohol to cool her down."

Faint alarm bells rang in Edie's ears. But why, when Bea could have something as simple as the flu? "Do the Barneses have any other kids beside Ernie and Bea?"

"Two." Gertie pulled out some cotton balls.

"Then I'm going with you." Edie held up one hand when Gertie started to protest. "Now listen to me. Everyone here has been so good to me. The very least I can do is take care of the other kids while you're working on Bea."

"I don't know, Edie. I couldn't stand it if something happened to you while you're staying with us."

"Nothing's going to happen. Like you

345

said, no one's going to come looking for me here." Edie sounded more confident than she felt. "And it's not like I'm parading through Marietta Square. We're just going two doors down."

Gertie leaned a hip against the side of the countertop. "And what about Abner Ellerbee?"

"I'll send a note with your dad."

Her friend snorted an indignant huff. "I don't like having my own suggestions flung back at me."

Edie walked over to where Gertie stood. She owed this woman — this community — so much. "Just let me help you."

"Fine, but only for a little while. And we're going to have to talk to Daddy and see if there's a way to sneak you on the bus later without anyone being none the wiser."

"Thank you. I'll go change."

"Be ready to leave in ten minutes."

Edie's lips twitched into a faint smile as she walked out of the kitchen, leaving Gertie to hunt down the rest of her supplies. She had accomplished something getting the best of her friend, not an easy feat. But Gertie might need help, especially if Bea was as sick as she sounded.

Fifteen minutes later, Edie stood in the doorway of five-year-old Bea Barnes's bedroom, Ernie and his two younger sisters, Ramona and Hessie, clinging to her as if they feared for their lives. She'd tried to interest them in a game of Old Maid in the tiny living room, anything to keep their minds busy and away from the pall hanging over the back bedroom of the modest house.

"She just had an upset stomach last night," Alice Barnes said, hovering over Gertie as she pulled the ear piece of her stethoscope from her ear. "So I put a cold rag on her belly to draw the heat out and she was better. Then this morning, I came in here to get the girls up for school, and Bea was gasping, like she couldn't take in her air."

Edie's throat tightened. Fever, stomach-ache, difficulty breathing. The diagnosis flashed through her mind.

Polio.

Pulling back the covers, Gertie lifted the child's arm. "Bea, I want you to lift your arm up for me, okay sweet girl?"

Edie held her breath, throwing up bits of prayer, hoping that she'd made the wrong diagnosis, that little Bea just had a cold or something. But when her arm fell like deadweight to the mattress, Edie knew she'd read the situation correctly.

Gertie pulled the covers back up around

Bea, tucking them in tight. "We need to get her to the hospital as soon as possible."

"My man is off fighting, Gertie, and I don't have a lot of money to be spending on hospital bills." Her low clipped words came out needy and nervous. "Can't you just doctor her here?"

But Edie knew the answer. If the paralysis had been contained in the arms or legs, then yes, they could do everything that the hospital personnel would do. But Bea's difficulty breathing meant the virus had infected her chest, and that called for an intervention.

Gertie stood, swinging her stethoscope around her neck. "No. Truth is, Bea needs help to breathe and that's not something I can do here. But if we get her to the hospital, they have machines there that will help her breathe easier."

A drop of moisture slid down the woman's cheek, her coffee-colored eyes swimming in unshed tears. "All right."

Gertie stood from her place beside Bea's bed, turned and hugged Alice. "We're going to take care of her, Alice."

"I know."

As Gertie headed in her direction, Edie looked down at the children. While Ernie and Hessie seemed fine, Ramona's cheeks had a bright flush that concerned her. "Ernie, why don't you take your sisters into the kitchen and write Bea a letter? I'm sure she'd love to read it once she gets better."

"Can we use crayons?"

Edie wasn't sure what Mrs. Barnes's rule was, but thought she would probably bend it if the kids kept their minds occupied on other things than their sister. "Just this once. But be very careful."

The children scooted off just as Gertie joined her. "Do you know how to drive a car?"

An odd question in light of the situation. "Yes, why?"

Gertie smashed her lips together. "We've got to get that child to the hospital because if we don't, she is going to die."

"Okay."

Gertie touched her arm. "Do you realize how much danger you could be putting yourself into? I don't want anything to happen to you."

She didn't, either, Edie admitted. But she was tired of running. If her father and his *Gau* wanted her, she would go — not willingly, but because she couldn't stand the thought of putting others at risk for her sake.

I know the plans I have for you, plans for good, not evil.

Edie nodded. God would work this mess out. She had faith in Him.

"Get her ready to go," Edie said, hurrying toward the front door. "I'll go get the car."

Edie slid her hand along the oak banister, slowly making her way down the hospital stairway, the cool air trapped in the cinder blocks a blessed respite from the continued heat. Gertie had told her to wait here, figuring that the stairwell was a safe place for her to hide while she got Bea Barnes admitted.

Was Beau taking care of the little girl even now?

Edie lowered herself to the stair. Why did her thoughts always turn back to Beau? Hadn't she learned anything after he pushed her off on Gertie and her family just to save his own? Wasn't valuing one person's life over another's just as morally wrong as what the Germans were doing in Europe?

And still, despite it all, she loved him.

"Edie?" Her name echoed down the serpentine line of stairs. "Are you down there?"

She tilted her head back and saw Gertie leaning over the banister. "Did you have any trouble getting Bea admitted?"

"It was like pulling donkey's teeth, but we managed to wrangle the last bed. We're still filling out some paperwork. You mind waiting a few more minutes?"

"Take your time."

"Thank you." Her friend threw her a brief smile. "I've got someone who wants to see you."

A few seconds later, the metal exit door slammed shut. A gallop of footsteps burst out overhead, growing louder until Beau came around the corner and stopped as if she might get startled and run away. "Hey."

She slid down on the step, her knees giving way. "Hi."

He took a cautious step toward her. "How have you been?"

"Fine. Busy. Lots of work at the plant." She paused for a moment, not sure what to say next. "How's my mother doing?"

"She's a lot better. Merrilee talked her into joining the Ladies Auxiliary. They've been keeping her busy rolling bandages for the troops."

She never thought she'd hear of her mother helping out the Allies' effort. "Merrilee and Claire. Are they okay?"

Before she knew what was happening, Beau plopped down on the stair beside her, his gaze studying her as if casting her to memory — every nuance, every curve of her face. "Missing you like crazy."

His words chipped away at the stony wall around her heart. She straightened. "I'm sure you explained everything to them."

"Claire's had a cold so she didn't ask a lot of questions." Beau gave her a sidelong glance. "I didn't have to explain much to my aunt."

Edie's head snapped around. "Did you think I wouldn't tell Merrilee about something as dangerous as my situation?"

"Honestly, no, I didn't think you would. But that's because I judged you against myself and realized I would have done whatever I had to save my skin."

"I don't believe that," she blurted out. "Not for one second." Her thoughts picked up steam. "You were a medic on the battlefield. You ran from one injured person to the next, trying to do what you could do to save lives, with little more than a pistol."

"That was my duty," he bit out.

"No, that's the type of man you are." Without knowing why, Edie reached over and covered his hand with hers, her heart doing little flips when his fingers automatically threaded between hers. "You've got your faults — we all do — but you're a good man."

"You think so?"

The question made her heart throb in

pain. Beau was a good man, but he had a troubling fault — placing the value of one life over another — that haunted her. She nodded, unraveling her fingers from his, pressing herself closer to the wall.

The door behind them slammed open. "Thank heavens, you're still here," Gertie said, a little bit breathlessly. "I was afraid you might have already left."

Why would she do that when Gertie was her ride to work? "What are you talking about?"

She took in another huge gulp of air. "Beau, you've got to get down to the emergency room."

"Why?" Beau caught hold of the banister and pulled himself up.

A gloomy pall fell over Gertie, chilling Edie to the bone. "Claire's being seen by Dr. Lovinggood right now. Merrilee says she's been trying to get Claire's fever down all morning and can't."

Oh, Lord, please heal Claire's body, give Dr. Lovinggood peace and wisdom in finding out what is wrong.

Beau's muscles tightened into a solid fortress beside her. He would do anything for his family. "What does he think it is?"

Gertie hesitated, just like she'd done a million times before when Edie had watched

her deliver bad news. "Dr. Lovinggood
thinks Claire might have polio."

CHAPTER NINETEEN

The kerosene lamp flickered in the corner of the hospital waiting room, the shadows dancing across the walls in a slow waltz of light and darkness. Beau leaned his head back, his eyes closed, exhaustion stinging the backs of his eyelids.

This was all his fault. If he hadn't taken Claire to the picnic with Gertie and her neighborhood, Claire would be up and getting ready for school now. But he'd been selfish, wanting to find a way to spend the day in Edie's company.

I broke my promise to John.

"Dr. Lovinggood should have been back by now. What's taking so long?"

Through tiny slits, he watched Merrilee pace back and forth across the room. Poor woman. Claire was her life. "I'm sure Dr. Lovinggood just wants to do a thorough exam."

She scrubbed her hand across her face in

a helpless gesture. "I just wish we knew something."

"I know." Sitting up now, he grabbed her hand when she made another pass by him. "Just remember that Dr. Lovinggood is a good doctor. He'll come out and talk to us when he's got news."

Merrilee squeezed his hand, as if drawing strength from him. "It's at times like this that I wish . . ." She broke off.

"What?" Beau tugged on her hand. She dropped down in the seat beside him. "What do you wish?"

But she just shook her head as she stood up again. "I wish the doctor would hurry up."

Beau watched his aunt walk to the other side of the room. Why did he feel like an opportunity to talk Merrilee about John had just slipped away? Maybe he could maneuver her into the discussion. "You know, I wasn't sure what to expect when I came home. But Claire, she was a complete surprise. She took to me like a frog to a lily pad."

Merrilee turned to him and smiled. "You took time with her, talked to her. Of course she loved you on sight."

"All she's ever wanted were stories about her dad."

His aunt crossed her arms over her waist. "I guess that's normal. Ever since she found out he bought us the house, she's been asking more about him."

His next question might be pushing things, but it was time Merrilee made peace with John, even if just for Claire's sake. "Don't you think it would be better if John told his daughter about himself?"

Merrilee closed her eyes, but not before a flash of pain raced across her features. "John chose not to be a part of our lives when he filed for divorce."

"Are you so sure about that, Aunt Merri?"

"Of course, I am. I wrote him letters and letters, telling him how much I wanted him to come home, how much I wanted us to be a family." She drew in a deep sigh that to Beau seemed almost pained. "But he never came back."

Beau pushed out of the chair and took several steps to stand in front of Merrilee. "What if things were different and John wanted to come home?"

"He made his choice, Beau." She gave a defeated little shake of her head.

"How would you feel if he changed his mind?"

"I don't know." A sad smile played along the corners of her mouth. "I've always wanted Claire to have some kind of relationship with her father."

She still hadn't answered his question. "But what about you? How would *you* feel?"

Merrilee dropped her chin to her chest, her eyes fastened to the checkerboard tile. "That doesn't really matter, does it?"

But Beau wasn't so sure about that. The man he'd known like a father had loved his aunt with a single-mindedness that he'd never understood, until now. Loving Edie had given him a new perception of John and Merrilee. Those letters he had mailed off might give his aunt a shot at the happiness she deserved. And he owed her the truth.

"I'm sorry, Merrilee."

The look she gave him was full of confusion. "Sorry for what?"

He explained about the letters he and Edie had found, the ones Merrilee had written to John and how James had stolen them before they made it to the post office. "Maybe if I had stuck around, Dad wouldn't have gotten away with it for so long."

Merrilee sat down beside him, her body angled to his, her fingers warm on his hand. "If you'd stayed, there's a good chance your daddy would have beat you to death. And if you had managed to survive, what kind of man would you have been? Bitter? Scornful?"

Just like his dad.

"I missed you like crazy all those years you were gone." Merrilee gave him a quick smile. "But I like the man who came home. He's loving and so protective. A real man of God."

Was he really the man Merrilee had described? "But I took Claire to that picnic, and now all the kids have polio."

"Aw, honey. That could have happened to anybody. And you don't know. She could have picked it up at school."

A door to the ward opened, illuminating the room in bright light. "Merrilee?"

Beau rose alongside his aunt, holding on to her elbow in case she needed him. "How is my girl, Doctor?"

He pointed to the chairs. "Please have a seat."

Once they were all seated, Lovinggood began. "Well, we got the fever down, and she's moving her arms and legs, though not as much as I'd like to see."

"So it is polio?" Merrilee's voice broke on the last word.

The portly older man leaned over and clasped Merrilee's hand between his. "I know it seems like a dire diagnosis, but the majority of our polio patients have no residual effects."

But Beau was worried. The lack of movement in Claire's limbs and the concern he read beneath the doctor's perfect bedside manner bothered him. How would Merrilee cope if Claire was left paralyzed?

"What can we expect next?"

"Well." The doctor leaned back in his chair, pinching the crown of his nose. "We'll be watching her condition closely for the next twenty-four hours, make sure she continues to improve on her own. Then we'll go from there."

"What if something goes wrong?"

Lovinggood patted her hand. "Now, Merrilee, there's no sense asking for trouble until it comes knocking on your door."

Merrilee gave him a noncommittal nod. "Can we see her?"

"Claire's had a rough night, and when I left her, she was finally falling asleep."

One look at his aunt's crestfallen face and Beau knew he had to make a case for her. But Dr. Lovinggood must have seen that same agony flicker across Merrilee's features because he relented. "Just for a moment then."

"Thank you!" Merrilee stood along with the doctor then looked back at Beau. "Are you coming with me?"

He shook his head. "Claire's had enough excitement for one day. I'll wait for you right here."

Merrilee hesitated for a moment then nodded. "I'll be back in a few minutes."

She followed the doctor into the ward, the door closing behind them casting the room in semidarkness, his conversation with Merrilee fresh on his mind. Was it possible that his aunt was still in love with John even now, all these years later? She'd talked of his decision to give up on their marriage, but what about her?

If only he could talk to Edie.

Beau stretched his legs out in front of him, crossing one ankle over the other. As soon as he got Merrilee settled for the night, he'd go over to the Stephenses' and help Edie and Gertie nurse their young patients through this epidemic. Not because he liked taking care of sick kids — though he had to admit, he did — but to be close to Edie. To work out whatever problem was bothering her.

And tell her how much he loved her.

"Beau?"

He lifted his head from his chest and watched Maggie, still outfitted in the jumpsuit she'd left the house in yesterday, cross the room. "Have you heard any news about Claire Bear?"

"Only that they finally got her fever down and she's resting. Merrilee's in with her now."

She sat down in the chair next to him. "Is it polio?"

Beau gave her a slight nod.

Maggie leaned back in her chair, her arms wrapped in a protective embrace around her waist. "How is Merrilee handling it?"

"You know Merrilee. She's probably been praying since Claire's temperature went up half a degree."

Maggie chuckled. "Probably before that."

Maybe his cousin could help him. "Could you take Merrilee home for me? I need to get out to the Stephenses' house."

"Is it true what I heard? That Dr. Lovinggood told Gertie not to bring anymore sick kids here because there are no more beds on the Negro floor?"

Beau thought he might snap his jaw, he was grinding his teeth so tightly together. "Where did you hear that?"

"One of Gertie's friends upstairs was getting off work and told me that. What are they going to do?"

Great, news of a polio outbreak in the Negro community would just fuel fires.

Well, maybe he could put them out before they got started. "We're going to move the sickest ones into the Stephenses' house so we can keep a closer eye on them. Edie's looking after the ones who aren't as ill."

A good plan, considering. Now to scour the hospital inventory for supplies before he headed over to the Stephenses' neighborhood himself. And if Dr. Lovinggood got in his way . . .

But it all depended on Maggie. "So will you stay?"

Maggie nodded. "I figured you'd want to get over there as quick as you could."

"First, I've got to get some things." Beau stood, eyeing the door to the ward with wariness. "Even if I have to march in there and punch the good doctor in the mouth to get supplies."

A giggle made him jerk his head toward his cousin. "Have I told you how glad I am to have you home?"

He smiled down at her. "Me, too, cousin."

"Now go!" Maggie leaned back in her chair to get as comfortable as she could. "And if it's anywhere near as bad as I've been told, let me know. I'll find you some help."

"I'm so cold, Ms. Edie." The little girl

huddled under the threadbare bedclothes, her tiny limbs shaking like leaves trembling in a tornado. Her dark eyes blazed up at Edie, bright with fever.

"Let me see if I can find you another blanket, Ramona dearest." Edie pushed up the thin blankets and tucked them tightly around the girl's small frame.

She flung the covers from her body, snatching Edie's hand in a tight hold. "Don't go. I'm scared."

Edie nodded, pressing her hand over Ramona's cool fingers. Of course the child was scared. The last of the Barnes children to come down with the virus, she'd been in the same bed when her older sister, Bea, had taken ill. Best to get her mind occupied with something else. "Would you like me to sing you a song?"

"Me and Bea like to sing 'Jesus Loves the Little Children,' " she whispered through chattering teeth. "Do you know that one?"

Edie answered by humming softly, recalling the last time she'd heard the song, of Beau reciting the verses to comfort her. Her lips tingled at the memory. In that moment, she'd had such hope that all would work out, that maybe she would get the chance to tell Beau just how much she loved him.

A moan from the bed drew Edie's attention back to the little girl. She'd hope that despite the fever racking Ramona's poor little body, the child might get some needed rest. Within a few minutes, the death grip the girl had on Edie's hand slackened. She studied Ramona for a moment. Although the girl still shivered, she took deep, even breaths.

Leaning her head back, Edie shut her eyes. The situation in Gertie's neighborhood had been far worse than anything she'd experienced at the hospital. Almost every child and several of the younger adults had been infected with the virus. And with no supplies and no available beds at the hospital, several of the sicker children hovered close to death.

Gertie stuck her head inside the room. "How are things in here?"

"I think Ramona's finally asleep." Edie extracted her hand from the child's grip. She stood, stretching her back out, moving from side to side to ease the vague ache in her muscles. "I only wish we had more blankets."

"Wait right here." Gertie left, only to return a few moments later with a beautiful quilt made from strips of royal blue and gold. "Ask and you shall receive."

Edie unfolded it, recognizing Merrilee's

tight, clean stitches. "Where did you get hold of this?"

Gertie shook out one corner of the quilt, unleashing a wave of blue and gold. "Captain Hicks brought a whole mess of them by when he dropped Beau off."

"Beau's here?" The thought woke her out of the working stupor she'd been in since the first child had taken ill.

"Not at the moment, but I'm expecting him back any time now." She tucked one edge of the quilt under the mattress. "He drove one of the more severe cases to the hospital."

But Dr. Lovinggood had refused any more of their patients, and the closest hospital accepting Negroes was in Atlanta. Edie grabbed one end of the quilt and tugged it tight. "I thought her parents didn't want to go to Crawford Long."

"They didn't." Gertie tucked the blanket around the little girl. "Don't ask me how, but Beau talked Dr. Lovinggood into moving some beds up to the Negro floor. From what I gather, he made a big stink about it."

Edie smiled to herself. Yes, that was the Beau she loved, always raising a ruckus. If given the right reasons, she added to herself.

"He also managed to squeeze some supplies out of the doctor — blankets, washcloths, aspirin, even enough rubbing alcohol to sponge down every feverish kid in the neighborhood."

"That's wonderful." And it was, but what had she expected from Beau? He might have reservations about helping Gertie's community, but it was because he feared for their safety, both the Stephenses' and hers. And now this. Why had she ever doubted him? Because she'd judged him against everyone else, against her experience with her father.

"Ramona can spare you for a while," Gertie whispered as she tucked the edges of the quilt around the little girl's shoulders. Ramona immediately snuggled into the cover's warmth. "I think you could use a little break."

Edie looked down at her small patient. Ramona only shivered slightly now, and breathed as if in a deep slumber. "I'm fine."

"Momma said you haven't eaten anything since this morning."

It had been a while since she'd had a piece of dried toast and a cup of coffee. Her stomach growled. "Maybe I could eat a little something, just to tide me over." She glanced up at her friend. "You'll send someone to get me if Ramona worsens, won't you?"

"You know I will," Gertie replied. "And Edie?"

"Yes?"

The brief smile was one of genuine appreciation. "You don't know how much you being here means to me. To all of us."

Edie smiled back at Gertie from the door. "I could say the same thing about you taking me in like you did. But I figure friends do things like that for each other."

"Get out of here before you have me squalling like a baby," Gertie grumbled, her voice breaking.

Edie turned and headed down the cramped hallway. Within seconds, she stood out on the Waterses' front porch, the hint of cool night air against her bare arms and legs refreshing. She stretched. Every joint in her body ached, and her stomach growled. Maybe Gertie was right. Maybe she did need a break.

She stepped off the porch before she noticed the man standing in the front yard, a baseball bat clutched in his right hand. The hairs on the back of her neck stood on end as he slowly ambled toward her. "You just couldn't leave well enough alone, now could you?"

Edie's heart jerked into a rapid beat. "Is there something I can do for you, sir?"

From the side of the house, another man, tall and wiry, his pressed shirt crisp even in the dim light of evening, climbed the porch railing. "You are Edie Michaels, right?"

Her stomach tightened into a painful knot. This couldn't be good. "Why do you ask?"

"Just interested." The man in the yard stepped up on the first stair to the porch.

Edie backed up. "Well, we have a polio epidemic going on here, so it might be best if you just go on home."

"But you're here." He flashed her a sickening grin that made her skin crawl. "A white woman exposing herself to these . . . diseases."

A spark of anger roared through her. "Black or white, polio is polio. And to think otherwise is just plain —" She broke off.

He cut the distance between them until Edie could feel his vile breath on her cheeks. "Just plain what?"

She gulped for air. She'd lived with fear, lived with the worry that came from running away from the evil her father had become, but never had she felt this jittery throb of terror coursing through her veins. Edie took another step back.

A strong arm from behind her wrapped around her waist and pulled her flush against a sturdy wall of muscle. Edie dug her fingernails into the corded muscles. She opened her mouth to scream, but her voice failed.

"It's okay, sweetheart. I've got you."

Beau! She relaxed against him, wrapping her arms over his.

"I didn't know you were here, Daniels." The man on the stairway stepped back. "This doesn't concern you."

"Anything having to do with Ms. Michaels or these folks concerns me." His arm tightened around her waist. "So go ahead and say your piece."

CHAPTER TWENTY

Every instinct in Beau's body clamored to slug the man. But he was determined to rein in his temper, to hear the man out, to listen to his pitiful excuses for confronting Edie when she'd only spent the last sixteen hours nursing sick kids.

Then he'd slug him.

"So." Beau drew Edie closer to his side. Her fist clenched the front of his shirt, and her body trembled. "Did you hear about the outbreak and decide to help out?"

The man's thick brows fused into a straight line. "Why would I want to help . . ." He paused, his mouth drawn up into an ugly smirk. "These people?"

At the man's words, Edie flinched beneath his touch. A few of the men in the neighborhood had gathered in the yard, but the man didn't seem to notice. Beau wouldn't have to raise a hand to him. If he kept talking such hatred, these men wouldn't think twice about beating him to a pulp. "Get out of here."

The man guffawed. "Well, you're not your father's son, that's for sure."

Best compliment Beau had gotten in a while. "No, I'm not. I believe in helping all of my neighbors like the Bible says."

"Your daddy's not going to be happy about this."

Probably not, but this was his life and he had to live it according to the conscience God had given him. "I think it's time you left. We've got sick children to tend to."

The man pointed at Edie. "This ain't over, kraut."

Fury roared through him like gasoline to the flame. He could threaten Beau all day long, but not Edie, never Edie. Pushing her out of his arms, Beau took off down the stairs, fisting his hands in the front of the man's shirt, glaring down at him. He didn't have time to react before Beau had his cocked fist aimed for the man's red nose.

Beau was close enough to see his pupils darken in fear. "You're going to pay a little visit to my friend, the sheriff. And if you ever so speak to Ms. Michaels again, I will track you down and make you wish you'd never been born. Is that clear?"

The man gave a weak nod before Beau

gave him over to two of the men gathered in the yard. "And just so you know, Sheriff Worthington knows about your friends, so if they so much as pass by this neighborhood again, they'll be keeping you company in jail."

The man fell back, his lips pressed against his teeth, caught by two of the men. The men parted to allow the group through the small crowd.

Beau glanced out over the crowd. "Go on home. We've got enough to worry about without standing out here, waiting for trouble to come back." He turned to Gertie on the porch next door. "Are we about ready to take those kids to the hospital?"

"Will be in just a few more minutes." Gertie's gaze slid from Beau to Edie and back again. "Enough time for a short break." She disappeared inside the house and shut the door.

Beau took the first stair, then looked up to find himself almost nose to nose with Edie. Even in the dim evening light, her eyes sparkled, the color of a late-afternoon summer sky. Soft and endless.

And looking only at him.

"You stood up for me. Again."

He nodded. Had she really expected him to throw her to the wolves? No, that's what experience had taught her. With her parents, with her friends. Even with him at first. She'd never be bullied again, not that she'd ever let that stop her from doing what she felt was right. Well, he was here now, standing in front of her, loving her.

She cupped his face in her hands. "Thank you."

Beau shook his head. "I'll always be here for you."

"Thank you for being here, helping us. I know you were worried about the Stephenses' safety, but you came anyway."

He covered her hands with his, bringing them to his chest. "I wouldn't be much of a man if I turned my back on people in need."

She gave him a tiny smile. "I should have had faith in you."

"Why?" Beau asked. "When everyone you loved had let you down?"

Edie leaned closer. "I can't wait to come home. Which will be very soon. Mack caught me as I was leaving the hospital today. Told me that the government had cracked down on the Bund. Most have been put into prison camps, but a few escaped to Germany."

Her body flush agaist his, Edie rested her head on his shoulder. Then she remembered. "How's Claire?"

"It's polio, but not as bad as we first thought. She's got a little muscle weakness in her legs, but Dr. Lovinggood seems to think that a little therapy will help her get her strength back."

Oh, thank You, Lord.

Beau pressed her palms against his chest, enjoying her touch even through the layer of cotton. "I have so much I want to tell you. But right now . . ."

"I know." She pushed away from him, putting some distance between them.

But even that was too much space for Beau. He clasped her chin between his fingers, lifting her head until his gaze met hers. "Soon, Edie." He leaned down, and brushed his lips against hers before he stepped back.

"Soon."

Now was not the time, not with all the sick kids who still needed tending. Beau forced himself to take a step back, but not before catching her hand in his. She nodded, the tender spark in her eyes giving him the confidence he needed. Yes, they would talk soon.

The next few days were a blur of alcohol sponge baths and stripped sheets. Beau made two more runs to the hospital, first to pick up supplies, then to retrieve the Waters baby. By the third day, the tide of illness seemed to have turned.

With one last check on her sleeping patients, Edie settled into the rocking chair with a scratch piece of paper and the pencil she carried around in her pocket.

She was lost in her sketching when she felt a warm hand on her shoulder. "What are you doing? Making a list of all the things you want to do once we get home?"

She glanced up at Beau. Even with three days of growth on his beard, she never tired of studying his handsome face. "I was thinking. The hospital was built when Marietta only had a few thousand residents, but with the bomber plant, there's almost four times as many people living here."

Beau squatted down beside her, leaning on the armrest. "So?"

"Marietta is going to need a bigger hospital." Edie swiped the tip of the pencil into a straight line across the white surface of the paper. "One large enough for everyone."

He leaned over and studied her drawing. "You mean one that can cater to both whites and Negroes in the community."

Edie held her breath. What if he couldn't see the value of this idea, the need to provide health care regardless of color?

But the broad smile lighting up his face told her he agreed. "It's brilliant."

"You think so?"

"Yes." Beau tugged on a loose curl, shifting it between his fingers before pushing it behind her ear. "If there's one thing I've learned from this war, it's that everyone willing to fight and die for this country deserves an equal chance."

Edie nodded, focusing on the drawing. Did that chance include her, or was she always going to be paying for the sin of being German?

"I went to see my father before I came here."

Her design for the new hospital slid from her fingers onto her lap. Beau had been so determined not to visit James in jail. What had changed his mind? "How was he?"

"As mean and stubborn as usual." Beau stared off into space as if reliving those moments with his father. "I expected him to be that way. That's who he is."

Her heart ached for him. "That's too bad."

Beau nodded. "Yeah, it is. But that's his choice." He paused, a vague sadness in his eyes calling out for her comfort. "I told him I'd be back."

That surprised her. What did Beau hope to accomplish in visiting his father? "Why?"

"Because that's my choice, Edie." His eyes met hers, his gaze staring down into the deepest depths of her being. "As much as I can't stand most of the things he's done, I can't hate him, Edie. I just can't."

The pencil fell with a soft clatter to the floor as Edie reached for him, curling her fingers around his forearm, hope flickering to life inside her heart for the first time in a very long time. "Of course not. He's your dad."

"I have to forgive him, or I won't be able to live with myself." Beau covered her hand with his. "You taught me that."

"Me?"

"Yes, you." He chuckled softly, his thumb stroking the delicate skin of her wrist before settling over the notch where her pulse drummed out a wild beat. "You didn't stop loving your parents even when they tried to force you into working for the Nazis. You left. You built a life for yourself."

She drew in a shaky breath. "You left home, too."

"I left out of anger, not beliefs." He let go of her, only to cup her cheek in the palm of his hand. "And when your mother showed up on our doorstep, you chose to forgive her despite what she had done." He looked at her with such incredible longing, Edie couldn't breathe. "I want to love people like you do, even when I'm not crazy about some of the things they're doing with their life."

Any doubts she might have had that Beau could love her despite who her parents were evaporated like the morning mist. She lifted her hand to his face, his beard stubble a pleasant rub against the sensitive skin of her palm. "I struggle with forgiving people too, you know. So I have to stay in constant prayer, asking God to let me love people the way He loves them. That's all any of us can do."

He nodded. "Gertie needed you, and you were right here, not worrying about what everyone else would think, just sure you had to do the right thing by God."

Her cheeks went hot. "The phone lines still aren't up."

"But they will be." He laughed, stroked his thumb across the arch of her nose. "And it will make it easier on the phone company when I want a line installed in my dad's place."

"Did you get a renter?"

"I figured I might as well rent the place myself. I can live there while I save up to go to medical school then maybe buy Dad out and set up my office there." Was it her imagination or was he suddenly closer? "Though it still needs a lot of work, particularly on that back bedroom."

"Back bedroom?" She leaned into his palm.

"I figured you'd need the best light if you're planning on drawing up plans for all the houses and new buildings Marietta's going to need."

Her heart tripped over in her chest. "You're teasing me, aren't you?"

But the expression on Beau's face was very serious. "I could spend a lifetime watching you."

Edie's breath caught in her throat at the love shining in his eyes. "You don't mean that."

"Oh, yes, I do. Every time I look at you, you know what I see?"

She shook her head, not trusting her voice to speak.

His face broke into the most beautiful smile she'd ever seen, one that burned a path all the way to her heart. "I see my future."

Any resistance she had left, melted at his words. Beau loved her. He wanted to make a future with her. And there was nothing standing in their way. "I want a future with you, too."

"I love you, Edie."

Her heart burst with joy. Beau loved her. As he closed the distance between them, she whispered against his lips. "I love you, too."

EPILOGUE

Edie stepped out onto Merrilee's front porch, drew in a deep breath of cool autumn air and smiled, joy running through her veins, infusing every part of her being.

A pair of familiar arms wrapped around her waist as Beau pulled her gently back against his warm welcoming chest. "What are you smiling about this morning?"

"How do you know I'm smiling?"

Beau's lips spread into a playful smile against her temple before brushing a kiss there. "You're always smiling here lately. Just like me."

She chuckled. The man knew her far too well! True, he had spent the better part of the last three months courting her while she wore his ring, but really! What kind of surprises would be left for them to discover for the next fifty or sixty years? Edie couldn't wait to find out.

She wrapped her arms over his. "It really

is a beautiful day for a wedding, isn't it?"

"Too bad it's not ours," he grumbled.

Her stomach fluttered at the frustration in his voice. "Maggie and Wesley offered to make it a double wedding."

Beau's chest pressed against her back as he drew in a deep breath, then released her. He walked over to the porch banister before turning to face her. "I know and that was very nice of them. But I still think it's best if we wait until after Dad's moved to the federal penitentiary before we start our life together." Beau leaned back against the railing. "I still can't believe he confessed."

Yes, James's confession had taken the whole town by surprise. But after the initial shock wore off, Edie wondered if it had been Beau's visits that had changed James's mind. Edie walked over to where Beau stood, marveling at the man she'd promised to marry. He'd kept his word to his father, visiting him week after week, sometimes spending the whole visit in silence. "Maybe your dad decided he didn't want to put you and the rest of your family through a trial."

Beau opened his arms. In one fluid movement, she moved, pressed against his side, her hand against his chest, his heart steady and strong like her love for him.

He looked down at her, a smile playing at

the corners of his mouth. "I was thinking it could be the answer to our prayers."

She lifted her face to him. "That's my favorite answer."

Beau lowered his head, his face going out of focus as he drew nearer. Her eyes fluttered shut, her breath caught in her lungs as his lips touched hers.

"Excuse me."

She jumped, but Beau held her flush to his side, the pulse at the base of his neck thundering at an erratic rate. She stifled a giggle when the tips of his ears turned fire-engine red.

Beau recovered his voice first. "Dr. Lovinggood, you're kind of early for the wedding."

"I thought I'd drop by on my way to a house call." The older man glanced from one to the other.

Beau shook his head. "Just spending some time with my fiancée before things go haywire this afternoon. What can I do for you?"

"Do you remember me mentioning my friend, Dr. Phillips at Emory University?"

"Vaguely," Beau replied.

"He's assistant dean over at the medical school. Anyway, he heard about the work you did during the recent polio outbreak and would like to talk to you about a scholarship." The doctor gave them a thoughtful smile. "He thinks he may have an opening in the upcoming class."

"Beau!" Edie pressed her face into his neck, her arms wrapping around him.

"Thank You, Lord," he whispered into her hair.

Edie smiled. *Yes, thank You, Lord, for this Godly man.*

"We're going to need more doctors to accommodate the county's growth," Lovinggood continued. "Even the mayor is talking about building a new hospital, one that can provide for all our new citizens."

Not surprising when Edie had given the mayor her drawings for a larger hospital herself. She turned her head toward the doctor. "Will it have more beds for the Negro population?"

Lovinggood exchanged a look with Beau, then shrugged. "I don't know, Edie, but with Beau in medical school and intending to practice here, he'll have a say in the matter."

She glanced up at Beau who gave her a slight nod. This would have to be a battle for another day.

"Dr. Lovinggood," Beau said, extending his free hand to the man, "I don't know how to thank you."

The man took Beau's hand in his grasp and shook it. "Just be the kind of physician I know you're capable of being." He tipped his hat to Edie. "See you this afternoon."

The doctor was barely halfway down the front walk when Beau pulled her into his arms, his laughter rumbling beneath her fingertips. "This has turned out to be a wonderful day!"

Smiling up at him, Edie laced her arms around his neck. "I can't wait to marry you, Beau Daniels."

He leaned toward her, resting his forehead on hers, his usually pale green eyes darkened by love and longing. "Soon."

How could one small word hold such promise of the future lifetime? But questions ceased to exist when he leaned forward to claim her lips. She returned his kiss, knowing Beau was only the beginning of the family they would build together in the years to come.

Dear Reader,

Thank you for joining me for another story set in World War II Georgia, and Merrilee Davenport's boardinghouse. Edie Michaels caught my attention as WASP Maggie Daniels's friend in *Hearts in Flight*. I hope you enjoyed reading how Edie found healing from her father's betrayal in God's love for her, and in Beau and Edie's blossoming love for each other.

I was surprised to discover how many German-American families were torn apart by the onset of World War II. While some young men and women chose to follow their parents' political leanings and traveled to Germany to serve in Hitler's army, many others, determined to stay true to their beliefs, left friends and family behind, in some cases never to see them again.

I love hearing from my readers and encourage you to visit me at my website, www.pattysmithhall.com, to learn more about my upcoming releases and events. Or if you love the feel of pen against paper like I do, write me at Patty Smith Hall, P.O. Box 2788, Duluth, GA 30096.

Blessings,
Patty Smith Hall

QUESTIONS FOR DISCUSSION

1. We first meet Beau Daniels climbing in the front window of his aunt's house because she always provided a safe haven after one of James Daniels's beatings. Have you ever encountered a child in an abusive situation? How did you react? Were you willing to open your home to this child, knowing the possible dangers?

2. Edie makes a snap judgment about Beau based on his father's recent arrest. Have you ever found yourself in a similar situation? How would you have reacted?

3. Beau reveals a secretive nature when he finds a letter from Edie's German grandmother and hides it rather than question her about it. Is he being protective of his aunt and cousin? Or should he have confronted Edie about the letter immediately? How much do you believe his

abusive past played a part in his decision to investigate Edie privately?

4. Edie is concerned about Claire Davenport's obsession with the father she'd never known. How would you handle someone's questions about a subject you found uncomfortable? Who do you believe made the correct choice — Edie for voicing her concern about Claire's questions, or Beau for encouraging his cousin's inquiries about her father?

5. Edie works as an architect in a time when men dominate the field. What do you think gave her the self-confidence to make such a bold career choice?

6. Both Beau and Edie hide their friendships with the Stephenses, an African-American family, because of the racial barriers at the time. Have you ever had to hide a friendship out of fear of what others would say or do? How do you think the other person in the relationship felt about being kept secret? How would you feel?

7. Edie's father is active in the German movement in the United States and is

determined to ship his daughter to Germany to further Hitler's cause. Yet Edie still loves and prays for him every day. Have you been faced with loving someone despite a sin they continue to commit in their life? How did you react?

8. Edie has to hide her father's secret, yet she judged Beau based on his father's past behavior. Do you find her actions hypocritical? Or was she merely protecting herself and the other residents in the house she'd grown to love? If you believe neither is true, what do you think caused her to behave this way?

9. Beau worries that the townsfolk will think he is just like his reprobate father, and is determined to prove himself as a better person. In what ways, good and bad, are you like your parents? What one trait would you change? Write out a plan of action.

10. Edie's feelings for Beau begin to change when she hears Beau pray. What can you learn about a person by praying with them? How important is prayer to a relationship?

11. Beau feels the need to thank Pastor Williams for preaching God's word, which set the foundation for Beau's faith. Who would you thank for helping you grow your faith if you had the opportunity? What can you do to show your appreciation for their following God's calling?

12. Pastor Williams tells Beau he sometimes dealt with discouragement when trying to reach people for God. Have you ever felt discouraged in a ministry you're working with? What helps you work through your discouragement? A kind word? Certain Bible verses?

13. Beau is shocked to learn he didn't play a part in George's decision to leave home. Have you ever taken responsibility for someone else's choices? How did it affect you? How did it affect your relationship with the other person?

14. Beau and Edie find letters James Daniels had stolen from Merrilee and John, letters that could have saved their marriage. What would you do with the letters if you were in Edie and Beau's place? Would you

forward them to John? Or return them to Merrilee? Why?

15. Edie's decision to forgive Beau, after he confesses to keeping her grandmother's letter and investigating her, surprises Beau. Do you think Beau has a problem with the concept of forgiveness because of his abused past? Name a time in your life when someone extended unexpected forgiveness to you.

16. Edie and Beau both have issues with their parents that could influence the way they handle their relationships with each other and their children in the future. What Bible verses could the couple study and memorize to help them in raising their family in the years to come?

ABOUT THE AUTHOR

A Georgia girl born and bred, **Patty Smith Hall** loves to incorporate little-known historical facts into her stories. Her writing goal is to create characters who walk the Christian walk despite their human flaws. When she's not writing, Patty enjoys spending time with her husband of twenty-eight years, their two daughters and a vast extended family.

Patty loves hearing from her readers! Please contact her through her website, www.patty smithhall.com.

ML   12-10